UGLY LITTLE THINGS

COLLECTED HORRORS

ALSO BY TODD KEISLING

THE SOUTHLAND MYTHOS

The Sundowner's Dance
Devil's Creek
Scanlines
The Final Reconciliation

THE MONOCHROME TRILOGY

A Life Transparent
The Liminal Man
Nonentity

COLLECTIONS

Cold, Black & Infinite: Stories of the Horrific & Strange

PRAISE FOR THE WORK OF TODD KEISLING

"Todd Keisling is a born storyteller, drawing the reader into artfully constructed narratives that scout the darker end of the literary spectrum with skill and bravado. A pleasure to read, his stories linger well after the last page has been turned. Excellent stuff." —JOHN LANGAN, author of *The Fisherman*

"Todd Keisling is already a mainstay of modern horror, and this book proves why. A wildly original and unsettling tale, *The Sundowner's Dance* is an unforgettable journey of grief, cosmic horror, and making the most of the time we've got left. Pick up a copy of this book immediately." —GWENDOLYN KISTE, Bram Stoker Award-winning author of *Reluctant Immortals* and *The Haunting of Velkwood*

"Filled with anxiety, anguish, and grief, *Cold, Black & Infinite* tips, bends, and spins reality. This is Keisling at his best." —CYNTHIA PELAYO, Bram Stoker Award®-winning author of *Loteria* and *The Shoemaker's Magician*

"Keisling writes in the shadows, his words like that first long drag on a cigarette after work. I couldn't help coming back for more, and before I knew it, that one story, that one cigarette, turned into the whole pack." —STEPHANIE M. WYTOVICH, author of *The Eighth*

"The author has a keen, lucid understanding of suffering, which lends each plotline extra heft and depth. These stories contain tenderly and humanely rendered characters who are drawn towards various forms of uncanny annihilation. After reading this excellent collection, I'm eagerly awaiting whatever Keisling produces next." —JON PADGETT, author of *The Secret of Ventriloquism*

"Todd Keisling's *The Sundowner's Dance* is a harrowing work of cosmic horror that masterfully inhabits a dark territory somewhere between John Langan and Bentley Little. Highly recommended." —BRIAN KEENE, author of *The Rising*

"Keisling is a cosmic cartographer forging through the darkest depths of our nightmares. He is a bard of the abyss, a voice from the void, and the horrors he's charted within this unforgettable collection will change the literary map for generations to come." —CLAY MCLEOD CHAPMAN, author of *Wake Up and Open Your Eyes*

"*Cold, Black & Infinite* is a compelling cocktail of American folklore, gothic hauntings, and urban myth, served up with Keisling's consummate flair and garnished with a swirl of blood. Resounds with everyday terror." —LEE MURRAY, four-time Bram Stoker Award®-winning author of *Grotesque: Monster Stories*

"*Devil's Creek* is the kind of book you have to read with your lights on. Hell, make sure your neighbors have their lights on too!" —S. A. COSBY, *New York Times* bestselling author of *Razorblade Tears* and *Blacktop Wasteland*

"Make no mistake. This is no imitation. This is original, fierce, and explosive writing [...] Keisling is a master storyteller." —ERIC LAROCCA, author of *Things Have Gotten Worse Since We Last Spoke*

"You're not going to hear me say this too often because it's pretty rare for a book to really scare me enough to lose sleep or be afraid to walk around in my house after dark, so listen carefully: This book scared me." —SADIE HARTMANN, Bram Stoker Award®-winning author of *101 Horror Books to Read Before You Die*

"*The Sundowner's Dance* weaves a compelling tale that explores the depths of human resilience when faced with mortality. Keisling's masterful storytelling choreographs grief, acceptance, and the unyielding spirit of life into a cosmic horror ballad for the ages." —AMANDA HEADLEE, author of *Madness and Greatness Can Share the Same Face*

"Reading *The Sundowner's Dance* is a bit like casting a spell to ward off existential dread despite the greatest terrors of the novel evoking this very thing; the beauty and hopefulness at the core of the story refuse to be stamped out by either the wrath of an alien invader or the ravages of age. It's Todd Keisling at his absolute finest: dark, unflinching, visceral, and innovative. His pitch-perfect prose and masterful storytelling will leave you, quite literally, breathless." —CHRISTA CARMEN, Bram Stoker Award®-winning and Shirley Jackson Award-nominated author of *The Daughters of Block Island*

"Keisling's finest tackles grief and aging in a way that compels you through the darkness. *The Sundowner's Dance* cements his status as the future of the genre." —ROBERT P. OTTONE, Bram Stoker Award®-winning author of *The Triangle*

UGLY LITTLE THINGS

COLLECTED HORRORS

TODD KEISLING

FOREWORD *by* MERCEDES M. YARDLEY

Crystal Lake Publishing
www.crystallakepub.com

This one's for my parents.
It's all gone dark.

TABLE OF CONTENTS

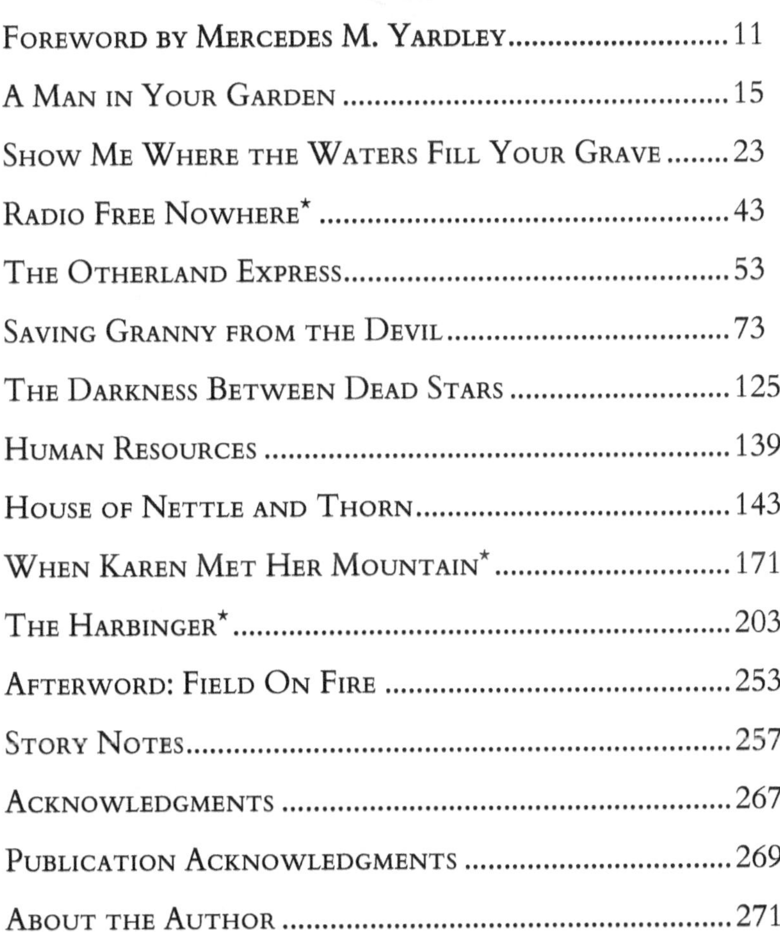

*story is part of the Southland Mythos

FOREWORD

Well, reader. Aren't you in for a delightfully disturbing ride? I first met Todd Keisling years ago on a rather uncomfortable broadcast. We were being interviewed about a book we were in. The interviewees eventually banded together to form our own online series, *Awkward Conversations with Geeky Writers*. Todd is our host.

He's gloriously deadpan. His sense of humor is wicked and dry. Nothing gets past him, and when he laughs, it's the most splendid thing. It's like watching a mountain weep. There's a sense of awe in seeing a force of nature moved.

He's the slow, creeping thing that is older than his years. He's the Green Man in the old fairytales that presents you with the bag of gold that never empties, or tells you how to defeat the monster. How does he have this knowledge? It's never revealed, but he simply knows. He's somehow privy to more than we are, understands things on a deeper level than most. It's a blessing and a curse for him.

You'll see that in this book. You'll read tales that will move you, will frighten you, and will literally take your breath away. Todd Keisling exposes our wants, wonders, and fears in this collection. There's the desire for acceptance in "House of Nettle and Thorn," and the loneliness in my personal favorite, "The Otherland Express." There's tongue-in-cheek humor in the soul-crushing story "Human Resources." You'll see old men who dance with the dead, the gorgeous horrors of space, and the disquiet that comes when you see a strange figure outside. These stories are unsettling. They're spun of everyday experiences and then infused with something else, something primitive and frightening and wondrous. There's a clean elegance to the written word that is so very much at the heart of Todd's work. The deeper emotions are uncovered with clever care. Even when there is bloodstained infection, it's conveyed with refinement. You'll want to wipe your filthy paws on your pants and then sit with a glass of wine. How can such a thing be?

The short stories are ugly little things of beauty, but then there's something more. Again, this is typical of Todd's fiction. Fathoms below the surface of the story, things breathe and writhe.

Let me introduce you to one of the most thrilling, most brilliantly paced takes on the King in Yellow mythos I have ever read: "The Final Reconciliation." This novella will catch your attention from the second Aidan reveals his fingernail-sized scars and won't let you go until you close the book and stare at the wall. The characters are fictitious, yes, but they're so very real. You'll be able to hear the beats of the music and be swept up in the delicious madness. The chapters themselves are presented as music tracks and that lends to an even more immersive experience. I wouldn't be surprised to find Todd himself standing behind you, strumming a guitar while you read. That's the type of personal and unsettling touch I've grown to expect from him. Most people look for monsters in their closet. After reading this collection, you'll imagine Todd tucked away behind your clean clothes, working diligently on his new book. This visual is equally comforting and terrifying.

I'm honored to write a foreword to a body of quality work that I found deeply enriching. Enjoy this now while Todd is still a relative newcomer to the scene. He won't remain our unknown gem for long. Soon his name will be everywhere and we'll have the pleasure of being readers, friends, and fans who knew him while he was still a secret treasure.

Mercedes M. Yardley
March 1st, 2017

A MAN IN YOUR GARDEN

There's a man in your garden. You're sure of it. You thought you saw him as you stumbled your way to the bathroom. What was it that made you look out the window? It's dark, raining, and the streetlight illuminates a billion water droplets across your corner of the block. Why would you dare look out on a night like this? No matter—you've looked already, and there's a man out there. You're sure of it.

You pause and look back at the window, trying to peer through the hazy stupor of a late night with friends, a late night at the bottom of not one bottle, but several. You look out, but now you can't see anything because you've changed placement. The dim hallway nightlight casts a reflective glow, but rather than try to find that magic place where you can see outside, you tell yourself it was your imagination, a phantom conjured from the tomb of sleep, given life by the bourbon soaking into your liver. You tell yourself it's just the booze whispering its wealth of dark secrets. It's just the curtain of sleep pulled oh so sharply away from your eyelids. All those ghosts summoned from the murky sludge of your mind.

So maybe there's nothing out there in your garden. No man.

No phantoms. No monsters. It's just you standing foolishly here at your window with a screaming bladder, so you do what you clumsily climbed out of bed to do. You wander into the bathroom and piss for a thousand years. Outside, the rain falls in heavy gusts, pattering against the glass of the tiny window over the toilet, and here in the dark, as you drain the last of your evening with friends, those beads of water look like bright, unblinking eyes. Millions of them, all staring back at you as they wriggle and slide across the glass like little slugs.

From outside, you're a pale face hidden in shadow, blanketed by a storm that rages forever. You're a lonely soul in a big, empty house. You went out with friends, hoping to return home with a warm body to keep you company for the night, the week, forever. Instead, you returned home alone, and now there's a man in your garden—

But there isn't. You tell yourself it was all a dream, that you were half-asleep as you stumble-walked down the hall. The shape was a trick of light and shadow, nothing more.

Awake now, your bladder quieted and empty, you decide that maybe you should eat something to soak up all that booze. Drinking always gave you an appetite, and though you know that you'll pay for it in the morning, the prospect of rummaging through your refrigerator is too enticing to pass up. You walk by the window again, refusing to look out this time because there is no man in the garden. And why would there be, anyway? It's just an old garden, one left by the previous owner, and you don't have a green thumb. You were going to tear up the old trellis and build a patio under the pergola. Maybe put one of those giant propane grills there instead of all those dead, withered plants.

So no, there's no one in the garden. No giant, hulking shape of a man, his neck as thick as a log, with arms tattooed like the fellow you pissed off at the bar while you were out with your friends. You're certain he wasn't there in your garden, looking up at you, the rain flattening his cropped, black hair. No, he wasn't there. Of course not. He was still at the bar, laughing and having a raucous good time, while your friends dragged you away.

Maybe it wasn't him. Maybe it was the guy you knew in college. The one whose tires you slashed because he slept with your girlfriend. He was big, too, just like the guy at the bar tonight. He never did figure out it was you. Not that it matters, really. That was fifteen years ago, and you haven't thought about him in nearly as long. You tell yourself you've lost your mind, shaking your head and snorting at your paranoia as you stumble downstairs to your tiny kitchen.

You stand at the sink and look outside, and—

Christ, there *is* a man in your garden. He's tall, broad-shouldered, built like a garbage truck, and could probably lift one too. He's got a clown mask over his face and an axe in his hand. He looks just like something from your nightmares. Not any recent nightmares, either, but the one from your childhood, when you were still in elementary school and your stepfather let you stay up late to watch that slasher film on TV. You can't remember if the film actually had any axe-wielding clowns, but you remember the nightmare, you remember the hulking monstrosity dragging the axe down the mirrored hallway of a funhouse, laughing hysterically while your legs refused to function, your bones suddenly gelatinous, rubbery, unable to support your body. You remember the teeth, the notch in the axe blade, the bloody red nose, the teeth, the piercing white eyes, you remember the teeth—*the teeth.*

Blinking, you realize you've been staring at the old trellis in your garden, and your throat is parched. You turn to the sink, reach into your cupboard, and fill a glass. You drink, washing down the metallic taste in the back of your mouth. Staring outside into the storm, you think the trellis doesn't look anything like that nightmare. You think, maybe, it looks more like a creature from one of your favorite horror novels. One of the slimy, slithery things with arms like ropes and snakes for a face, born from an ageless chasm beyond the scope of human understanding. A thing indescribable yet standing eight feet tall right there, *right there*, in your dying garden, its feet coiled with dead foliage.

A thing so indescribable, so impossible, it infects time and space. You think, maybe, it infects perception as well because you realize you're still standing at the sink, the water is still running, and there is nothing out in your dead garden except the old trellis, husks jutting across the failed flowerbed, withered old hands slick with rain and clutching for the sky to pull it down around you.

You blink, roll your eyes, and tell yourself to stop. You take another drink and shut off the faucet. The water gurgles as it rolls down the drain, and you reach for a towel to wipe your mouth. As you do, lightning shatters the sky, illuminating the entirety of your backyard, and there, standing not under your trellis but just beyond it at the edge of your garden, is the darkened shape of a person. Male or female, you can't tell, but it doesn't matter because there *is* someone in your garden. Your heart climbs into your throat and pulses so hard you can barely breathe. The shape is there, it's standing *right there*, and what is that in its hand? You can't tell, but it's certainly holding something, beckoning to you from beyond the safety of your home, daring you to step across the threshold into its domain.

This impossible phantom, this formless beast, it wants you to come outside. To come and play. And somehow, beyond all manner of reason, you decide you're going to. Never mind the games your imagination is playing with your head. Never mind the itchy fear lurking at the back of your throat, pushing you away from the backdoor and toward your phone to call the police, the fire department, the National Guard. No, dammit, it's time you make a stand and confront this intruder. How dare they climb your fence and trespass on your property. No, you'll show them. You'll make them sorry that they ever set foot in your domain.

Heart racing, your mind still clouded from the booze of a night with friends that seems as though it happened years ago, you step into a pair of flip-flops, grab the flashlight from the top of the refrigerator, and head out into the storm.

Rain beats at your face, punishing you for even thinking about stepping into the night, but you push on, into the garden. Grass and mud seep between your naked toes as you follow a pale beam across the yard toward the phantom shape. It's still there, refusing to move, defiant even now as you approach.

You clear your throat and raise the flashlight. The beam is filled with sheets of rain, each one a universe of tiny stars falling to earth in unison, and beyond the light is the shape, the intruder, standing before you.

As you prepare to speak, you realize you haven't thought this far ahead. What can you say? What should you say? So you blurt out the first thing to come to mind: *Can I help you?*

The intruding shadow says nothing, and for the first time, you realize your flashlight isn't illuminating its features. It's a void in the shape of a person, holding something in its blank hand. You raise your free hand to shield your eyes from the rain and discover you're shaking. Even on a warm summer night like this, you're freezing in the rain.

The shadow says nothing. You take another step. You say: *You need to leave!*

Another step. Another. You're nearly face to face with the shadow—and you realize it's just that. A shadow. There is no shape. No monster. No beast and no evil clown dredged from your nightmares.

Relieved, feeling extremely stupid, you chuckle to yourself and catch your breath. It's the booze. Of course it is. Why else would you be out in a storm like this, walking through the garden in the middle of the night?

Just before you turn, something catches your eye. A glint of light caught in the naked beam of the flashlight. Something metallic at your feet. You reach down and pick up the hatchet. There's a notch in the blade. You can't remember owning a hatchet, and even if you did, you wouldn't leave it lying in the grass to rust in the rain.

Confused, you turn back toward your house, and your heart stops. Upstairs in the window. A pale face pressed against the glass. Looking down at you.

Standing in the garden, you peer up at the intruder, wondering why they would dare look out on a night like this. You wonder what makes them think they can break into your house.

How dare they break into your home and trespass on your property. No, you'll show them. You'll make them sorry they ever set foot in your domain.

You frown, tributaries of rain running down the contours of your pale face.

It's a good thing you found this hatchet.

SHOW ME WHERE THE WATERS FILL YOUR GRAVE

The rain's come again, and this time Jonathan is ready. He's spent weeks preparing for this moment, days and nights glued to the fancy thin television his son bought him last year for Christmas, endless hours watching the pretty young lady on the weather station. He's learned to tune out the commercials and advertisements. Though his body is withered and spent, Jonathan Crosby's mind is still sharp. He still has his wits, knows how to define right from wrong, and determine safety from danger. He's cognizant of his choices and fully aware of their repercussions.

So today, when the weather alert buzzes across the screen in a thick red band, bisecting the pretty girl talking about the non-stop rains in the northeast, Jonathan doesn't pay attention. He doesn't have to. He knows he's in danger. The promise of doom and rainfall is what he's been waiting for all summer long.

Last time the waters along the river rose high enough, he was still submerged in a different kind of mire. Glenda's passing had filled his head with the worst kind of depression, the sort that seeped down into the roots of the heart and stayed there. She'd been gone less than a week, and he'd spent the following days in a kind of stupor, wandering the rooms of their house, noting the lack of color, the absence of warmth. His joints sang together in a chorus of misery, a funerary ode to the moisture in the air.

The rains had started the day after they buried her and did not stop for a full week. Insult to injury, he supposed. When the world lost a soul like Glenda, he figured that shedding a few tears was to be expected. God knew he'd wept for days; why shouldn't the world? Her absence had left an aching void in his life, an open wound of the spirit that would never truly heal. A wound that was always at risk of being pried open by the most innocent of queries from friends and strangers.

"How are you today, Jon?" was the most common. Their neighbor, Sarah, was the most recent perpetrator of such an infraction. Of course she was only making idle chatter. Of course her heart was in the right place. But oh, the pain, how it seeped back into that wound, festering with a different kind of infection that would take weeks to cleanse. Sarah didn't know any better. She was half his age, with a family of four to tend to, and wouldn't learn the agony of losing a spouse for some years yet. Lying to her was one of the hardest things he'd done that day, next to getting out of bed and wandering outside for the mail.

Those early days, he kept to himself as much as possible, a heartbroken hermit locked away in a cave of perpetual melancholy. Although Glenda was entombed just a few miles down the road, their house had become her memorial, and he was its caretaker. He forced himself to pick up her routines, dusting the mantle and framed photos hung on the walls, feeding their pet guppies in the aquarium, and making the weekly grocery trip every Tuesday morning.

A few weeks after the funeral, Sarah's husband, Donald, invited Jonathan over for dinner and beers. Jonathan acquiesced, mainly to stem the tide of their incessant requests, and over the course of the evening proceeded to drink a number of Donald's brews. By the time the sun had set, Jonathan was two sheets to the wind, as Glenda would say, and confessed to Donald that he was just biding his time.

"For what?" Donald asked.

"For the rains," Jonathan slurred. "Ain't you ever heard that old saying?"

Donald shook his head and finished off his beer. He crinkled the can in his fist. "What sayin's that, Jon?"

"Sorry, Don. I forget you didn't grow up here." Jonathan sloshed the last gulp of beer in the can, made to take that last drink, and then thought better of it. "This whole area's in a floodplain. When I was just a boy, the gang down at Miller's Bar where my daddy used to while away his evenings, they'd always joke around with me 'n say that you know it's rainin' rough when your grandma comes to visit."

"That's kinda grim for a joke, ain't it?"

Jonathan shook his head. "Those were different times. We weren't as sensitive to things then. Anyways, the first time I heard it, I asked my daddy what it meant, and he told me that the flood of aught-nine caused all the coffins to rise. Took 'em weeks to round up and sort out all the caskets."

Donald uttered a low chuckle that gave way to a belch. He excused himself and frowned as he put the pieces together. "So when you say you're waitin' for the rains… Aw, shit, Jon, I'm sorry."

"Nah, no need for that, Don. It's just the beer talkin'."

But it wasn't. Jonathan thought it was, but when the rains came again, they made a liar out of him.

To tell the truth, Jonathan hadn't given much thought to that old joke in decades. Not until the storms that followed Glenda's funeral. He was standing on his back porch and watching the world fall down in thick white sheets when the warning buzzed across his TV. The steady drum of raindrops on the porch roof masked the harsh buzz, and Jonathan almost didn't hear it. When he turned back and looked through the window at the red band on the screen, he sighed and shook his head. After four days of rain, the weather station's announcement was obvious: water levels were rising.

He closed his eyes and listened to the rapid beat of rain overhead. *God's playing the drums again.* Glenda always said that. Now that she was gone, he'd grown conscious of the way her words haunted his lexicon. She was a part of him even in speech, living on as a linguistic phantom that could not be exorcised. Not that he wanted her to be. Painful though it was, Jonathan took comfort in knowing she was still there somewhere, living on in his words. He need only speak to bring her back to him, if only for a fleeting moment.

"God's playing drums again," he whispered. "Signalin' your arrival to His kingdom, darlin'. I hope you're having a hell of a party."

He wondered if that was true. Sure, he was raised in church, but in his adult years, he'd wandered off the path. All that fire and brimstone didn't suit him—there was enough of it on the nightly news—and besides, he'd rather enjoy his time instead of dwelling on his transgressions. He and Glenda saw eye to eye on that matter, so they'd lived their lives the best they could. Now, though, Jonathan's imagination ran wild with possibilities. Was she watching him from heaven? Was she really up there, sitting on a cloud and laughing at every little thing he did while he waited his turn to shuffle off this coil?

A slow, cold sensation slithered into his gut, carrying with it an alternate thought. *What if she isn't up there?* he wondered. *What if she isn't anywhere? What if she's just gone? What if…*

"Stop it," he told himself. The truth was, he had no way of knowing, and he was better off not dwelling on it. Easier said than done, maybe, but he didn't have much of a choice but to try.

He locked away those troubling thoughts and leaned forward against the porch railing, watching the churning waters of the river slowly surge and creep over their banks. Most folks would've found the rising waters to be cause for concern, but not Jonathan. He and Glenda had lived in their home for over thirty years before she passed, and not once in that time had the waters ever reached their foundation. The rising tide would break at the foot of his driveway, just like it had all the other years.

He watched until late evening when, in the failing light, he saw the river had crept high enough over the bank to kiss the edge of the road. By that point, the winds had picked up, slapping the branches from one of Glenda's dogwoods against the siding and reminding him that they needed trimming. He'd forgotten to do that this year, preoccupied with his wife's illness.

It'll keep until the storm passes, he thought, listening to the steady clap of limbs and pitter-patter of rain. *Maybe tomorrow. Couple days at most.* His vigil concluded, Jonathan turned away from the porch railing and retreated into his house.

Satisfied, his joints aching from the damp air, Jonathan curled up on the sofa and took his evening deluge of prescription pills. Cholesterol, arthritis (one for inflammation, one for pain), thyroid, and the latest to join an all-star cast: anxiety. He'd kept this last one a secret from Glenda in the final months of her life. She was already down on herself; he didn't want to burden her with his stress. "Just something to take the edge off," he'd told his doctor. "Until this ride is over."

The ride had ended, but Jonathan was still hanging on. He liked being leveled out. The pills made the nights a bit easier to bear.

He washed them down with a mug of cold coffee, lowered the volume on the TV, and wrapped one of Glenda's handmade blankets around him. He hadn't slept in their bed since she'd passed, couldn't bring himself to do so. Sleeping there seemed wrong somehow, as if the act might disturb some sacred oath he'd sealed with her in her passing. That if they could not lie there together in union, so shall the bed remain cold and empty, a monument to the time they spent together as husband and wife. And beneath that sense of marital duty, Jonathan supposed it just hurt too goddamn much.

Another weather update buzzed from the television, but he didn't bother reading it. Instead, he reclined on the sofa, closed his eyes, and listened to God play drums.

He waits at the bottom of the stairs, dressed in his Sunday best while reports of a perfect storm creep into the foyer. "Seek higher ground," they say. "If you need assistance—"

But Jonathan tunes out the meteorologist, focusing instead on his silver cufflinks. They're miniature books, a gift from Glenda on his thirtieth birthday.

"*Because you love reading,*" she'd said, "*and because you lost your old pair.*"

Jonathan traces his thumb across the smooth rectangle and smiles. The last time he wore them was at her funeral. The same as his suit, as a matter of fact, and for a moment, he wonders if his attire isn't appropriate for the occasion. After all, a three-piece suit and tie isn't practical when dealing with rising floodwaters, but he reminds himself that today is special. Concessions must be made in the face of extraordinary situations.

Elsewhere, the pretty weather lady says to expect another surge of rainfall by noon, with no signs of slowing down by nightfall.

He checks his watch.

Jonathan smiles. Not long now.

Three slow knocks woke him from his sleep. The first knock was loud enough to rouse him from his slumber—a troubled sleep of dark dreams filled with lily pads and koi fish and a cluster of small hands lurking beneath the surface. The second knock pulled him through the twilit veil of sleep into a world of consciousness.

Jonathan opened his eyes and stared at the ceiling. The room was filled with the bluish light of dawn, the sun just a promise beyond the horizon. Had he dreamed those two knocks? Could they have been the rain? He held his breath and waited, listening. The rain had stopped, the winds finally quieted, and the earth was still around him.

Just a dream, he thought, and closed his eyes.

The third knock came at last. Jonathan sat up, rubbed the sleep from his eyes, and squinted at his watch. Not even 5 A.M. Who the hell could it be at this hour?

He climbed to his feet, ignoring the fire in his joints and the urge to take his pills. They could wait. This stranger at the door, however, could not. Someone knocking on his door at this hour would have a good reason. They could be hurt. They might need help.

As he stumbled across the living room to the foyer, his mind raced with possibilities of who it might be or what might be wrong. He thought of his neighbors, Sarah and Donald and their two little ones. Had the waters risen too high in the night? His house's foundation sat at a slightly higher elevation, only by a few inches, but those inches could make all the difference in a flood.

Jonathan resisted the urge to peek out the window. Instead, he twisted the deadbolt and opened the door.

The floodwaters crested just beyond the edge of his driveway and were already receding, a dark oily border illuminated in the dawn by a pale streetlight overhead. The water, however, was not what held his attention.

The woman in his driveway wore a sapphire evening gown with jewels sewn into the trim. She shimmered when she moved, the jewels reflecting the light overhead, enhancing the curls of wet, silvery hair draped over her shoulders. The hem of her gown fell at an angle just below her knees, revealing pale legs that had danced the nights away in their younger days. Her bare feet slapped across the water as she approached his doorstep.

"I was wondering if you'd answer, love."

Jonathan's knees gave out, and he collapsed at the threshold. "Glenda..." Words failed him, their syllables like dry air through empty cornhusks. "Why...h-how...?"

Glenda Crosby tiptoed along the pavement of their driveway. A slow trickle of water followed behind her, an inky black umbilicus stretching back to the ebbing tide below the drive. The longer he watched, the less Jonathan could tell which direction the water flowed. The dark stream followed her footsteps, surging forward in time to her movement, his queen marching along a wet carpet of foam and errant leaves caught in the tumult of the night's storm.

She paused where the sidewalk met the driveway. The water stretched thin, barely more than a trickle at that distance. Her safety rope would let her go no farther; he would have to meet her halfway.

Jonathan remained on his knees, befuddled by what he was seeing, his eyes encased in tears. How was this possible? How could she be standing here when she was buried over in Morningside? Was this a dream? A phantom? Any possible answers were swept away in the maelstrom raging within his head, his heart.

"Don't weep, my darling."

Now that she was closer, he could hear the lilt in her voice, a gentle rise in pitch that might accompany a tickle in one's throat. The sound of talking when water's gone down the wrong pipe. His mind flashed with the image of a gutter spout clogged with twigs and acorns, and he cleared his own throat instinctively. His mouth filled with phlegm, but he resisted the urge to spit it out. Grimacing, he swallowed back the filth.

"Glenda," he said finally, bracing himself against the doorframe before climbing to his feet. His knees sang together in a chorus of damp agony. "This can't be. I watched the life go out of you. I watched them put you in the ground, for Christ's sake."

A smile spread across her damp, pale face. She held out her arms. "And yet here I am, my darling. Come to me."

He took one step across the threshold onto the sidewalk but couldn't bring himself to take another. *No, he reminded himself, everything is wrong about this. Glenda's dead and buried, Jon. She can't be here.*

She lowered her head and peered up at him. That look made his heart flutter. Her bedroom gaze. He'd teased her about it for years, when they were still young and virile. Even after their son grew up and moved out, she still gave him the stare from time to time. "*I'm yours,*" it told him. "*And you're mine.*"

Staring into her sapphire eyes, Jonathan felt compelled to join her. And why not? The one thing he'd desired most—to be with Glenda once again—had been granted to him. He'd won some sort of cosmic lottery, the recipient of a gifted miracle of nature. His wife, once deceased, now stood mere feet away from him, awaiting his embrace. How he'd longed for her, to hear her voice again, to hold her hand. All the nights he'd slept without her, even before her passing, raced back to him in that moment. Every night without her touch was another quiet reassurance from reality, a coarse blanket pulled over him that was too scratchy, too short to truly bring him any comfort. He feared those nights would define the rest of his life. One lonely evening of depression would bleed into the next, counting down to the day that he, too, would wither and fade away into the great big nothing beyond.

But now, somehow, beyond all hope and reason, here she was again. And she was waiting for him. Beckoning for him. Yearning.

"Come to me," she said. "Dance with me one last time."

And he wanted to. God, how he wanted to, his aching knees be damned. He took one step across the threshold, and then another.

Glenda turned away and gazed up at the side of their home. She smiled faintly. "You forgot to trim the dogwood again, love."

Jonathan choked back a humorless laugh. There was nothing funny about her statement; quite the contrary, her words all but confirmed that what he saw before him was truly happening. Only Glenda would give him grief about those damn branches. His heart climbed into his throat. "Is it really you?"

She looked back at him, reached out, and took his hand. Her skin was wet, cold, and touching her gave him goosebumps.

"Dance with me," she whispered, and leaned in to kiss him.

He's drifted off to sleep when Donald pounds on the door. The sound startles him so bad he bumps his head against the staircase banister. Dark, muted colors explode before his eyes as he clamors to regain his composure, pressing his hand against the back of his skull to dull the pain.

"Jon? You in there, old man?"

Old man. He hates when Donald calls him that, even if the name is apropos. Grimacing, with one hand clasped to his head, Jonathan staggers forward and opens the door. Donald peers up at him from beneath his poncho's hood. The rain's coming down so hard he can barely hear his neighbor's voice.

"Didn't you hear the emergency siren? The whole neighborhood's being evacuated. We gotta go." Donald pauses, confused by the old man's attire, and for a moment, there is a flash of understanding on his face. Jonathan can see the young man's epiphany through the downpour, tinged with a hint of sadness. *He thinks I've gone senile.*

"Yeah, I heard it," Jonathan says. "You get your family out of here. I'm staying. Go on."

He's about to close the door, but Donald holds out his hand to stop him, and for a moment, Jonathan sees red. He sees himself slamming the door in his neighbor's face. He wants to growl and shout and tell Donald to mind his business, but the anger is displaced in an instant as the shrill horn of Donald's SUV tears through the storm.

"Don't make me leave you here, Jon." Donald turns back and waves to his family in their vehicle. It's time to go. Past time, really. Jonathan can see the water is almost to the edge of his driveway. *Just like last time,* he thinks, and struggles to contain his smile.

"You aren't leaving me. This is my choice, Donald. Go take care of your family. It's your duty."

Jonathan makes to close the door, and this time Donald slams his palm against the barrier to stop him.

"She isn't coming back, Jon. Your duty is to keep living. So help me—"

Donald doesn't finish his sentence. He's stunned into silence by the barrel of Jonathan's revolver, held a mere six inches from his face.

Jonathan keeps his head, maintaining an even tone and a poker face to match. He clears his throat, licks his lips, and speaks steadily: "I know what my duty is, young man. Now I'm giving you until the count of three to get the fuck off my doorstep. One. Two."

He doesn't get to three. Donald steps back with his hands held out, either in defeat or confusion, Jonathan will never know. He opens his mouth to speak but thinks better of it, offering Jonathan one more glance before turning away and sloshing back across the yard.

Jonathan watches long enough to see Donald climb into his SUV and drive his family to safety. He places the revolver—a gift from his daddy, many moons ago—back into his pocket, and reminds himself to load it. Glancing up at the dark clouds overhead and the sheets of rain pouring down from them, Jonathan smiles. Soon, now.

Soon, he can do his duty too.

Glenda led him down the driveway toward the waterline, her damp hand slick in his, their fingers entwined in a lover's knot.

"Dance with me," she said again, and this time he didn't protest. He was so lost in her eyes and her leaking smile that he didn't notice when she stepped onto the surface of the churning waves. Sickly yellow foam collected around the tops of her pale feet as she walked, and Jonathan had taken three steps with her before he realized that he, too, was suspended above the surface. *Another miracle*, he thought dreamily, but the act of walking on water was nowhere near as fantastic as Glenda's reappearance.

Somewhere in the back of his mind, Jonathan supposed this was a dream. This was the only way it all made sense. People didn't come back from the dead. Not since Jesus, by his count, had anyone truly come back from the dead. Glenda had been in the ground for six days at that point, twice as long as their savior, and he suspected that if they were to walk the waters all the way to her grave, they would find the headstone undisturbed.

Because this was a dream, he reasoned. Because this wasn't really happening.

Glenda pirouetted on the water, her soaked dress flapping behind her like a limp tail. She came to rest before him and laughed. Water trickled down from the corners of her mouth.

"Do you remember the steps? One-two-three?"

He placed his hand on the small of her back, and took her other hand in his. "I remember enough, I think."

Years ago, in the months leading up to their wedding, Jonathan took a series of dancing classes with Glenda. He was never a fan of dancing, had never had the rhythm for it, really, but Glenda insisted he learn the basics for their wedding. "I want to dance with my husband," she told him with her bedroom eyes, and how could he say no to that? He took those lessons and learned enough to get by, but he never did feel comfortable enough to say he enjoyed dancing. The night of their wedding, he stepped on her feet twice, but she just laughed at his embarrassment, slowly turning in time to Etta James singing 'At Last'.

"I can't fault you," she later said, after they'd made love in their hotel room. "I've seen you try to drive a stick shift. You're not much better at that, either."

She was right. Jonathan never did have much rhythm, but after her passing, he would've learned to tango if it meant being with her another day.

Later, Jonathan supposed the miracle of her resurrection wasn't the only miracle God handed out that day. For the first time since their wedding night, Jonathan danced again. He only stepped on her feet once, but he didn't care, and she didn't seem to mind. They had no audience in the dawn. There was only them and the flood, the detritus from the road and ditches, and a low breeze roiling the waters beyond the tree line.

She led him in the dance, the water spilling over the feet as they moved in counts of three. Jonathan tried not to question the logic of walking on water—after all, he was dancing upon the surface with his deceased wife. Instead, he tried to enjoy the moment and privilege to be with her once again, no matter how fleeting it was. If he was meant to wake from this dream soon, then he would enjoy it for as long as he could even if he knew the memories would haunt him for years to come. The worst dreams always did.

They danced along the surface, first across the road to the river and then along the shoreline. Glenda kept time for them both, humming a tune he didn't recognize. Every now and then, the air in her throat would catch, punctuating her song with a seeping gurgle of water and phlegm. Jonathan didn't mind the noise. He'd spent nearly a year listening to her hack up the remains of her lungs after the chemotherapy had done its damage. She was choked on the water, was all. Why wouldn't she be? Her grave was no doubt flooded.

A low fog creeped along the surface of the water, silhouetted against fragments of morning light poking through the canopy of gray clouds. Those thin sunbeams fell upon both of them, and in that moment, Jonathan saw the faint trickle of water dribbling from the corner of her lips, down the side of her cheek. When she leaned in close to him to put her chin on his shoulder, he glimpsed something else slipping out of her mouth: a black, viscous sludge.

Embalming fluid, maybe. He wasn't sure what else they pumped into her body at the mortuary. An assortment of chemicals for preservation, perhaps. Who was he to judge the finer intricacies of coming back to life?

But something about that thick, licorice blackness made a part of him grow cold. Glenda sensed his unease, pulling back long enough to look him in the eye.

"Is something wrong, my darling?"

"Nothing, dear." He looked away, already knowing that she knew better, but too ashamed to say anything on the contrary. "Hold on to me. Don't ever let go."

Glenda smiled, tightened her grip on him. "Never." She leaned in, put her chin on his shoulder once more, and he felt himself go ten degrees colder. The whole world around them had dropped in temperature. Jonathan peered out over the surface of the river at the rolling fog bank. Glenda was leading them right for it.

Later, after he'd collapsed on the doorstep of his home, Jonathan would recall that it was the fog that woke him from her spell and made him realize he wasn't dreaming. The cold moisture in the air made his knees scream. Until the drop in temperature, he hadn't noticed their stark agony; he'd been too lost in Glenda's emergence to think of much else. Now, though, the cold was what sobered him up, and he gasped at the sudden jolt of pain shooting down his legs.

He was about to ask if they could stop and sit for a spell when Glenda spoke: "We're almost there, my darling. Not far now."

"Where are we going?" he grimaced.

"To my grave. Where the waters are waiting."

The mere thought of that empty hole in the ground made him shiver. His whole body quaked, and she squeezed closer to him, yet her body offered no warmth. She was soaked through to the bone, her pruning skin like congealing fat on an old hunk of meat left out to spoil. In a warmer climate, Jonathan was certain that flies would've accompanied their dark, impossible dance across the surface of the flooded river.

"I… Glenda, honey, I need to rest a moment. My knees—you know how bad they get."

"Shhh," she said. "I'm so cold there in the deep, my darling. When the waters fill my grave, I get so cold. Won't you keep me warm?"

Her voice was almost apologetic, as if she could not help herself despite what came next.

Jonathan turned for the shore and tried to pull away from her grip but found he couldn't. Her pruned fingers clasped around him like handcuffs, and when he met her gaze again, her blue eyes did not greet him.

Black slime leaked from her sockets, mingling with a twin stream gushing out her nose. The skin around her face sagged, and for one horrifying moment, Jonathan realized that this thing was wearing his darling Glenda's face as a mask. He screamed, a hoarse cry for help that sounded too thin, too distant for anyone to hear.

The cold fog inched closer, threatening to envelop them. Jonathan pulled once more, resisting his late wife's grip.

"Keep us warm in the deep," the Glenda-thing gurgled at him. Flecks of that blackened ichor spotted his cheeks. Jonathan struggled to find his footing and brace himself against her, only to find that he had no footing to gain. He was slowly sinking into the depths of the river, the freezing waters thick, gelatinous, a sudden bog in the middle of a churning stream.

A sandbar, he thought. *Just get out of this mess, Jon. Just—*

He looked down. What he saw aged him by a decade, maybe more. His heart paused for a full beat before painfully chugging to catch up with itself.

Hands.

Dozens—no, hundreds of bloated hands reached up from the depths of the river, their fingers entwined with the tendrils of the looming fogbank. They clamored for him, gripping his shoes, pulling at his pant legs, dragging him down to the dark depths of the floodwaters inch by cold, agonizing inch.

He twisted around, back to the Glenda-thing to make a desperate plea for his life, and discovered that her form was collapsing into itself. Her face dripped like warm wax, slowly melting into a dark blob that sank into her torso. Within seconds she was nothing more than a puddle of the black ooze, oily and dispersing into the roiling waters before him.

"No," he cried as the hands slowly pulled him down. "No, Glenda, no!"

Jonathan struggled against them, fighting against the pain singing in his knees to lift one leg. Just one. Just enough to break free.

One-two-three, he thought, only he heard Glenda's voice in his head. *You remember how to count, don't you, darling? Keep the rhythm. There's nothing to it.*

He leaned forward, clenched his teeth, and flailed his arms into the water, pulling himself against the current. Still the hands pulled, yanking and pinching at him, pulling at his groin, his thighs, seeking any piece of him that could be held, gripped, and dragged down to them. For an instant, he speculated what might be at the other end of those bloated limbs, but the impossible things that stretched out from his imagination made him go numb. Instead, he focused his efforts on freeing himself and swimming to safety.

Jonathan slowly lifted one leg, crying out in pain as the tendons around his swollen knees flared and sang a tune. As he did, he pulled one arm toward him, then the other. He kicked his other leg, pushing off the cluster of hands beneath the surface. Still they gripped him, but less so, and slowly—*one-two-three, that's it darling, keep your rhythm*—moment by moment, Jonathan freed himself from their pull.

One of his shoes came off in their grip. A disappointed sigh breathed across the water's surface. The hands pulled his second shoe free from his foot, and he shot forward into the current. A cold wave slapped his face, stealing his breath for a precious second. *You're free, darling. Keep going. One-two-three.*

Jonathan swam. He swam harder and faster than he'd ever done before, his weak knees be damned, his old heart racing so hard he feared he might die of an attack right there in the river. *Wouldn't that be something*, he thought idly, *to drown after all this?*

But no such thing happened that day. Jonathan reached the shore, collapsing at the foot of his flooded driveway in time to watch the sun break through the overcast sky. The fog on the river had dispersed by then, and though the temperature had risen a few steady degrees, he found he could not keep warm. Out there on the water, he glimpsed a cluster of darkened, bloated hands for just a moment before their fingers slipped slowly beneath the waves.

Somewhere beneath the surface, he knew, Glenda was there. For the second time in his life, he'd lost his wife, and when the realization struck him, Jonathan Crosby turned away from the river and sobbed.

Jonathan waits at the foot of his stairs, ruminating on that bizarre morning after the flood four years ago. He runs his hand over the curves of the revolver. Every day since, he's watched the weather, waiting for the moment when the weather is right.

Every night since, he's suffered from dreams of drowning, of Glenda returning to drag him down to the cold stillness of her grave. He can't bring himself to visit her anymore. The last time he went to the cemetery was after the flood, to make sure she was still there and that her casket hadn't floated to the surface. It hadn't, of course. Deep down, he knew that thing that led him out to the water wasn't his wife, but the promise of her return—oh, it's too much to bear now. He prefers not to dwell on such things.

Instead, Jonathan passes his time watching the weather. He waits for a day just like today, when the rains will not let up. He waits for the conditions to be right. And when the sky opens up to let loose the furies of heaven, he remains steadfast in his resolve.

After he turns Donald away, the waters continue to rise, reaching record heights by mid-afternoon.

He doesn't know what she really was, or why he was chosen to be her prey. He wonders if maybe there's more to that story his daddy told him about the flood of aught-nine, but he will never know. Daddy's long gone, for decades now, and all that's left is speculation on Jonathan's part.

So Jonathan waits. He sits at the foot of his stairs and watches the floodwaters rise high enough to trickle under the doorway. He looks at the revolver in his hand, runs his thumb along the length of the barrel, and wonders if she really was Glenda. And if she was, can he do what he needs to do? Can he do his duty and put his wife to rest?

He waits, and the waters stream into his home.

He waits. There's a knock at the door. *One-two-three.*

He smiles.

The rain's come again, and this time Jonathan is ready.

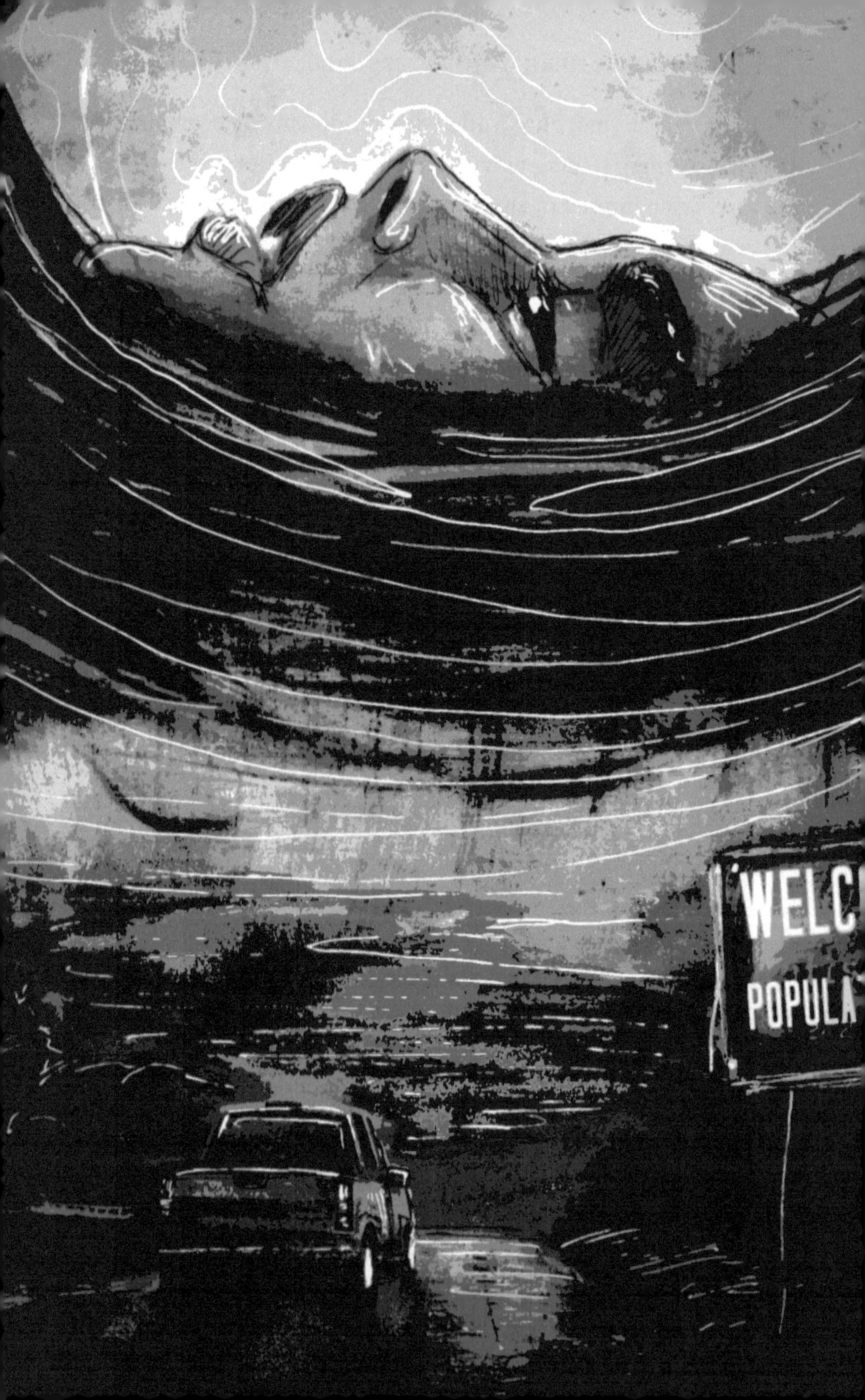

WELC
POPULA

RADIO FREE NOWHERE

"What about this one?"

Conrad paused the radio scan, settling on a country station. Ashley clenched her fingers around the steering wheel and shot him a quick scowl before returning her eyes to the highway.

"I didn't realize you had a death wish, Connie."

He shook his head and held out his hands in defeat. "Come on, Ash. You don't like Top 40. You don't like country. You don't like *classic* rock. You're not leaving us much choice."

"Relax," she said, grinning. "And that's not fair—I do like classic rock. Everybody likes classic rock."

"Yeah, but we're driving through Radio Free Nowhere right now. It's a goddamn dead zone. We'll be lucky to pick up anything between these mountains." He tapped his knuckle against the window. "So if I've gotta suffer through this shit, you should too. *I'm* not the one who forgot the iPod."

He had a point, but she didn't think he had to know that. Truth was, she enjoyed driving in silence, listening to nothing but the hum of the engine and tires on the road. They were six hours into their road trip, having just crossed over into West Virginia courtesy of

I-68, and still had another eight hours to go. She would've been content with spending the entire trip in silence if Connie would let her, but he insisted on making playlists for the drive.

Playlists he wouldn't have a chance to broadcast. Her iPod was sitting at the back of a drawer in her bedroom. She knew this because she put it there. Connie was a sweet guy and she cared about him—maybe even loved him, but let's not be hasty about things. And yet he had terrible taste in music.

The country station's pop and twang gave way to static interjected with commentary from another station bleeding through the airwaves. She smirked.

"So much for that."

"That's enough out of you, smartass." Conrad seemed angry, but when she glanced to her right she saw he was smiling, and she felt better about leaving the iPod. He twisted the radio dial. "If only we had one of those satellite receivers."

"You know," she began, "you could always try the AM band. Maybe listening to those holy rollers would do you some good, you godless heathen."

He put his hand on her thigh and gave her a light squeeze. A pleasant chill worked its way down the back of her leg. "What, because we're living in sin? Baby, if sleeping with you is wrong, then I don't want to be right. Send me to the lake of fire—at least I'll go with a big smile on my face."

Ashley laughed, her cheeks flush with a sudden heat. *Eyes on the road*, she told herself. She lifted Conrad's hand and put it back on his lap.

"Down, tiger. Wait until we get to a hotel."

"You're no fun, lady."

"I'm plenty fun and you know it. Why don't you check the GPS and find us a place to stop for the night?"

A smile slowly spread across Conrad's face. "I like the way you think," he said.

Conrad was still fiddling with the GPS when they pulled off the highway for gas an hour later. They drove for a few miles into the wilderness, following promises of a BP station back at the exit ramp. The gas station emerged before them like a petroleum oasis in a desert of trees, and when Ashley saw the gas pumps she breathed a sigh of relief. The fuel gauge teetered on empty. Getting stranded out here was the last thing she wanted.

Ashley parked alongside one of the pumps and shut off the car. She yawned and blinked away her fatigue, wondering how truckers managed to drive for such long hours.

"This damn thing…"

"Still no luck?"

He shook his head. "No. There's something wrong with it. Like it picks up a signal but it won't give me directions to anywhere but the destination. Everything's locked out."

Ashley took the device and pecked at the screen, but it remained frozen on the map, outlining their path in purple.

"Weird," she said, handing the GPS back to him. She opened the door and climbed out. "Keep trying. You have better luck with gadgets than I do."

"No shit," he mumbled, tapping heavily at the screen. "I don't need you to lose this too."

"I heard that."

She was filling up the car when she heard the music, a gentle tune carried on the back of a soft breeze. The trees rustled, and her hair was blown back over her shoulders. That faint sound tickled her ears, a light melody hummed by a voice too far away to be just a whisper, and yet its singer could have been no further than a few feet away. Ashley turned, surveying the parking lot and expecting to see another car with its windows down and radio on, but they were alone.

The soft music lilted along the air for just a moment longer before the breeze died, its abrupt end accented by the loud clunk of the gas pump shutting off. She screwed on the gas cap and made her way into the station.

"Evenin', miss."

The attendant tipped his hat and leered at her. He was middle-aged by the look of him, with a patch of silver stubble covering up dry, leathery skin.

"Pump two," she said, placing two bills on the counter. When the attendant turned toward the register, she noticed a yellow ear plug stuffed into his ear.

"Here's your change, miss. And a little somethin' else, too." He slid a few singles and a packet of ear plugs toward her. She looked at him for a moment, unsure of what to say. "Go on," he said, "take 'em. On the house. You ain't from around these parts, so it's best you wear 'em."

"I don't—"

That faint music rose up in the station, bursting out of the speakers with a hiss of static. She could hear the music more clearly this time, its steady beat more pronounced with the old-time swagger of a piano tune, and the achingly sweet voice of a woman singing in a language she'd never heard before.

The leathery attendant nodded. "As I was sayin', darlin', you best put those in yer ears. Some people go a little funny if they listen fer too long." He twirled his index finger beside his ear. "That purdy lady'll lead you places where you don't belong. There ain't no light down in that murk."

But Ashley wasn't listening. She was too caught up in the sound, trying to decipher the beautiful language enunciated by its singer's silky voice. Outside she could only hear a ghost of that melody, but in here the sound was given flesh, its tune agonizingly vivid.

"Miss?"

She blinked, realizing for the first time that she was crying. The attendant only smiled at her and pointed to his ear plugs.

"As I's sayin', you'd do best to put 'em in."

"But…why? It's beautiful. It's—"

The attendant shrugged, suddenly dejected by her inquiry. He snatched the ear plugs off the counter. "Suit yerself. Take yer change, lady. And don't say I didn't warn ya. I hear the water's quite fine this time of year anyways."

Ashley scooped up her change and shoved it into her pocket. She left the station in a daze, carrying that haunting melody in her head while trying to work out the singer's puzzling language. Conrad set down the GPS when she climbed back into the car.

"Damn thing's busted," he said. "Fuckin' Garmin. I tried every—hey, are you all right?"

She looked at him, puzzled. "What do you mean?"

"You're pale and—" He leaned over, frowning. "Honey, you're crying. What happened in there? Did someone say something to you?"

Ashley shook her head. "No, Connie." She put her hand on his cheek and smiled. "I just heard a beautiful song, that's all. I'll try to find it on the radio. I want you to hear it."

Conrad gave her a hard stare while chewing his bottom lip. "You're sure nothing's wrong?"

"I'm sure. Let's go find us a place to stop for the night."

They followed the road back through the forest and found the highway once more. Conrad kept toying with the GPS, too focused on the device's stubbornness to notice Ashley's preoccupation with the radio. She twisted the dial, searching the stations, looking for that wonderful song. Thirty miles after leaving the gas station, she set the radio to scan and left it there, humming what she could recall of the tune while the evening sun extinguished itself behind the mountains.

They were on the road for more than an hour without seeing a sign for a hotel, and aside from the occasional tractor trailer, their car was the only one on the highway. Conrad stirred in his seat, snoring. Ashley leaned back and yawned.

The GPS startled her with its chime, directing her to take the next exit ramp on the right. Ashley glanced down at the device, frowning at the purple line veering off into the cartographic wilderness. She was about to reach down and tap the screen when the radio locked onto a station awash with interference. Static swarmed the car.

"Turn that down," Conrad mumbled. Shaking, Ashley reached out to turn down the volume when—

Yes. The song. There it was again, clearer than it had been inside the gas station, rich with sound, and full of even more instrumental accompaniment. And there, bellowing over that music, was that blessed singer's soulful voice, silky-smooth and crooning unknown words that filled Ashley's heart to its brim. Tears clouded her vision, and she blinked them away just as the GPS chimed the turn-off.

Ashley wiped the tears from her cheeks and flipped on her turn signal. She guided the car down the exit ramp, wondering only for a moment why the device was leading them off the highway before the song reached its crescendo, the singer belting out a cry that bordered on orgasmic. Ashley brought the car to a stop at the bottom of the ramp, sobbing into her hands as her heart continued to ache.

The song slowed, fading off into white noise before beginning again, its lulling notes building up to that mysterious singer's first few bars. Ashley thought about waking Conrad so he could hear the song's beauty, but he was resting so peacefully in his seat. And why bother waking him? She knew he wouldn't appreciate that beautiful voice or the subtle nuances of the backing band. No, she would let him sleep and keep the secret of the siren's song to herself.

The car's headlights pierced the shadows ahead, illuminating an empty two-lane road that curled its way around a mountain. Ashley drove with the radio off and the window down. The static was distracting, and besides, she was so close to the source now she could hear the music in the wind. The song was louder, gaining volume as they snaked their way along the road's curves. Her heart thudded to the rhythm and her chest swelled with each chorus, those strange words punctuating the cool night with a bittersweet warmth. Even the crickets were silent, allowing the siren to grace their stage.

Ashley wondered what she was singing about. The GPS chimed once more for her to take a left at an upcoming junction, and a glance at the small screen revealed she would find out soon enough. Their destination was just a few more miles away.

She slowed the car and turned left down a gravel road, forging a path into the dark, filled to the brim with a dangerous sort of wonder. Every muscle ached and her head pounded, but oh God, did she need to get to the source of that beautiful voice. Nothing else mattered.

The lake stretched out before them, its shores lined with the cars and trucks of other lucky listeners. The moon shimmered on those gentle waters, looking back at her like a single, pale eye. *Come*, it said, *cleanse yourself, child. Baptize yourself with the siren's voice.*

Ashley parked the car and got out. She didn't bother closing the door, fearing the noise might wake Conrad. She glanced back at him, yearning for his touch, some part of her resisting the song that played overhead like the voice of God. She heard herself cry out, telling herself to wake up, but the song kept playing and that singer's voice was *so* beautiful and serene.

She turned toward the lake, slipped off her shoes, and waded into those murky waters.

Conrad woke in the low light of dawn. He sat up, cringing at his stiff neck, and took a moment to get his bearings. Their car was parked between two old, rusty trucks. Beyond was the shore of a lake, its body obscured by a hazy fog, and the sky was overcast.

The driver door was open.

"Ash?" He sat up and unbuckled his seat belt. "Ashley? Where the hell are we?"

He became aware of a low, subtle drone permeating the air. The noise made his head hurt. He turned, surveying the shore of the lake. Hundreds of cars were parked along the water, some old, some new. All were abandoned.

"Ashley?" His voice echoed across the water, accompanied by the slow lapping of the waves. "This isn't funny. What are we doing in this place?"

"Beautiful, isn't it?"

He turned toward her voice, and when he saw her, his stomach tumbled to the ground. Ashley emerged from the lake. She was naked except for strands of a black sludge that wrapped around her arms, between her breasts, and curled down between her legs. Open sores dotted her forehead, and when she smiled at him, one of her incisors dropped to the dirt.

Conrad's gut lurched again, and he was torn between running *to* her and running *away* from her.

"What—what happened? What did you do?"

"The siren told me you wouldn't hear it," she said, lurching forward with one bloated hand stretched out to him. "You always had bad taste in music, Connie. But that's okay. We forgive you."

Dark hands emerged from the water, groping the air, clenching, eager for something to grip. Conrad reached out and took her hand.

"We have to get you to a hospital." He was crying now, unable to process what had happened. He was so lost in his sorrow that he didn't feel Ashley's hold on his arm. Not at first. He turned to her, recoiling as one of her eyes slipped from its socket.

"I'd rather stay. Come take a dip with me," she said, tightening her grip. An army of bloated, darkened hands rose from the water, beckoning to them, and Conrad began to scream. Ashley smiled. "The water's fine this time of year."

THE OTHERLAND EXPRESS

Gregory Simmons was nearly asleep when his iPod battery died. He looked away from the window and frowned. Without music, there was nothing to keep the Greyhound's ambience at bay. He could already hear the other passengers murmuring to themselves over the engine's white noise.

He'd left his charger back at his old man's place. The AC adapter was still plugged into the wall socket next to his bed, one of the few belongings he'd left behind in haste, and he didn't have enough cash left to buy a new one.

So much for that. He coiled his earbuds, stuffed the iPod into his backpack, and leaned his head against the window, watching as the world rolled past in a darkened blur. Miles away, lightning arced across a cloudbank, turning the hills into silhouettes and his thoughts into fears.

What if his old man came after him? Unlikely, but plausible. Then again, Gregory doubted his old man had even noticed he was gone. These days, the only time Eddie Simmons paid his son any attention was when he wanted a beer or when he wanted something to beat on.

Light from a passing car filled the cabin, and for an instant, Gregory saw his reflection in the glass. The bruises were still fresh, but the swelling had gone down. That was good. People wouldn't be so keen to notice or stare. The last thing he needed was for some Good Samaritan to ask if he was okay, where was he going, where were his parents, and so on.

In Gregory's rush to escape from his father's apartment, he'd not given much thought to a cover story should a stranger inquire about his travels. "Traveling to visit my mom" seemed too cliché; "Traveling to my mom's funeral" was far more accurate even if it was just a few years too late. Both stories made his heart hurt for the same reason.

No one bothered to ask though. It was a fact that might have irritated him under different circumstances, but today he was grateful for the anonymity. Today, he was a seventeen-year-old nobody, just another kid with fresh bruises on the run from the bad cards life had dealt him. A couple hundred miles back, his father was probably arriving home with a fresh buzz from the bar, the old bastard's knuckles still raw, ignorant of Gregory's absence or the money missing from beneath his mattress.

His father's drunken slurs echoed in his head: *Should'a kicked yer ass out years ago, ya worthless punk! Yer a parasite, that's what you are. A worthless faggot parasite.*

The old man's words always did more harm than his fists, but years of suffering through both had tempered Gregory's wits, and he wouldn't let himself be frightened into returning home. Eddie Simmons crossed a line this time, and Gregory had had enough.

A bolt of lightning lit up the night, fracturing the skyline into a thousand jagged pieces. Gregory's bruised reflection stared back from the window, and he was about to turn away when something else caught his eye: the reflection of a man sitting in the seat across the aisle. He was staring at Gregory.

Or *was* he? Gregory couldn't tell, and the lightning had ceased by the time he looked over his shoulder. There was only a bus filled with shadows, its occupants marked as silhouettes against the glare of headlights from passing cars. The man across the aisle turned his head slightly and offered a short nod.

Gregory returned the nod instinctively, more as a reaction than out of good manners, and turned back toward the window. Heat flooded Gregory's cheeks and he tried holding his breath to slow his thudding heart. What if the stranger *knew* he was a runaway? What if Gregory had given something away in his appearance or maybe even through his mannerisms?

Stop it, he told himself. *The guy's just being nice. You're the one who turned around and stared, remember?*

He glanced back across the aisle. The stranger had turned away, staring out the window at the passing storm. Gregory leaned his head against the glass and closed his eyes. *Just my imagination. The real monster's a few hundred miles back. Keep it cool until the next stop. Call Tommy when you get there. He'll be worried. Just don't draw attention to yourself.*

The thought of his boyfriend—*was* he a boyfriend? Could he call Tommy that now?—set his heart at ease, but the lingering fear that this stranger somehow knew what he was doing kept Gregory awake for the next fifty miles.

The phone rang three times before a voice said, "Hello?"

"Hey Tommy, it's me."

"Greg? Are you okay?"

The surprise in Tommy Keegan's voice made him smile. "Yeah. A little bruised, but the old man's done worse. I missed you."

His cheeks flushed. Speaking those words aloud filled him with a giddiness he'd not felt since he was a child, and the smile on his face felt so alien that he didn't recognize the sensation at first. His stomach tumbled and rolled, held adrift by the butterflies inside, finally free of the stone he'd carried. He had *missed* him.

Gregory was so caught up in his elation that he didn't notice the long pause on the other end of the line.

"Tommy? You still there?"

"Yeah, Greg. I'm here. Listen, I'm not supposed to talk to you anymore. My mom…well, your dad called my mom after…you know. She knows all about us. About what we were doing."

That familiar heat clung to Gregory's cheeks but for different reasons. No matter how far he ran, he couldn't escape his father's shadow.

"You don't…regret what we did, do you?"

"No. Yes. I don't know, Greg. I'm just confused, y'know? I mean, I don't even know you, and you're on the other side of the country. It was fun chatting with you online, but now things are so serious, y'know? I think I just need some time to get my head straight."

Gregory didn't know how to respond. The elation he'd felt only moments before had completely drained from him, and the butterflies in his gut had all but flown away. He felt as though he'd taken one of his dad's sucker punches, his lungs deflated, his head lost in a daze. The bruise on his cheek throbbed. He squeezed the payphone against his ear and leaned against the wall.

"You don't mean that, Tommy."

"I think I do, Greg. We're just names in a chat room, man. It's not like we'll ever meet face to face. We just met the wrong people is all."

He squeezed the receiver until his knuckles popped. *The wrong people.* Those were his father's words. A voice boomed overhead from a loudspeaker, announcing the next bus was boarding.

"What was that? Greg, where are you?"

Gregory clenched his teeth as his vision went cloudy with tears. "It doesn't matter. I'm sorry I bothered you, Tommy. I'm sorry—"

—*I ever met you,* but he didn't say it. The words hung there on his tongue, weighted down by the pointless anger of heartbreak. He closed his eyes, trying to hold back the flood building up behind them. His face burned.

"Don't be like this," Tommy said, but Gregory was already hanging up the phone. Just before he set the receiver back in its cradle, he thought he heard Tommy say they could still be friends. That was a lie, though, just like everything else.

Gregory slung his backpack over his shoulder, took a breath, and found a quiet corner at the far end of the terminal. He sat down, drew his knees to his chest, and allowed the levy to break behind his eyes. The floodwaters rose. He hoped he would drown in them.

Tommy had only ever asked once about Gregory's family. After a few months of chatting online, they'd swapped phone numbers so they'd have a voice to match their text. Gregory's father was still working third shift at the factory, so he had free reign of the phone in the late hours—which was great because Tommy lived on the west coast where everything was three hours behind. Gregory missed those early days. He slept better.

"There's not much to say. My mom died of cancer a few years ago. And my dad..."

As far as Gregory was concerned, his real father had died in an accident after he was born. That's what he told himself to deal with the monster wearing his father's face. When he was younger, he made up stories about how his real father died while committing a heroic act, like saving a group of children from a burning orphanage. Sometimes, he told people his real father died in a car accident. And sometimes, when he was feeling particularly cynical, he told people the truth: The man he lived with really was his father. Sometimes, when the old bastard had had enough to drink, Eddie Simmons beat up his only son to make himself feel better.

That first night they spoke, Gregory chose to be honest with his friend.

"Your old man sounds like a real asshole."

"He is," Gregory said. "One day, I'm going to pack up and leave."

"You could always come out here," Tommy said. "We've got a spare bedroom. It would be nice to meet you face to face."

Gregory smiled. "I'd like that."

After a long pause, Tommy let out an exasperated sigh. "I think I would too."

Their calls were infrequent at first, only once or twice a week, but as their relationship grew, so did their desire to speak to one another. Tommy asked his mom for a webcam for his birthday, and Gregory managed to scrape together enough spare cash to buy a cheap camera for himself. The resolution was shitty, but he could finally see Tommy's face, and that gave him something to look forward to every day.

Looking back, Gregory knew that was the beginning of something he wished he'd never started. The low ache in his cheek—and the pain he felt in his heart whenever he thought of Tommy—simply wasn't worth it. Now, he was stranded in a bus terminal hundreds of miles from home, caught between two dead ends.

"**Y**ou okay, son?"

Gregory opened his eyes, squinting at the dark figure standing over him. He squeezed the strap of his backpack to make sure it was still there.

"Dangerous, you know." The stranger stepped back and offered his hand. "Sleeping in the terminal, I mean. All manner of folk come through here at all hours. Lost and found, they all come through here."

He eyed the stranger's gesture with caution. After a moment, his vision cleared, and Gregory saw the man's odd face with harsh clarity. The stranger wore a dusty old suit with fraying seams. He was older, with shiny salt and pepper hair slicked back and tucked behind his ears. The skin of his face was leathery, stretched tight over bone, and his eyes were like two gray pearls submerged in darkened sands.

"I'm fine," Gregory said, licking his lips. His gaze fell upon a pair of soda machines on the other side of the terminal. How much money did he have left? He couldn't remember.

The stranger twiddled his fingers in the air. "I won't bite. Just want to help."

Gregory hesitated a moment longer before taking the man's hand. The stranger helped him to his feet. "Thanks," he said, looping his arm through the backpack's strap. He checked his iPod for the time but remembered the battery was dead. He looked at the odd man with the sunken eyes. "Do you have the time?"

The stranger pulled back his jacket cuff and checked his watch. "Quarter past two. You were asleep for an hour."

Gregory nodded, took two steps, and stopped. He turned and looked back at the man with the leathery face.

"What did you say?"

"You were asleep for an hour. I was watching from over there." He pointed to a bench fifteen feet away. "Here's some advice if you're going to run: you can't be invisible to everyone all the time. Someone's always watching." The stranger held out his hand. "Name's John."

Gregory gaped in stunned silence. His first impulse was to tell this man with the weird face to piss off, but there was distinct calm in John's voice that disarmed Gregory's mental alarms. John didn't mean him any harm; if he did, he would've already made his move while Gregory slept. That thought gave Gregory some comfort.

He reached out and shook John's hand. "I'm Greg."

"Greg, it's a pleasure to meet you. Always nice to meet another wayward soul at a bus terminal. By the look of you, I'd say your reasons for running are about as good as they get."

The flush of Gregory's cheeks prompted his bruise to throb, and he put his hand to his face instinctively. "Yeah," he said. "Nice to meet you too."

John nodded. "I'm sorry, son. I don't mean to offend, but that is quite a shiner you've got."

Gregory blushed. "It's…it's a long story."

"Hey, I understand. Listen, we have a rule where I come from: Always look forward. Never mind what happened. It's in the past, so let it stay there, you know?" John pulled back his sleeve and took another look at his watch. His knuckles were badly wrinkled, almost as if he'd suffered severe burns in the past. "I've got about an hour to kill before my ride shows up. What do you say I buy you a snack?"

Gregory reached into his pocket and frowned at the loose

collection of nickels and dimes. Sixty cents in total. He met John's gaze and nodded. "All right," he said. "You're on, mister."

"Wonderful," John said, his leathery face wrinkling at his cheeks.

Gregory followed his newfound friend across the lonely terminal, picked out something from the vending machine, and sat down on a nearby bench. He opened his pack of crackers and took a bite. John watched with unblinking curiosity. The way the stranger stared with those sunken eyes unnerved him, and he had a sudden flash of recognition: the man on the bus.

Gregory swallowed too fast, wincing as the bits of cracker scratched the back of his throat. He coughed, spraying crumbs across the floor. John chuckled.

"Not all at once, son."

"Sorry," Gregory rasped. He cleared his throat. "Where did you say you were headed again?"

John smiled. "I didn't."

"Oh."

"Is there something you want to ask me?"

Gregory took another bite of cracker, but not because he was hungry. No, the feeling of hunger had passed moments before, displaced by a leaden weight in his gut. Heat clung to his cheeks now, threatening to suffocate him as he struggled to find the right words. *Be cool*, a voice spoke in his mind. *Just be cool.*

There *was* something he wanted to ask this strange man, and the words were right there, ready to be given voice, but he was so afraid. He felt like he was in the presence of his father, too afraid to speak, too afraid to *move*.

John put his hand on Gregory's shoulder. "I won't bite, Greg."

Gregory chewed the cracker and swallowed. He took a breath. "Are you the man who was staring at me on the bus?"

"Of course I am."

John spoke so matter-of-factly, so disarmingly that Gregory almost accepted the statement without question—but the look in the stranger's eye was too gleeful and eager to set his mind at ease. A chill crawled down the back of Gregory's neck.

"You—you were watching me?"

"I was."

"So you followed me?"

"Only as far back as the last stop. You caught my eye immediately. I know a runner when I see one, son. Old John Doe used to be one himself."

Gregory blinked. "John Doe? Seriously?"

"Yes, sir." He rose to his feet and offered Gregory a short bow. "A genuine Nobody, at your service."

Gregory squeezed the strap of his backpack. All of his belongings were in the pack, and if he needed to run—and he might—he didn't want to leave them all behind. Not that keeping the backpack would do him much good. Aside from his ID, all he had was a change of clothes, an empty wallet, and a dead iPod.

"Relax," John Doe said, recognizing the boy's apprehension. "I'm not going to hurt you."

"Isn't that what you *would* say if you were going to hurt me?"

"Touché." John returned to his seat, leaving a wide space between them. Gregory gripped the backpack, ready to run at the first sign of trouble. "Despite what you may think of me, I have helped thousands of others suffering from the same plight as you."

Gregory scoffed. "Same plight? Mister, you don't even know me."

"This is true," John Doe said. He reached up and scratched at his face. The flesh around his eye sagged from the pressure and made a strange squelching sound which twisted Gregory's stomach into knots. "But what I do know is enough. I know your name is Gregory Simmons. I know that you're on the run from your father because he beats you on a daily basis, and last night, he went a little too far because he caught you masturbating to your boyfriend over the internet." John Doe smiled, revealing yellowed teeth and spotted gums. "Would you say that's enough? Or should I go on?"

An icy serpent coiled around Gregory's insides, squeezing the last breath of air from his lungs. He exhaled in a low, raspy heave as the cloud of heat returned to his face. He suddenly felt like a child lost in the wilderness, yearning for the comfort of his home no matter how broken it was. And yet here he was, hundreds of miles from his comfort zone, facing the real world head on for the first time—and feeling helplessly terrified.

Gregory stared into John Doe's sunken eyes. "Who are you?" He swallowed back the ball of cotton in his throat. "*What* are you?"

"I told you, Greg. I'm a genuine Nobody. I help all the other Nobodies get from here to there, and sometimes I find Nobodies who don't realize they're Nobodies. Sometimes, I find people who want to *become* Nobodies just like the rest of us."

"I don't understand," Gregory said, shaking his head. "What do you mean you're nobody?"

"Ask yourself something, son. Where are you going to go after tonight? Back to your father's home? Or to your boyfriend's house? Neither one of them want you. All you have is a pocket full of loose change and a bus ticket to the west coast."

Gregory turned away. "How do you know that? This doesn't make any sense, you fucking weirdo."

"I know because it's my business to know. Because it's my part to play. I help others disappear, and sometimes that means finding those who don't realize they want to. People like you, I can almost smell your desperation. It's like overripe fruit, just a bit too sweet and a bit too bruised. No one wants you the way you are. So I'll ask you again, son: Where are you going to go?"

He dropped his smile and stared. Gregory looked down at his backpack, running his fingers across the fabric of the strap while a number of sarcastic replies ran through his mind. What could he say? He hadn't considered Tommy backtracking on everything, and he'd not yet given himself time to grieve over that particular loss. Going back home wasn't an option now, especially since he'd stolen his old man's rainy day savings to buy a one-way bus ticket. He could already hear Eddie Simmons shouting loud enough to shake the heavens.

Like it or not, he was on his own now, and this strange man with the squelching face had a point: No one wanted him. He wished his mom were still alive. She might've been upset over what he'd been doing with Tommy, but she wouldn't have hit him. She would've made an effort to understand.

But that didn't matter now because she'd been dead for years. Now he was alone, and no one wanted him. No one except Mr. Doe.

John checked his watch. "In about five minutes, a bus full of other Nobodies is going to pull up to the station, and I'm going to climb aboard. If you come with me, no one's going to ask for your ticket. You'll be welcomed. If you join me, Greg, I can make you two promises." He climbed to his feet and once again held out a wrinkled, leathery hand. "The first is that you can be whomever you want to be, and no one will judge you for what you choose."

Gregory wiped tears from his eyes and looked up at John Doe. "And the second?"

"The second is that everything you are now will never be again.

Gregory Simmons will cease to exist. Who you become afterward is up to you, but you can never be you again."

Gregory took John Doe's hand and rose to his feet. "You mean I'll have a new identity? New ID, name, address?"

John Doe smiled, and his lips clicked when they slid across his teeth. "Something like that."

The bus arrived on time just as John Doe said it would, and a voice filled the terminal from a series of loudspeakers announcing its departure time. They had ten minutes to board. Gregory stood with his companion on the sidewalk, shivering in the breeze. The storm had let up over an hour ago, but the damp air carried a chill that nipped at his ears.

John Doe took a breath. "Last chance to change your mind, son. Once you board the Otherland Express, you can't go back. Everything changes from here on out."

"You were right," Gregory said, clenching his jaws to keep his teeth from chattering, "when you said no one wants me the way I am. I don't know how you knew, but you were right. There's nothing waiting for me now."

"Have you thought about where you'll go? This bus will take you wherever you like."

He hadn't, but the answer came easily enough. "I'd still like to visit the west coast. See the ocean. You know, where it's warm."

"West coast it is, then." John Doe held up his hand and the bus door folded open. He stepped across the sidewalk and stuck his head inside. "Just two tonight, Joe." He turned back and motioned to Gregory. "Right this way, Mr. Simmons."

Frowning, Gregory slipped his arms through the straps of his backpack. "Don't call me that," he said. "That's my father's name."

John Doe nodded. "My apologies, Greg. After tonight, you won't have to worry about that anymore."

A series of overhead dome lights stretched to the back of the bus, illuminating rows of smiling faces. Men and women of varying ages filled the cabin, and despite the poor lighting, Gregory could see their eyes were sunken into their skulls just like his strange host. Several of the passengers turned to watch as he followed John Doe down the aisle toward the back of bus.

After he found a seat near the back, Gregory realized his heart was racing, and he wasn't sure if it was from fear or excitement. He thought about what he would tell Tommy, but his heart sank when he remembered how their last conversation had gone. And what was it that John Doe had said? He wouldn't be himself after this?

Not that he'd want to pay Tommy a visit anyway. Even though Gregory's heart ached, somewhere deep down, he knew Tommy lacked conviction. Gregory wasn't ashamed of what he'd done. It felt good and right, and he'd do it again if given the chance. He wished his old man was there so he could say it to his face.

But all that will be behind me, he thought. *It's time to look forward.*

John Doe took a seat across the aisle. He raised his hand again, and the bus shuddered into gear. The driver, Joe, came over the loudspeaker. "Good evening, fellow Nobodies. We've got some miles to go before our next stop, but before we make our way through the Otherlands, please put your hands together for our newcomer, Greg. He's the latest to join our tribe!"

Gregory looked at John and mouthed, *Tribe?*

John winked and joined in the applause. "Welcome, Gregory!"

A pair of older men turned in their seats and congratulated him.

"We've been Nobodies for more than a decade," they said. "We joined together, and we make the exchange every few years. It's great to shed the skin. You'll love it!"

Gregory offered a polite smile, unsure of what to say. Joe's voice boomed from the speaker above: "Now you all know the rules: no shedding until we've crossed the boundary lines. We've got a long stretch through the Otherlands tonight, so that means you've got more time to make your exchange. Until then, find someone you like, someone who's your type, and get to know them. And remember, people: John Doe gets dibs on the newcomer."

He turned to John Doe once more, but his strange friend was conversing with a pair of young women in front of him. Gregory sank back into his seat and watched with mounting trepidation as the bus terminal grew smaller in the distance. Soon, the bus was back on the highway, headed west toward America's enigmatic Otherlands.

They were on the road for an hour before John called out to him. Gregory lifted his head from the window pane and looked across the aisle at Mr. Doe's silhouette.

"We're almost there," John said. He shuffled across the aisle and sat next to Gregory. "Before we get there, I need to explain something."

Gregory sat up in his seat and rubbed his eyes. He'd almost dozed off, lulled to slumber by the rock and hum of the Greyhound. "What is it?"

John Doe leaned forward and rubbed his hands absently, his head bowed as if in prayer. "The Otherlands is a special place. Things are different there."

"Different how?"

"Different…in a lot of ways. You'll see it. More importantly, you'll *feel* it. It's like being drunk. Your senses are numbed. This place is where you'll become someone else."

Gregory leaned over and whispered into John's ear, "Are you going to tell me what the hell is going on? Whatever it was that Joe was talking about back at the station?"

"I'm getting to that," John said. "But I think it may be best to show you. Do you feel that?"

He wasn't sure what John was talking about at first, but the sensation that came over him a moment later told him all he needed to know. He lost the feeling in his lips and tongue, followed by the tips of his nose and ear lobes. His fingertips tingled, and his toes were tickled with dozens of phantom pinpricks. Gregory blinked lazily, marveling at the strange purple glow spreading across the sky.

Outside, the highway melted into an alien landscape pockmarked with gray craters and dotted with maroon vegetation. Trees curved from the earth like tentacles, their branches writhing with wildlife too small to be seen, but somehow, Gregory could sense them, could almost see the vibration of their tiny wings beating the air. He remembered something Tommy had said about experiencing acid for the first time, and he wondered if John Doe had drugged him somehow.

"Is this—?"

"It's real," John said. His lips peeled back into another toothy grin. "This is where the Nobodies of the world come to commune, Greg. Out here, we get to frolic backstage while the world carries on with its self-importance and loathing. Out here in the Otherlands, we're free to be ourselves."

The bus slowed to a stop in the middle of the gray desert. As if on cue, the passengers erupted into cries of jubilation. The two men in front embraced while the women across the aisle kissed. Gregory marveled at the landscape, wondering how such a place could ever exist, and he was so caught up in the sensations in his body that he didn't notice the articles of clothing flying through the air.

John Doe rose from his seat and raised his hand to calm everyone.

"Friends and fellow Nobodies, tonight we inaugurate a new face into our tribe. He's a little nervous, but I think that once we strip off our earthly burdens, he'll feel right at home. After all, we're all the same beneath the flesh!"

What happened next left Gregory's mind reeling, and for the first few terrifying moments, he questioned what he was seeing. The other passengers climbed out of their seats and stripped out of the remains of their clothing. Their naked silhouettes were cast in the dim, purple glow of the world beyond, and when the dome lights came on, Gregory saw that John Doe had joined them.

"Let me show you," John said. "Let me show you how to shed the old you."

So he did, and Gregory bit his cheeks to stifle a scream.

John reached up, found a seam behind his ear, and peeled back the mask of his face, revealing the sinuous meat and muscle beneath. He lifted underneath his chin and yanked, stripping the flap of his face from his skull with a single motion. The sound that met Gregory's ears reminded him of Velcro, and the gaping stare of John Doe's skinless face made his stomach crawl into itself.

He watched in sickening horror as John Doe peeled back every bit of himself like a piece of fruit, moving on to his arms and hands, then on to his chest, gut, and groin. Every fold of skin peeled away with that same scratchy, squelching Velcro sound, and now Gregory understood the odd noise he'd heard back at the bus station.

He looked away from the stranger and recoiled in disgust as he witnessed others doing the same. The men in the next row helped each other peel away their flesh, one working his hands under the wrinkles and folds of the other, inching the skin away from the meat underneath like stripping back a sticker from plastic. The women across the aisle were already exposed. They ran their hands across their sinuous folds, exploring their anatomy, and Gregory realized with sickening horror that he couldn't tell if they were smiling anymore because their lips were gone.

"This is what it is to shed your skin," John said, offering his hand. "We come here to the Otherlands to strip away our burdens and trade faces. Here, we are free to be whomever we wish. Tonight, you will become me, Gregory. And I will become you. Forever one with the Nobody Tribe."

Gregory's mind buzzed. Was this what he wanted? Was this the price he had to pay to become someone else?

John Doe slicked his leathery tongue across the top of his brittle teeth. "Remember what I told you, Greg. It's too late to go back, but I promise you'll thank me when it's over. I keep my promises."

Gregory reached out and took John Doe's hand for the last time. "Will I remember anything? Will it hurt?"

"You'll remember everything." John squeezed Gregory's hand. "And yes, my friend, it will hurt. The pain will be transcendent, the most glorious thing you have ever felt in your life."

John Doe's fingers sank into the boy's flesh, and Gregory knew his friend wasn't lying.

One day later, a man no one had ever seen before stepped off an unmarked Greyhound bus in Long Beach. He wore a dusty black suit that was nearly a size too big, and his youthful eyes betrayed the mess of salt and pepper hair sitting atop his head. No one paid him any attention, and at another time, in another life, this fact would have bothered him.

He smiled, feeling his cheeks wrinkle back. His face was too big, but that was all right; his friends in the tribe told him he would grow into it.

He walked over to a nearby trash can, reached into his back pocket, and pulled out his wallet. He thumbed through until he found his old ID and looked at the smiling face of a young man who would never again know the force of his father's fist.

Gregory Doe tossed the ID into the trash, grimacing as his muscles ached. The other Nobodies on the bus told him aspirin would be his best bet until he got used to his new skin.

A breeze blew past him, filling his nostrils with the scent of the salty Pacific, and he thought of Tommy. Tommy Keegan, with his sun-bleached hair. A fluttering ache rose up within his chest, and he frowned.

The other Nobodies didn't have a remedy for that. Heartache was something he couldn't shed, something he couldn't throw away.

Can anyone?

SAVING GRANNY FROM THE DEVIL

I remember when Granny had her first stroke. I was there with her, and I thought she was going to die. She didn't, though. Granny was from strong stock, and it was going to take more than one stroke to keep her down. She had physical therapy for several months before a bigger stroke partially paralyzed the left side of her body. Even then, she slowed but did not stop. Four strokes couldn't hold her back, and I think that if age hadn't been a factor, she would've kept on going.

But I'm getting ahead of myself. I want to tell you about Granny, first.

I don't even remember why I called her "Granny," she was just Granny to me. Granny Mildred. She was my dad's grandmother, but after my parents divorced, she gave my mom and I a place to live. She didn't care about how awkward the situation was—she just cared about me having a roof over my head. That's what I remember most about my early childhood: growing up at Granny's house. Her home was my world, and she was one of the only constants I had in my life.

While Mom worked during the day and went to school at night, Granny took care of me. Mom was around when she could be, but most days belonged to Granny and me. She took me shopping or out to run other errands, showing me off to all her friends.

On Friday mornings I accompanied her to Arlene's Beauty Shop, where she sat underneath a hair dryer for an hour before having her head meticulously sculpted into a pristine, silver bouffant right out of the 1960s. Afterward, we'd get drive-through for lunch, and then I'd spend the rest of my afternoon crashed out in front of the TV with a pad of paper, doodling whatever spilled from my imagination.

This was my early life. Just Granny and I versus the world. She was my best friend before I understood the importance of such a title. Before the strokes got the best of her. Before the Devil paid us a visit.

I was eight years old when I first met the Devil, although I didn't recognize him at the time. I thought he was my friend back then, but that's not quite true.

He was just a messenger.

"Kiss it."

Gerald presented his mud-covered sneaker. I tried to squirm away, but Brent's weight was too much. He held me down in the grass and twisted my arm behind my back. Pain burst before my eyes like phantom fireworks.

"We'll let you go if you kiss his shoe."

"No," I groaned. I didn't want to cry, but the tears were there, waiting. Brent bore down on me, pushing the air out of my chest. He was big for an eight-year-old—easily the biggest kid in our class—and I felt every pound of him compressing my insides. When he shifted his full weight against me, I squealed in pain.

"Hey, I think this fag's gonna cry."

That did it. The comment wasn't even the catalyst—I was still too young to know what that word even meant. No, what made me cry was the fact that they knew I couldn't help myself. Every kid has their limit, and they'd just pushed me to mine. I started sobbing like the baby I really was.

Struggling, taking big panic breaths, I searched the road for someone—anyone—who might help me, but there was no one around on that Saturday morning. Mom was at work, and Granny was back at home cleaning up after breakfast. I'd told her I wouldn't venture too far, but that was just an innocent white lie.

Gerald shoved his shoe against my chin. The acrid stench turned my stomach. There was more than mud on his sneaker.

"Kiss it, or else."

These two inseparable bullies were always picking on the quiet kids. I'd kept my distance—even eight-year-olds understand a pecking order—but this morning I was careless. I wasn't allowed across the street, but I'd explored every inch of my granny's yard long ago, and there was only so much in that plot of land to occupy my imagination.

Fancying myself an explorer, I'd waited until Granny was finished in the kitchen before wandering around the corner and beyond the row of trees marking the edge of Mr. Fuson's yard. I'd overheard my mom talking to Granny about the neighbor's plan to tear down the old dog kennel at the edge of his property just a few days before.

After exploring most of the neighborhood, my curiosity was working overtime, an itch in the back of my brain that I couldn't quite scratch. If I didn't explore the kennel soon, I'd never get the chance—and now I regretted that decision.

I happened upon Gerald throwing stones at the windows of the old building, and like the idiot I was back then, I yelled for him to quit it. Gerald wasn't much bigger than me, and in a pinch, I figured I could outrun him. When Brent emerged from the old kennel with a rotted piece of wood in his hands, I knew I'd stepped into a hornet's nest.

"Now he's crying!" Gerald's shrill voice whined in my ears. "Look at the little baby cry!"

"Kiss the damn shoe," Brent grunted. "Do it, or we'll lock you in there."

I knew where he was talking about, and I wanted to protest but all my words came out in pained sobs. Hot needles stabbed into my arm as Brent held me there, and I had to fight the urge to vomit. I remember thinking how perfect this would be if I threw up all over Gerald's shoe, but knowing those boys, I think that would've made things worse.

"Screw that," Gerald squealed. "Let's put him in there anyway. With the dead dog!"

My eyes grew wide when I heard that. I immediately regretted not kissing Gerald's shoe. Before I could protest, Brent pulled back on my arm, yanking me to my feet. Dark spots burst in my vision as the bullies shoved me into the decrepit kennel. I stumbled to the dirt floor, gasping for air and fighting the rising desire to retch. Turning back, I saw the door close behind me and heard my captors cackle in triumph.

Banners of light filtered through the broken windows like pale, crooked arms. Motes of dust wandered lazily in the musty air. I wiped tears and snot on my sleeve, climbed to my feet, and pushed against the door. The sturdy wooden frame wouldn't budge. I imagined Brent pressed against the door, bracing his hulking mass against my puny resistance. I kicked at the door and beat my fists against it. I was angry and humiliated, afraid of what they'd say at school the following week. Even at eight, I knew how vicious rumors were—especially the true ones.

"Let me out!"

Brent and Gerald chuckled at my distress.

"What do you think, Brent? Should we let him out?"

"No, let him sit in there. He's got company anyway."

The dead dog. In that moment I became aware of the stench, and this time I couldn't hold back. I turned away from the door, doubled over, and threw up. Outside, Brent's baritone chuckle punctuated the gaps between Gerald's gasping, shrieking laughter. Wiping my mouth, I realized I hated them, even though I didn't fully understand that hate.

"Shut up," I rasped, grimacing at the raw sensation at the back of my throat. I spat bile on the ground and reached out into the shadows to brace myself against the wall. The branches of sunlight only lit up the old kennel so much, leaving the rest bathed in a dim haze.

"Shut up," Gerald whined. "Shut up, guys. I'm scared. What a stupid baby."

Brent grunted. "A stupid fag-baby."

They erupted into new fits of laughter, rising and falling in waves that accented my shame. *I'm such a chicken shit*, I thought. *I should've stood up to them. I should've—*

"You should have, child, and you didn't. Why not let me?"

I held my breath. That was a grown man's voice. Deep and confident, the voice spoke with authority. I became aware of a different smell in the kennel: a pungent stench of eggs overpowered the rotting dog.

"It's quite all right," spoke the man. "I'm not here to hurt you, child. I'm not like them."

My heart thumped in my throat, and the burning fire in my lungs reminded me to breathe again. I exhaled slowly, listening to the pounding in my ears, feeling lightheaded and hoping that I'd imagined everything. Outside, the bullies continued their incessant banter, rapping against the door, calling me "fag-baby." The smell filled the room, thickening the air, and I felt it clinging to my skin like a slim film. I wanted to throw up again.

Movement stirred at the far end of the kennel. My head thumped to the beat of my heart as I searched the shadows, trying my best to seek out the shape of the man. I saw nothing but empty stalls and rusted wire fencing. The dull, rapid tapping of knuckles against the wooden door echoed in the empty chamber, providing a chorus to the pounding in my ears.

"H–Hello?" I wanted to cover my mouth, but my hands wouldn't cooperate. I stood there in the dark, petrified by what I could not see.

Something shifted at the far end. Closer now. Heavy steps moved slowly toward me, and when the bulldog stepped out of the shadows, my vocal cords finally woke up. I uttered a scream not out of fear, but of shock and disgust. The dog's stomach was bloated, its fur coated in a dark ooze that dribbled down its side. The creature's paws were covered in the stuff, and when the dog shook its head maggots flew out of its ears.

Something lurched in my gut and I heaved, but nothing came up.

"I detest that reaction."

I looked down at the rotting canine. Thick strings of blackened goo oozed out of its nostrils and limp jaw. A maggot writhed across its snout. Part of its front leg was stripped bare of fur, revealing raw, swollen flesh. What captured my attention, however, was the piercing blue glow emanating from the dog's sunken eyes. They resonated with life inside the dead creature's husk.

"Do you want out of here?"

The man's voice echoed under the kennel's tin roof, and the dog stared at me, waiting for a reply. The bullies kept up with their mockery. I looked away from the dog toward the door.

"Don't worry about them," spoke the dead dog. "Just tell me, child: do you want my help?"

Confused, my heart booming in my chest, I lowered my eyes to the dead animal. I stared into those unsettling sapphire orbs and nodded. My cheeks flushed, filling up with the shame of not being able to fight my own battles. I really was a chicken shit.

The dog shook its head again, flinging a clump of maggots to the dirt. A string of congealed blood dripped from the animal's left ear, pooling just beside its paw. "This will only take a moment."

The dog lowered its head, baring its fangs for the first time. Blood oozed between yellowing teeth, dribbling out of its mouth in thick clumps. For a moment I feared the animal was going to attack me, but when I heard the door creak I realized the dog was not growling at me.

"Hey, wait a sec," Gerald said. "What's happening to the—"

The kennel door swung open, flooding the dingy chamber with morning light.

"What the hell?" Brent stuck his head inside the doorway. "I don't know how you did that, fag-baby, but we didn't say you could leave—oh shit."

The dead dog snapped at the air, uttering a growl so fierce that I had to step away for fear it might turn on me. Brent's startled face went pale, his eyes wide and mouth frozen in shock. His lips moved but no words left them, and for the first time, he was absent of witty remarks.

The bulldog took a step forward, and then another, leaving behind a bloody trail of writhing maggots. The creature snapped again, letting loose a bark that was neither canine nor human. The sound was akin to crackling fire and wind, like kindling crumbling to ash in a bonfire. And those eyes—God, even now, I can't get that look out of my head. Those piercing blue eyes shimmered with life like a newborn baby, cutting through the gloom of the kennel and reflecting back on Brent's terrified face. Tears streamed down his cheeks.

"What is it?" Gerald's voice carried from beyond the doorway. "What's wr—"

He didn't get a chance to finish his sentence. The dead dog snapped once more, and this time Brent reacted, pulling back from the doorway just in time. The animal bounded after them, and in the moments that followed all I heard were the sounds of fire and wind punctuated with the screams of two bad kids. I stood in the shadows with my hands to my ears, shivering in the warm morning air.

"**C**ome on, child. Out you go." I opened my eyes to find a dark figure standing in the doorway. He offered his hand to me, but I hesitated. The screams of the bullies had faded away mere minutes before, but I feared they might still be out there, lurking, waiting for me to emerge. I pictured Brent and Gerald dragging me back here and locking me away again. The thought gave me a chill.

"Don't worry," spoke the man. "You have nothing to fear from them. I chased them off."

Timid, I walked to the entrance, squinting at the sunlight. As I neared the man, I could smell that same overwhelming stench as before: eggs. The stranger was pale with dark hair cropped closely to his ears. A thin, dark goatee accented his smile, and his bright blue eyes shimmered even in the light. His slender figure filled out the contours of a black suit. I'd never seen clothes so fancy. There was nary a speck of dust or lint on the fabric. He even had shiny gold cufflinks shaped like goat heads.

The dark man looked down at me, grinning. I stared up at him in awe.

"Did you chase away Brent and Gerald?"

"I sure did, kiddo. I've not much use for bullies. Parasites, they are."

The logical question of "Are you a talking dog?" hung on my lips, but I was too embarrassed to ask. I didn't want to be rude.

"Oh, please," the man said, waving his hand through the air. "That isn't a rude question to ask. In fact, it's the right question to ask. Yes, I was the dog. I heard you needed help, and I happened to be wandering by. Now here we are."

I suddenly felt dizzy, the morning air thickening in my lungs.

"Thank you," I whispered. He waved my gratitude away, producing a cigarette from his pocket. He held it to his lips and snapped his fingers, making a spark that set the cigarette ablaze. I was so entranced by his display that I almost didn't notice his long, black fingernails. They looked like claws.

"Are you a magician?"

He took a drag from the cigarette, exhaling a plume of smoke that stank of tobacco and cloves. The aroma did little to cover the smell of eggs. My stomach had settled itself over that smell, but I'd hardly grown used to it. I never did, either.

"A magician?" He shook his head. "No, Toddy. Magicians use magic. I just use what comes naturally."

He flashed a smile as his words sank in. *Toddy*. No one called me that. Well, no one except for Granny and my mom.

"How do you know my name?"

The dark man grinned. "I know a lot of names, kiddo. I speak a language of them, but right now, yours is my only tongue." He produced a small, black notebook from his back pocket and flipped through its pages. "Says it right here, as a matter of fact. Toddy. Don't you go by that?"

Frowning, I stood on my toes, trying to get a glimpse of the page's contents, but he was just out of reach. "No one calls me Toddy—"

"Except for your mother and your great-grandmother."

"Right."

"Right then. I'll amend that." He pulled a pencil out of his other pocket and scribbled a note on the page. When he was finished, he shut the book and looked down at me with an odd, light smile that made me want to laugh. Thinking back on it, I shouldn't have laughed. No, I should've run away, following in the footsteps of those bullies. But I didn't. The curiosity of an eight-year-old knows no bounds and no fears; it only knows wonder, and mine was about to get me into a lot of trouble.

"Now, let's get down to business," he said, extending a pale hand. "Pleased to meet you. Can you guess my name?"

I shrugged. Harvey came to mind. He looked like a Harvey. That was a city name. He spoke with a city accent, enunciating all his words properly, and he carried himself with a "city" demeanor I'd seen all too often on the TV. A name formed in the back of my mind, crawling out of the shadows like an animal on the hunt.

"Harvey J. Winterbell?"

The man blinked, seemingly amused. "That's a new one. Harvey J. Winterbell? That will take some getting used to, child, but if that's my name, that's my name." He stuck out his hand again. "Harvey J. Winterbell, at your service."

I reached out—but hesitated, suddenly remembering what I'd learned about talking to strangers. But what if a stranger came to my rescue? Surely he was a good guy, right? I mean, he was a professional, what with his fancy suit and speech.

"I won't bite," he said, smiling. "And we're not exactly strangers, are we? In fact, I have a feeling we could be best friends."

I reached out, took his cold hand, and shook. "Nice to meet you, Harvey."

Harvey J. Winterbell licked his thin lips, smiled, and spoke in a hushed tone. "No, child, the pleasure is all mine."

My new friend accompanied me on the walk back to Granny's house. I babbled on about school, about the neighborhood, and about that time I found a dead bird next to a nest of smashed eggs.

"They were bloody," I told him.

"I'm sure they were," he said, nodding politely. I realize now he was rather gracious, listening to a kid trail on about nonsensical childish things. I suppose that was part of his ruse to win me over, and to his credit, it worked.

Granny's house fell into view as we turned the corner. Her home was a humble two-story with white siding. Two red storage sheds stood adjacent to the driveway, obscuring the bottom portion of a tall oak. Dew glistened in the morning grass as we walked. Harvey

J. Winterbell slowed as we neared the driveway. I turned and looked up at him, smiling ear to ear.

"Will you come in? I want you to meet Granny. When she hears what you did for me, she'll pour you some cereal. We have Raisin Bran and Cheerios, but I ate most of the raisins."

Harvey smiled softly. "I would love to join you. Lead the way, young sir." He held out his hand in an advancing gesture, but paused for a moment, regarding me with those curious blue eyes. "You don't know me, do you?"

"Sure I do," I said. "You're my friend Harvey."

He nodded. "I suppose I am. Well, let's go tell your granny hello, shall we?"

Granny sat at the kitchen table, sipping from a cup of coffee while reading the Saturday newspaper. I held open the screen door for my friend, walked to the table, and pulled out a chair.

"Here you go, Harvey."

Granny lowered the paper and smiled. "Who's Harvey?"

"He's my friend, Granny. Say hello!"

She smiled and shook her hand up and down. "Pleasure to meet you, Harvey. Any friend of my Toddy is a friend of mine."

"He's over here, Granny." I laughed, moving her hand. Harvey sat upright in his seat, grinning.

"It's quite all right, child. She can't see me."

I turned back to him, my brow furrowing in confusion. "She can't?"

Harvey shook his head. "I'm afraid not. I only appear to special people in their time of need, and she's not ready to see me yet. Let's just pretend I'm imaginary. It'll be our little secret."

I nodded, listening intently. Everything he said made sense, and I spied Granny from the corner of my eye. She watched in amusement. I turned back to her and shrugged.

"Harvey says you can't see him yet, but that's okay. He's just my imaginary friend anyway."

"I'll declare, your imagination is something else." Granny brushed her hand through my hair. "So what did you and Harvey do this morning?"

"We met just a little while ago, and he helped keep those bullies—"

I paused, my cheeks flushed with heat. I'd forgotten that my encounter with Gerald and Brent had taken place in an area of the neighborhood that was strictly off limits. Granny's eyes narrowed, a funny, knowing smirk hanging low on her face.

"Toddy, I told you not to play with those boys. They're pure meanness." She looked down at my jeans. "I see you managed to get your new clothes dirty, too."

I lowered my head, ashamed. "I'm sorry, Granny."

Harvey leaned forward in his seat, his blue eyes shimmering even in the bright kitchen light.

"Tell her you won't do it again. Tell her you'll pray for forgiveness. She'll eat that right up."

I spoke Harvey's words, turning on the charm as best I could, giving her the pouting doe-eyed face that she fell for every single time. She pulled me close and kissed me on the forehead.

"You're such a good boy. I know you won't do it again. Why don't you run on into the living room so I can finish the paper? I bet your cartoons are still on."

"Oh, right!" My chubby face beamed. I took Harvey's hand. "Come on, Harvey. Let's go watch cartoons!"

Harvey rose from his seat, but he did not follow me to watch cartoons. Instead, he walked toward the door, peering outside for a moment before turning back to me. "I'm afraid I need to get going, kiddo. But don't worry, I'll be back."

"No fair," I said. "The day was just getting fun."

"No pouting, child." He knelt before me, just behind Granny's chair. "Tell you what. I'll give you this. You won't be able to see it, but it will follow you wherever you go, and wherever you go, there I'll be—even when I'm not. Give me your hand."

I did as he asked. He took my hand and traced one black claw in a star pattern along the backside. The long talon burned a little, but I bit my lip to keep from crying out. The pattern itself didn't leave any mark, but I felt it there even after he was done. My hand was hot to the touch.

"There. Now we'll never be apart."

"Okay," I said, rubbing the back of my hand. "Thanks, Harvey. Will I see you later? Maybe tomorrow?"

"Maybe," he said. "Maybe the day after. Say, what's that?"

He pointed toward the dining room, and I turned but didn't see anything. When I spun back around, Harvey was gone. Granny finished her coffee, set down her cup, and sniffed the air.

"I think the eggs are starting to go bad," she mumbled. "I only just bought them, too."

I don't remember much else about that Saturday, except that when I slept that night, I had terrible dreams. I remember being chased by dark, monstrous things lurking in the shadows of a tunnel that stretched on forever. There were creatures hanging above me, watching, laughing as I struggled to get away.

One creature was a dead dog the size of a school bus, its maggot-filled ears flopping in the air as it bounded after me. Black ooze gushed from its snout in thick, bubbling strings. Large stars burned in its dead blue eyes, and a voice echoed from the shadows: *I know a lot of names, kiddo. I speak a language of them, but right now, yours is my only tongue.*

I woke with a start, my heart racing in my tiny chest. I heard my mom stir in her bed, and after a moment, she flicked on her bedside lamp. Dim light filled the room we shared.

"Are you okay, honey?"

I looked over. Mom sat up in bed with the blankets bunched around her. She looked worried.

"I'm okay, Mommy."

"Go back to sleep, sweetie. Church tomorrow."

"Okay," I said, rolling over. I pulled the blanket up to my chin, absently rubbing at the back of my hand where Harvey had traced his mark. My skin felt sunburned in that invisible pattern, and I nodded off while tracing its outline along the back of my hand. Harvey's words followed me back down into my dreams, but the dog was gone, left to rot back in Mr. Fuson's old kennel, food for a new generation of flies.

Woodbine Baptist Church seemed like a million miles away from home, and the ride there was dreadful if only because of the anticipation of boredom. The church itself was picturesque in some ways, like something out of a Norman Rockwell painting—a white, medium-sized building standing alone atop a hill, its steeple painted black and poking the sky.

I remember the pastor as an older man wearing wire-framed glasses, his balding head adorned with strange brown spots and a permanent glow of reflection from the lights above. I once asked Granny why his head glowed like that.

She smiled at my innocence. "That's his halo, honey. He's a good man."

I remember thinking I didn't want my head to glow like that when I got older.

We shook hands. The pastor—I think his name was Thurmond—bent down and smiled at me.

"And how are we this morning, Mister Todd?"

"Sleepy."

"Sleepy?" He laughed and tousled my hair. "We'll have to wake you up with the Spirit!"

I didn't understand what he meant, so I just smiled and moved on after Granny into the church. We took our seats in a pew, Mom gave me a piece of peppermint candy, and several minutes later the service began. Once the singing was over, Pastor Thurmond took his place behind the lectern and called for a prayer. Everyone bowed their heads except me, and Mom tugged on my sleeve.

"It's time to pray."

"I don't know how," I told her.

"Just bow your head, close your eyes, and think about God."

So I closed my eyes and bowed my head and thought about God, but all that really came to mind was the darkness behind my eyelids, and for the next two minutes while the pastor asked the Lord to give everyone a fruitful day, I watched as colors swirled and danced in the dark.

They moved in odd, erratic patterns, blinking and streaking across that black expanse behind my eyes. Soon, strange shapes began to take form, and at first, I didn't think anything of them, but then I saw a dog limping across the darkness, with a weird red swirl pouring out of its ear. Behind the maimed animal was a tall man, vacant but for a thin, red outline and two sapphire eyes.

You don't really know me, he said, grinning with red swirling teeth. *But you will, kiddo. You will, and when we meet again, you'll understand what I am.*

"Amen."

My eyes snapped open, startled by the abrupt movement stirring within the congregation while my heart raced a marathon. Granny looked down at me, frowning.

"What's wrong?"

I shook my head. "I think I had a nightmare."

"You're okay now. Come on, honey," Granny said. "It's time for Sunday School."

Granny and I took our seats at the back of a small classroom, and after the other kids found their way into the room, class began. We learned about the Devil's temptation of Christ in the desert. Something about the scenario depicted in one of the Bible's more famous scenes piqued my curiosity, if only because the Devil just seemed like he wanted to help.

I ruminated on that dilemma for the duration of the class, and when we went back upstairs for the morning service I took the problem with me. While Pastor Thurmond worked his way up into a holy crescendo, decrying the wages of sin and warning of eternal damnation wrought in hellfire, I rolled the conundrum over in my head. The Devil was the bad guy, but he was trying to help Jesus in the desert, right? Wouldn't that make him a good guy instead?

Pastor Thurmond gave his cue for the choir to start singing "Just As I Am" while he called for sinners to repent at the pulpit, but I didn't pay him much attention. I was too busy trying to unravel the conundrum that had knotted itself in my brain. I carried that dilemma through the remainder of the service and back to Granny's car. My mom had some errands to run and agreed to meet us back at Granny's house for lunch. I was okay with that.

We were on our way home when I asked Granny about the Devil and Jesus.

"Granny," I began, "you know lots about the Bible, don't you?"

She brought the car to a stop at a red light and glanced at me, smiling. "I guess so. I guess I should—I've been reading it for most of my life, and I still read it, in fact." She did, too. Just about every evening before going to bed.

"So…what we learned in Sunday School today, about the Devil suggesting Jesus turn the rocks to bread so he wouldn't starve, I don't get why that's bad."

"Because the Devil tempts, honey. He tries to make men lose their way. Jesus went into the desert to pray and understand his purpose, and the Devil tried to tempt him away from his purpose."

I thought about that for a while, staring out the window as the countryside gave way to Corbin's Main Street storefronts. At the next stop light, Granny looked over at me, watching as I worked everything out in my head.

"Penny for your thoughts?"

"Still thinking about the Devil."

"He's a bad thing to think about, honey. Why not think about Jesus instead?"

"Because Jesus was dumb."

"Now Toddy," she scolded, "that's blasphemy. Jesus is our Lord and Savior. He died for your sins because He loves you. You can't talk about Him like that."

I looked at her, smiling to hide the shame burning away at my cheeks. "He went into the desert and starved himself on purpose. The Devil tried to help him, but he turned it down."

"You don't understand," Granny said. She pushed down on the gas and we sped through the intersection. "The spirit of God led Jesus into the desert to fast for forty days, and the Devil was trying to tempt Him and stop Him from doing that. He even offered to give Jesus dominion over the world if He'd only bow down to worship him."

"But...*why?*"

"Why what, honey?"

"Why would the Devil do that?"

Granny opened her mouth to speak, stopped, started to speak again and then paused once more. She was frustrated—more so with herself than at me for not understanding the lesson. Finally, after a moment of silence, she tapped the steering wheel and spoke with pursed lips, "Because he's the Devil. He's a tempter, a snake, the enemy of God. Everything he does is meant to hurt mankind, even if it doesn't seem like it. He's evil. That's just what he does."

"Okay, Granny." I let the subject drop. I could tell I'd agitated her, and I spent the rest of the car ride staring out the window, watching the small town of Corbin drift by. I didn't stop thinking about the Devil, though. Not for the next twenty-two years.

A couple of fading events defined my early childhood when I still lived at Granny's house. This was in the year following my first meeting with Harvey J. Winterbell, after he gave me his mark. The first event wasn't really a specific happening, but an ongoing phenomenon that occurred throughout most of my young life.

Drawing was my favorite hobby next to playing with Legos, and in fact, some of my first publications were stories I'd written and illustrated. One story, about two boys going fishing, was published by the Corbin Times-Tribune and hung from Granny's refrigerator door for years. She also had a copy framed and hung on her living room wall.

I drew my pictures and made up stories for them. Somewhere along the way, however, Harvey J. Winterbell began appearing in those drawings. He was subtle at first—an extra shadow here, a faint outline there—but soon enough, Mom and Granny began taking notice. So did my teacher at school, and one day Mrs. Leigh sent home a note with my latest artistic endeavors. I gave it to Mom, who read it with growing concern before perusing my most recent creations. We sat at the dinner table, my artwork spread out before us. Across all of them was a tall man in a black coat, with black claws and bright, blue eyes.

"Who's this person here?"

Mom pointed to the tall, dark man standing behind a tree in the background. I'd drawn a picture of Granny, Mom, and I in front of Granny's house. Behind the oak tree was Harvey, and I told her so.

"Who's Harvey?" Mom asked, her brow furrowed, seemingly concerned.

"That's his 'friend,'" Granny said. She gave Mom a wink. I just smiled, not catching the significance.

"I see," Mom said, nodding. She stared at the dark figure lurking in the background. "What about your friends at school, honey? Why aren't they in this picture?"

"Because it's just us, Mommy. Us and Harvey."

"I don't know how I feel about you drawing pictures of this Harvey character. You've been having bad nightmares as it is, and he doesn't seem like a very nice guy here."

"Oh no, Mommy. He's a good guy. He protects me."

"If you say so, sweetie." She leaned down, kissed my forehead, and affixed the drawing to Granny's refrigerator. "I'll give Mrs. Leigh a call and have a talk with her."

So I drew my pictures, and Harvey would show up somewhere in them, always watching from the background, always standing and smiling with those big blue eyes. Sometimes I couldn't remember drawing him, but there he'd be, watching me from beyond the page. Over time I came to use the drawings as a way of predicting my nightmares, because whenever Harvey *didn't* appear on the page, he would show up after I went to sleep. I dreaded those nights, throwing tantrums when Mom tried to put me to bed.

The dreams were usually the same: the dead bulldog with glowing blue eyes always gave chase, and Harvey's voice called out to me from the shadows. I'd usually awaken in a cold sweat, my blankets twisted up at the foot of the bed, my heart threatening to burst, and the back of my hand aching like a bad sunburn. The nightmares led me to question Harvey's intentions. If he was my friend, why was he haunting me? Surely he didn't mean me any harm, right? After all, he'd saved me from those bullies all those months ago.

I kept on drawing my creepy pictures during the day and running from that rotting dog at night. Soon the terrors began to manifest in other ways.

One particular weekday night, while Mom was at one of her night classes, I was alone upstairs watching a movie on TV. Granny was downstairs reading her Bible, and I was supposed to be asleep already, but with the nightmares and the fact that Mom wasn't home yet, I begged Granny to let me stay up.

"Granny, I'm afraid if I go to sleep that dog will get me. Please let me watch another movie. Please please please."

"Sweetie, you need to rest. Your mommy will be home soon, I promise. You won't even miss her."

I wrapped my arms around Granny's waist and closed my eyes. "Please, Granny. Don't make me run from that dog again."

She ran her fingers through my hair and sighed. "One more movie, and then you need to sleep. Yell for me when it's over and I'll come tuck you in. Okay?"

"Thank you, Granny." I kissed her cheek.

"You're spoiled rotten, you know that?"

I nodded, grinning. She walked over to the VCR and put in my favorite Disney cassette, *Bedknobs & Broomsticks*. She stayed with me for a while—the film was one of her favorites, too—but soon left to return to her Bible study. I curled up on Mom's bed, watching as Ms. Eglantine Price tried to conceal her interests in witchcraft from three orphans, transfixed by the mixture of magic and realism, and I was so absorbed in the movie that I didn't notice the movement to my right.

Back then, we had a three-tiered Pepsi display used to hold 2-liter bottles of soda. This display shelving stood to the right of my mom's bed and had been repurposed as a shrine to my favorite stuffed animals. Sitting in the middle of the top shelf was my favorite out of them all: a beige monkey with dark brown paws and black marble eyes.

When I was younger, I carried this monkey with me everywhere. I slept with it and ate with it. The poor thing had permanent stains around its snout where I'd tried to feed it. The top tier of that shelf was reserved for the monkey and nothing else. He sat in the middle like a king. I hadn't played with him in at least a year.

When the movement finally caught my attention, I turned to find the beige monkey crawling toward the edge of the display shelf.

"I'm comin' for your Granny, kiddo. Coming to get her and there's nothin' you can do about it."

I screamed, trying to scramble my way out of the nest of blankets—but my foot was caught, and I fell to the floor with a startling thump. I screamed again, this time accompanied by a stream of tears from the ache in my arm from my landing.

"*GRANNY!*" I shrieked, clamoring to regain my footing. She met me at the bottom of the stairs, almost as panicked as I was. I wrapped my arms around her, sobbing into her nightgown.

"Shhh, it's okay, I'm here." She gave me a squeeze, knelt down before me, and wiped the tears from my cheeks. "What happened, honey? What's wrong?"

"My monkey," I choked out. "It was coming after me."

She tried to keep from laughing. "Oh, sweetie. You were just dreaming."

I shook my head. "I wasn't dreaming. It was moving, Granny. I promise you it was."

"Well, let's just go have a look."

But I held her hand. I couldn't let her go back up there. Not after what the monkey had said. *I'm comin' for your Granny, kiddo.* I shivered, trying to hold her in place, but she resisted.

"Come on," she said. "Nothing's going to hurt you."

More tears gushed as my heart continued to race. I followed her up the stairs, panicked that something terrible would be waiting for her at the top. I waited on the landing, still crying, fearful that the monkey would attack—but all that followed her ascent was quiet laughter. She emerged from the room, standing at the top of the doorway holding the monkey in her hand.

"Honey, look. You had a bad dream. That's all." She held it out to me. "It's just your monkey."

I recoiled from that stuffed abomination, its dead eyes burning a hole right through me. I shook my head, crawling backward against the banister.

"It's a monster," I sobbed. "I don't want it anymore."

She gave me a puzzled look, then stared at the monkey for a moment. "If you say so, honey." She tucked the animal under her arm. "Scoot on up to bed and I'll tuck you in."

Reluctant, my heart still racing, I retreated back to Mom's bed. I made Granny leave the lamp on and the bedroom door open. I stared at the top shelf of the Pepsi stand, wondering if any of my other toys were going to spring to life and attack me. The monkey's words crawled through my mind.

I drifted off to sleep and dreamed I was running from the monkey while it swung from invisible branches. Harvey's voice echoed in that dark dream chamber: *Comin' for your Granny, kiddo.*

And when he finally did, I thought I would be ready for him.

We didn't tell Mom about the monkey incident. She was worried enough, what with my drawings and strange dreams. The word "doctor" got tossed around a lot in those days, usually accompanied by furrowed brows and concerned glances when they thought I wasn't looking. At first, I pretended not to notice their attempts at secrecy, but one day while playing with my toys I overheard Mom and Granny discussing the dark man in my drawings.

"—who do you think that's supposed to be?"

I turned away from my Legos. Granny stood at the edge of the kitchen table with her back to me. Mom was sitting down, around the corner where I couldn't see her. Granny had one of my drawings in her hand.

"He says it's his friend Harvey," Granny said. "It's not uncommon for kids to have imaginary friends."

"I know that, Granny, but this is a little scary, don't you think? I mean just look at this guy. Is he supposed to be a ghost? Or the Devil?"

I turned away, suddenly very interested in the red Lego brick in my palm. The sound of shuffling papers trailed down the hallway. The Devil? No way. Harvey wasn't the Devil. He was—

He's a tempter, a snake, the enemy of God. Everything he does is meant to hurt mankind, even if it doesn't seem like it. He's evil. That's just what he does.

The red Lego brick fell from my hand, clattering against the pile of multi-colored bricks spread out before me. Granny's words echoed in my head, and I was startled when Mom called out to me.

"You okay in there, honey?"

"I'm fine, Mommy."

A silence followed my words, and for a moment I was alone with just my thoughts. Was Harvey the Devil? No, he couldn't be. He just couldn't. The Devil was a big red guy with a tail and horns. He carried a pitchfork and poked people in their butts to make them fall into a big flaming hole in the ground.

And yet the nightmares hadn't started until I met him. The strange burning sensation in the back of my hand hadn't started until he left his mark on me. What if Harvey wasn't my friend? What if he just said that so he could come inside Granny's house?

"Doesn't look like the Devil to me. You know Toddy's got a big imagination. You've seen the other things he draws, sweetie. He could've picked this up from something he saw on TV somewhere. Why's this one any different?"

Mom sighed. "I don't know, Granny. I just—I'm just worried about him, that's all. Between his nightmares and this dark man he keeps drawing, I'm just scared. For no damn reason, I guess. Maybe I'm crazy."

"You're not crazy. You're just tired. Stressed. You've been working too hard, and..."

She trailed off, stopping mid-sentence as that last word lingered in the air. I turned around, eager to hear what else Granny had to say, but she never finished. She slowly bent forward, her arms pressed against the edge of the table, and I heard her say something that sent a chill crawling across my skin.

"It's dark," she groaned. "Oh Lord, it's all gone dark."

Granny's voice was all wrong. She sounded like she was in pain and maybe a little scared, too. I stared at her, unable to move.

"Granny?" I heard Mom's chair scrape the floor as she rose from the table. It clattered backward, and in a moment she was at Granny's side. "What's wrong?"

"All gone dark," she said, "'cept for those blue eyes." Her head rolled to the side, turning to stare at me. "It's going to be okay, honey. I just need to go rest..."

Her knees buckled and her arms went limp as her eyes rolled back into her head. Her mouth hung open in a confused gape, and had my mom not been fast enough, Granny would've hit the floor hard enough to crack her head open. Mom caught her, bracing herself against the dead weight.

"Granny!" Mom was crying now. She knelt and let Granny slide to the dining room floor. I broke free of my trance and went to her.

"Mommy, what's wrong with her?" Jaw quivering, I tried hard to hold back tears. I wanted to be brave for Granny, for my mom. "Is she dying?"

"Baby, I hope not. Stay with her. I'm going to call an ambulance."

So I stayed with Granny, watching beads of sweat form on her forehead and roll backward into her signature bouffant. For the first time I recognized the signs of her age, noting the wrinkles and spots in her skin and the slight sag of her cheeks. Until that moment, Granny had been just a big kid in my eyes, far removed from the other adults in my life, capable of a kindness and love rivaled only by my mother. She'd been there for as long as I could remember, and until I watched her sink to the floor, I was certain she would *always* be there.

Now I wasn't so sure, and that epiphany shook me to my core. I couldn't hold back my tears any longer.

"Don't go," I whispered. "I'm still not done building a robot with my Legos, and you promised we'd go for a milkshake later, so you can't go. I won't let you."

Mom's voice carried from the living room. She was panicked but trying to remain calm. I heard her giving someone on the phone our address.

Granny slowly opened her eyes, her lips twitching and the muscles in her face tightening. I didn't understand it at the time, but she was trying to speak. The stroke had taken that privilege from her temporarily, and all she could do was stare up at me, at the ceiling. After a moment her face relaxed, and she held my gaze, watching me cry over her.

"Don't go," I said. "Please don't go. Don't."

The effects of Granny's stroke were immediate and invasive. Although she regained the ability to speak several hours after being admitted to the hospital, the left side of her face remained oddly paralyzed, slowing her speech to a collection of slurred, agonizing syllables. When she spoke, she seemed to do so with a mouth full of rocks.

She also had trouble with her hands. Maintaining a consistent grip on anything was laborious, and for the first few weeks she had to test her strength with a handheld device that looked like it had been ripped from one of those arcade machines at the supermarket, except this one didn't take quarters.

Mom and I spent our evenings with Granny in her hospital room, watching game shows and then the nightly news. We stayed until visiting hours ended, and then we'd say our goodbyes until the next day. This was our routine for a week before she was discharged from the hospital. Her doctor said he expected full recovery within six months, provided her physical therapy went well.

Three times a week, a nurse came to our house to help Granny with her hand and speech exercises and little by little she regained her strength. More importantly, she got her voice back. Toward the end of her rehab sessions, Granny was her old self again, that spark in her eye burning brighter than ever. When she received her doctor's approval to drive again, the first thing she did was head off to Arlene's Beauty Shop. Her hair hadn't been touched since the stroke and was long overdue for that signature 1960s styling.

Life slowly crawled back to its normal pace. Mom went to work and I went to school. I drew a portfolio's worth of pictures for Granny's refrigerator door. She cooked for us and laughed with us. We watched movies together and played together. My friend was back. Everything was perfect.

Mom eventually remarried, and we moved out of Granny's upstairs bedroom to go live with my new stepdad. Those days, I didn't get to see Granny much, but I always called her in the afternoon when I got home from school. We'd talk about what I was learning, what games I was playing, if I'd drawn her any new pictures for her refrigerator, and how Mom was doing.

I missed Granny so much sometimes that I'd ask to spend my weekends with her, and that's how time passed for a while: me living at home during the week, going to school, counting down the days until I could spend the weekend with Granny. Then Friday would come around and Granny would pick me up from school. We were like a dynamic duo, me and Granny, making an escape from Corbin Elementary like a pair of wild bandits riding off into the early afternoon sunshine in her forest green Cadillac.

Several months later, just a few days before the fourth of July, a second stroke tore our return to normalcy out from underneath all of us.

I was there with her when the stroke happened. She was lying on the couch, and I remember her saying those same three words.

"All gone dark," she said. "All gone dark."

"**H**oney, don't do that."

I looked up from my pad of paper. Granny sat in her armchair, a small stack of newspapers and magazines on one side and a beige ottoman on the other. She was staring at the window to her left, frowning.

"What, Granny?"

She glanced at me for a moment and shook her head. "Not you, sweetie. The little girl in the rocking chair right here. She's rocking too fast."

Smiling and trying to hide my confusion, I climbed off the couch and walked over to the window where she was staring.

"Granny," I said, "it's just us here. There's no little girl. You don't even have a rocking chair."

I'll never forget that look of surprise on her face as if I'd slapped her across her cheek. She was absolutely dumbfounded, stunned into silence, and for a few minutes afterward, whenever she looked at me, she did so out of spite. My face flushed with heat, bearing a shame I didn't quite understand. Had I done something wrong? Why was Granny mad at me?

Except she wasn't. Minutes later, she asked if I'd refill her water glass. She had a grin on her face like she was the keeper of a big secret. I did as she asked, and when I gave her the glass I walked over to the telephone and called my mom's work number.

"Is something wrong? Is Granny okay? Are *you* okay?"

"I'm fine, Mommy," I whispered. I didn't want to rouse Granny's attention. "But Granny's starting to scare me."

"Oh, honey, you remember what we talked about? Remember what I said about how strokes can affect the way you think?"

"I do, but this is different. She's seeing things again, and when I told her so she kinda got mad at me."

Mom sighed. "Honey, you need to remember that when she does those things, it's because she's confused. You know Granny loves you and that she wouldn't do anything to upset you."

"But what if she stays mad at me?"

"Toddy, don't be silly. I'll be home in just a few hours, okay? Promise me you'll be patient with her?"

"I promise, Mommy."

"I love you, sweetie. See you soon."

I hung up the phone and looked back at Granny. She was slumped back in the chair with her head to the side. Her chest rose and fell in slow, measured swells. Granny napped a lot—something she never liked to do before the strokes happened. "They're a waste of the day," she always said, rising early to make the most of her time.

And yet as I stood there, I couldn't shake the feeling that this person had replaced my Granny. This woman was old and confusing and scary. She looked at me with anger sometimes, and other times she was too happy, seemingly in a perpetual state of giddiness. Sometimes she said things that didn't make sense, and sometimes she saw things that weren't there.

This doppelgänger had taken my friend away from me and replaced her with a hollowed-out husk of a human being. I wanted Granny back.

I'll give anything, I thought. *Even all my Legos.*

Defeated, I wandered across the living room toward the couch—but something caught my eye halfway there. I stopped in the middle of the room and turned toward the window. The back of my hand began to itch, and I scratched at it idly as I approached the glass pane. Outside and across the street, just beyond a row of trees in Granny's front yard, I saw a man in a black suit standing with his hands in his pockets. He had a black goatee and black hair cropped close to his head. I could see his glowing blue eyes even from across the street.

My hand stopped itching and started burning.

For the second time, almost a year to the day, Harvey J. Winterbell had decided to pay me a visit. This time we weren't friends.

"Are you the Devil?"

A thin smile spread across Harvey's face. "Do you want me to be?"

"*Are* you?" I stood at the edge of the grass, mere feet from him. The warm afternoon air was thick with the stench of rotten eggs. "Is your name even Harvey?"

"*You* gave me this name, child. I have many. Harvey is just one of them."

"I thought you were my friend, but ever since we met I've had nothing but terrible dreams about you and that dead dog in the kennel, and one night when I was trying to go to sleep my favorite monkey attacked me and..."

I gasped for breath, the words coming faster than I could breathe. I was so angry my hands were shaking, and the smile on Harvey's face just made me even madder still.

"Side effects of the mark I gave you, kiddo. Dreams, delusions, drawings—I manifest in many different ways, from person to person, especially with young ones like you. It'll go away when you get older, though. You'll be haunted by different demons by then." He paused, frowning. "Don't look at me like that, Toddy. I can be your friend when I have to be. You needed me that day when those two boys locked you up in that dog kennel. Who else would've let you out?"

He waited. I wanted to say something, but no words came. I just stood there, shaking and glaring at him as if that might make a difference. "See? You needed me, and I was there for you. And now I'm here again, but not for you."

"What do you mean?"

He took out a cigarette and lit the tip with a snap of his fingers. He took a long drag and exhaled a cloud of smoke.

"I think you know," he said. "You're a bright one. I'm sure you can figure it out."

My heart sank. He'd warned me months ago. The monkey's silent words were forever etched in my brain. How could I forget? Comin' for your Granny, kiddo. Coming to get her and there's nothing you can do about it.

"Bingo," he said.

"But you *can't!*" I took three steps forward and glared up at him. Tears lingered in the corners of my eyes, but I wouldn't let him see me cry. I had to be strong for Granny. "I won't let you, Harvey."

"Come on, kiddo." He reached down and tousled my hair, just like Pastor Thurmond used to do. "You think that's your Granny in there? She's a shell of a person. Whatever years she has left will be spent in a wheelchair, in a nursing home. I'm doing her a favor by taking her now. You think she wants to spend the rest of her life as a vegetable?"

His words made sense. I didn't want to grow up watching Granny grow older and slowly lose her identity. I didn't want to watch the embers in her eyes die one day at a time until there was no light left to shine. But I remembered what Granny told me about the Devil that Sunday morning, and I did the only thing I felt I could do: I pushed him.

My palms burned when I pushed against his stomach. I cried out in pain, freeing the tears in my eyes. I looked down at my hands. Blisters formed on the tips of my fingers.

"You should put some ice on that," he said. "Looks painful."

"Shut up," I grunted. "You're not taking Granny, and that's that. Now go away!"

Harvey J. Winterbell leaned back and let loose a wild cackle that shook the world. The air stirred in a warm, bitter wind that flattened the grass and swayed the trees. Branches tore from their trunks and clattered to the ground. When he spoke again, he did not sound like the man I knew. His voice was gruff and guttural, a voice of inhuman nature loosed from the heavens and given dominion over the kingdom of man.

Harvey's eyes bled thin trickles of blue down his cheeks, and when he opened his mouth to speak, I glimpsed crackling flames of hellfire in his throat.

"I will take what I wish, child. Now be gone."

Only I didn't listen. The words were out of my mouth before I could stop them, and at the time they seemed like the only words worth speaking. The only words that mattered. Sometimes words are all a kid really has, and if I'd ever said anything worthwhile in my life up to that point, this was it.

I looked Harvey in the eye and said, "I'll do anything to keep you from taking her."

And then, like a switch, Harvey's demeanor changed. He was his old, magically jovial self again. He'd heard exactly what he wanted to hear.

"Anything?"

I nodded, feeling a sudden weight in my stomach. My Sunday School lessons came racing back to me. The Devil made deals all the time, and his only currency was human souls.

Reluctant, yet scared for Granny's life, I looked the Devil in the eye and nodded.

"Anything," I said.

"I don't know," Harvey said, rubbing absently at his goatee. "What could you possibly have that I would want?"

I shrugged. "My soul?"

"Oh, there's that, but what's the soul of a child worth these days?"

He clapped his hands. "I've got it. Instead of your soul, I think I'd rather have your life."

I took a step backward in fear. "You're going to kill me?"

"No, no, no. In exchange for not taking your Granny, your life will belong to me until the day she dies. From now until then, you are mine."

"You mean I won't go to Hell?"

"That's not for me to say. That's up to you. But you will be bound to me from this day forth until she leaves this earth. This is my price. Pay it, and I will leave your Granny be."

He stuck out his hand. I'd like to say I hesitated, maybe contemplated just what I was agreeing to, but being only nine at the time, I didn't do anything like that. I did what Granny would've told me not to. I did what I felt I had to do, what my heart told me was right.

I looked him in the eye, reached out, and shook the Devil's hand.

I'd like to say Granny recovered after that, but I can't, and she didn't. Granny's condition grew increasingly worse. The day I saved Granny from the Devil, I lost a piece of myself that I knew I would never get back, and for a long time I lived in fear that I was damned to spend my afterlife in eternal agony, burning forever in the fires of Hell. Even if my heart was in the right place, even if I'd sold my most prized spiritual possession to God's greatest enemy to keep Granny alive, I knew I would suffer for it. Even the purest act of love couldn't outweigh the laws of a cruel, jealous god.

I paid for my sin by watching Granny lose herself one day at a time. She deteriorated to a point that she couldn't take care of herself, and without Mom and I there, my dad's family decided to have Granny put in a rest home. She spent the rest of her days there, in a hospital-like building with lifeless white walls and a stench of ammonia, bleach, and urine.

Visiting her was always awkward. There were other old people there, forgotten and left to rot by families who either didn't care or simply couldn't handle the stress. Most of them sat in a commons area, dressed in sweat suits and gowns, their hair unkempt, lethargically staring at a TV tuned to a channel of never-ending game shows. I hated the smells and the sounds. I hated the apathy of the nurses and doctors.

I tried to visit her as often as I could, but as I grew older my life took on its own schedule. I was busy with school and friends, busy with other things. I realize now I told myself these things to justify not going to see her. Because I was afraid. Because looking at her was a reminder of the price I'd paid. Even then I knew how selfish I was.

My nightmares continued, but instead of being chased by a dead dog or a silent monkey, I always found myself in an observation room of some kind, with a pane of one-way glass separating me from the cell beyond. In the middle of that blank room was a chair, and sitting in that chair was Granny, her wrists and ankles tied down. She was always struggling, always trying to free herself, crying out to God to save her. "Water," she'd rasp, and I'd bang on the glass, screaming for someone to please, please give my granny some water.

No one ever came, and I'd wake up shivering and covered in sweat, Granny's cries still echoing in my head.

I was twelve when I stopped going to see her at the nursing home. Mom and I rode the elevator up to her floor, wandered our way through a series of hallways filled with the lost souls of generations past, and found Granny sitting up in her bed, staring vacantly at the television.

"Hey there," Mom said, pulling up a chair beside the bed. "How are you today?"

Granny didn't respond. I shuffled my weight from one foot to the other and sighed. Mom knew I didn't want to be there, knew how uncomfortable I was in that place, but she'd mandated I come along. I hadn't seen Granny in several months, and the last time Mom visited she said Granny had asked about me.

Except when Granny took her eyes off the TV and looked at me, she didn't react like she used to. Her eyes didn't beam like they used to. She didn't smile. Instead, she looked at me with that same accusing stare from years before. Her eyes narrowed, and she drove her gaze away from me, focusing on my mother.

"He wanted to come see you," Mom lied. "He sure is growing, isn't he?"

But Granny shook her head. "I don't know this boy. Who is he?"

Those words pierced me like bullets. My breath caught in my throat, and even though I'd built myself up to believe that I resented her, I still felt as though I'd been cut down on a distant battlefield. I stepped backward, blinked away my tears, and walked out of the room. I never returned.

My teenage years were a tumultuous time, and although I don't think I was a bad kid by any stretch, I had my share of transgressions. High school brought its own troubles to accompany the storm raging inside me, fueling the anger in my heart that had been threatening to bubble up and explode since that day I shook the Devil's hand.

The longer I spent away from Granny, the longer I resented her for everything that had happened. After all, I never would've had to make my deal if she hadn't had her strokes. Everything had been fine until she collapsed into Mom's arms. My resentment was fueled by a deeper loathing that I didn't understand at the time, but that I now know was my own selfishness. I wanted to keep her around and was willing to sell my soul to do it, but all I got in return was a husk of a great-grandmother, her spark faded, dimming, dying—and a lingering shadow that followed me everywhere.

I had friends in school, but none of them were as close to me as Granny had been, and the innocent eyes through which I'd once viewed that sacred pact of friendship were tarnished by the harsh realities of adolescence. Children may be cruel, but teenagers are sadistic.

I was quiet. I wore black T-shirts. I carried with me a persona of mystery, and as I blossomed into a young man I began to grow a goatee just like Harvey. I figured that if I were damned, I might as well fit the part and walk that walk. My teenage arrogance was palpable. I suppose it was only a matter of time before I accumulated a rogues' gallery of enemies within the walls of Corbin High.

A rumor began floating around during my freshman year that I was a Satanist. A fitting rumor, to be honest, but at the time I was troubled with my convictions and struggling to find a place in the greater Christian scheme. I was anything but a Satanist, but trying to explain that to a group of teenage boys who hated my guts was out of the question. I weathered that storm for a while, ignoring their snide comments in class and the notes they passed around school. I tried to ignore the pentagrams I'd find drawn on my locker—and I did, for the most part, until one day I reached my limit.

I'd never been in trouble at school before. Teachers always had good things to say about me and my work. But one day, while standing in line at the cafeteria, one of the boys who perpetrated that rumor of Satanism made one smartass quip too many. I was suddenly eight years old again, locked away in that dog kennel by two bullies who were bigger than me, stronger than me.

This time I had the Devil on my side.

I was a tall kid for my age, and this punk who'd spent weeks sniping at me was a little on the heavy side. I spun on my heels, planted my foot behind his, took him by the throat, and shifted my entire weight against him. He teetered backward, falling flat on his back, and I went with him, a victim of my own gravity. I held him by the throat as students called out for a teacher. He stared at me, stunned, afraid, and I remember feeling alive with electricity, a powerful surge of vindication. I felt his fear.

"*You will leave me alone or I'll tear out your goddamn throat.*" I squeezed his neck, digging my fingers into his reddening flesh. Two teachers had to pull me off him, dragging me out of the cafeteria toward the principal's office while the kid curled up on the floor, gasping for air. He never bothered me again.

The principal called my mom, and she came down to the school to get me. This was before the days of shootings and bomb threats. I faced in-school suspension—the first reprimand I'd ever had, for that matter—and during the entire car ride home, Mom alternated between yelling at me and crying. I remember feeling remorse to an extent. Not for the kid, of course—he deserved what I'd done—but remorse for how I made my mother feel.

I stormed off to my room when we got home, wanting nothing more than to be alone from the world to shut out everything I'd done. Mom wasn't having any of that, and she followed after me.

"We're not finished here, young man."

"I don't want to talk about it."

"But you're going to talk about it," she said. "I don't know what to do with you anymore. You never talk to me. You come home and shut us out of your life. You never go to church with us anymore. And now you're wearing these dark clothes and the music you're listening to honestly scares me. Is it any wonder those kids think you're a Satanist?"

"I don't care what they think."

"That's bullshit. If you didn't care, you wouldn't have nearly choked a boy to death."

Mom sat down at my desk, planted her elbows on her knees, and buried her face in her hands. She sobbed for a few minutes, and I just stared at her, not really feeling anything. How could I expect her to understand? I could barely communicate what I felt with my drawings. Giving voice to what was going on inside my heart was beyond my ability. Instead, I sat there with a ball of cotton in my throat, watching my mother cry with the same grief she had when Granny collapsed that day.

After a few awkward minutes, Mom wiped her eyes and stared at me. She shook her head.

"What *happened* to you? You aren't the same child I raised."

The Devil happened to me. The words were on the tip of my tongue but I couldn't bring myself to speak them. I might have said the Devil made me do it. Except he didn't. He didn't make me do any of it. All of this was my own doing—the regret, the anger, the resentment. Everything I felt, everything that happened to me, including the Devil's shadow that followed me every step of the way and the dreams that haunted my sleep, was all a result of my own behavior.

I had chosen my path by shaking the Devil's hand. My actions were my own, pieces of a greater whole. Sitting there, looking at my mom's mascara-streaked face, I realized the picture I was drawing of myself was bleak: a sketch of scratchy lines and incomplete shadows.

I still couldn't bring myself to answer her, though. She grounded me for a month from TV and video games. All I had left were books and my drawings. I didn't understand it at the time, but Mom grounding me was one of the best things she ever did.

Harvey J. Winterbell was right: the mark went away as I got older, and I was haunted by different demons. Harvey was still with me, of course—not in physical appearance, mind you, but in the metaphysical sense. The creative sense. He was always there in my drawings, somewhere, even if I didn't give him shape or form. His demons were now mine, and I took to the page with my pencils and pens, scribbling away, trying to free myself of them. But they were still there—dark shapes lurking in the background, between the lines, always watching. Accusing me. Mocking me.

My drawings became more erratic in that month-long purgatory. Every face looked evil. Every eye was blue, every chin covered in a closely-groomed goatee. Any outsider would've assumed these drawings were a series of self-portraits—after all, I had fashioned myself to look just like my tormentor in a sick form of Stockholm Syndrome. No matter how hard I tried to break free of that cycle, every time I put pencil to paper, Harvey and his demons were there.

Frustrated to the point of tears, I ripped up that last drawing and threw the pieces into the air. I'd hit a wall, questioning my sanity in the process. Was it normal for a teenager to lose his mind? I can't say. I heard my mother discussing the possibility of taking me to see a "professional," much in the same way as she'd done with Granny when I was a child.

My therapy came in a different form. I'm not sure if the books or the writing came first, but halfway through that month of confinement to my room, I started using a pencil to draw letters instead of pictures. I had a small library of books, mostly leftovers from my younger years—books by R.L. Stine and Ray Bradbury and John Bellairs—but my mom also had a cache of grown-up novels by Stephen King and Dean Koontz. I procured a copy of *Intensity* from her bookshelf one afternoon after school when she wasn't home and hid it in my room.

I read the story at night, long after my parents expected me to be asleep, devouring its pages and living through the author's words. I found a strange sort of peace within my own head while reading that book. More importantly, the demons weren't there. The nagging, mocking weight that sat upon my shoulders was lifted for a brief time, leaving me with nothing more than the magic of mere words. I'd found a way to escape my demons. To run from them.

But to chase them? That was something infinitely more difficult—yet I had to try.

So late one night after my parents went to bed, I crept out from under the blankets, turned on my desk lamp, and began writing a story. Harvey wasn't in it, and neither were our demons, and for the first time since I'd given myself to him in order to save Granny, I found some semblance of peace within myself.

I kept writing. I kept chasing my demons. And Harvey didn't follow.

Life went on for me even after serving my month-long sentence. I grew up. I finished high school and enrolled in college. I wrote stories about bad things happening to even worse people. I became defiant, determined to go against my family's wishes. We argued and we fought. We turned our backs on one another, and by the time I finished college, I'd had enough of the small town in which I'd spent most of my life.

I packed up my things and moved almost a thousand miles: far enough to get away from my past so it couldn't haunt me anymore. Far enough that no one could touch me. I left everyone behind, including my granny.

Granny, the woman who had raised me, who was my best friend, the woman who had died to me the day I gave my life for hers. I'd finally found a way to escape the mess I'd made for myself, carving my thoughts into empty white paper one word at a time. I shirked my responsibility in exchange for what I thought was self-fulfillment. Once again, I thought I was doing something right, but in reality, I was being just as selfish as ever.

I moved away, leaving behind someone who I thought didn't mean anything to me anymore.

Six months had passed when I got a call from my cousin. I hadn't spoken to anyone in my family since I'd left, and even then our words had been sour, tainted. I was visiting a fellow writer at her home, hanging out and listening to music, talking about our current works in progress and exchanging the woes of a writer's life. Agents and publishers. Editors and being edited. I was far away and living in my element, exorcising those demons one by one, and meeting others who were doing the same thing. For the first time in my life, I felt like my own person. A *new* person, removed from his past. Free.

My phone rang, and I excused myself from the room. I walked outside into the dark, sucking in the crisp autumn air, and examined my cell phone. My heart skipped a beat when I saw it was my cousin.

We'd not talked all that much after I'd gone to college. My curiosity got the better of me, and I answered. The world dropped out from beneath me.

"Listen," my cousin said, "you need to come home. Granny passed away tonight."

I've made some long drives in my life. The drive from Pennsylvania to Kentucky is anything but short, and the time of day is a determining factor of its length. The day I left for Kentucky, I had to work first shift at my crappy retail job. My wife Erica (she was my girlfriend at the time) picked me up from work because we only had one car. We left from there, driving through the night across the mountains of Maryland and West Virginia. Erica slept, and I had a lot of time to myself to think about everything.

I hadn't seen Granny since that day in the nursing home when she didn't recognize me. I couldn't bring myself to face her after that. Now here I was, returning home to pay my respects to the woman I had shunned during my teenage years. I'd left her behind like the detritus of my past, scraps of paper crumpled in a wastebasket, filled with the lines of incomplete drawings.

We'd just crossed the Kentucky state line when I realized the pact was complete. Although I'd spent the last several years ignoring the nightmare of our agreement, chasing away Harvey's demons with every single written word, I had failed to recognize Harvey's absence. To be fair, I hadn't drawn anything in years, so if he was still with me in the form of his looming shadow, I didn't know—or maybe I refused to see him. Maybe I couldn't. Maybe I'd grown blind to him like any other child does to an imaginary friend.

To my surprise, I felt nothing. No sorrow, no fear, no relief. I was going back home exactly how I wanted to be: a clean slate.

We arrived at my mom's house around five in the morning. The funeral visitation wasn't until that evening, so we had time to catch up on our sleep, but I tossed and turned in my old bed. Everything was smaller than I remembered. To be back in my room felt like a dream in which everything is familiar and somehow foreign at the same time, slightly off, with memory and reality colliding. I spent most of the dawn trying to justify my actions of the last ten years, worried that the peace I'd worked so hard to find would suddenly leave me.

When I finally slept, I did so deeply and without dreams. After I woke, I spent the hours leading up to the visitation composing my thoughts, preparing for an onslaught of nasty looks and remarks. As the black sheep of the family, I suppose that was to be expected, but it didn't stop me from asking if I could say a few words. I felt that was appropriate—even if they didn't—and nothing they could do would stop me. I only asked to be polite.

Truth is, though, I had no idea what I'd say. Not until I put pen to paper. How arrogant I felt, composing something for a woman who I had all but abandoned—but that was all the more reason to do it. I owed her. She didn't have to be a Granny to me but did so anyway.

I felt ashamed, scribbling my words onto paper. Memories of all I'd felt, done, and said over the last ten years washed over me. A tsunami raged in my head, and I expected Harvey to resurface, but he didn't. I was alone with my thoughts. Just as I'd always been.

I stepped outside the funeral home for some air. Members of my family lingered inside, shaking hands, thanking longtime friends for showing up to pay their respects. I hadn't yet read what I had to say, struggling with the right time, struggling with the fear that what I had to say would be taken out of context. Everyone was civil to me that night, leaving me to wonder if the scorn I expected was nothing more than a projection of how I felt about myself.

Standing under the awning, watching cars drive by on Master Street, I fell into my own thoughts. My heart was racing and my hands shook. Had I grown into the man she always wanted me to be? Had I made her proud? That was a laugh—there's no way I possibly could have. I wasn't worthy of her love. I was a selfish child. I wanted her for myself, even if it meant her suffering through the last of her days. I condemned her to that nursing home, and for that, I was damned.

"Not necessarily."

I looked to my left. Standing in the shadows was the figure of a man. The cherry ember of a cigarette glowed in the darkness.

"Can I help you?"

"You already have, kiddo."

My heart climbed into my throat as I recognized that familiar voice. The lingering stench of sulfur rose with the breeze, causing my stomach to tumble into itself.

"Harvey?"

He stepped out of the shadows and gave a shallow bow. "In the flesh, child. I would have it no other way."

"Why are you here?"

"To honor our agreement. I told you I would own your life until the day your Granny passed on. That day has come, and here we are. Your life is now your own—just as it always was."

"What do you mean?" I stared hard into his glowing blue eyes. "It was never my own. I ruined my life the day I gave it to you. And I ruined hers."

"But she never stopped loving you, kiddo. You may have stopped loving yourself, but she never did. She never gave up on you."

I wiped tears from my eyes. I wouldn't let him see me cry. Standing there in the dark, I suddenly felt empty, a husk of a man, drained of everything. There was nothing left.

"She always told me you were a tempter, a liar. That you were the enemy of man."

"Perhaps," he said, puffing on his cigarette, "but I'm more of a mirror than an enemy. I'm here to show you who the real enemy is."

I thought about that for a moment, twisting his metaphor around in my head. I was about to respond when he held out his hand and looked at his watch.

"I need to be going. Enjoy your life, kiddo. Keep writing those stories, too. They might take you somewhere someday."

"You didn't come for her, did you?"

"Hmm?"

I took a step forward, so close I could smell his burning breath. "This was never about her, was it?"

Harvey J. Winterbell, the Devil of my life, tilted his head back and laughed. "You're just now figuring this out? Of course, it wasn't about her. This was about you. It always has been. I was there for you, child. To measure you. To teach you and test you."

I scoffed at that. All he'd taught me was anger and resentment.

"Don't look at me like that, kiddo. You know I'm right. You were given a choice, and you chose. But it wasn't about the choice so much as what you did with it." He paused for a moment, snuffing out his black cigarette beneath the sole of his shoe. "You once asked your granny why I tempted Jesus in the desert. You remember that, don't you?"

I nodded.

"Right," he went on, "and the answer is quite simple. I tempted Him because I had to, because that's what I was made to do. I am what I am because I have to be, because sometimes the Old Man Upstairs needs a measuring stick. I measured Jesus just as I measured you, and sometimes I have to cut people down to do that. I separated Jesus from His human pride, measuring His resolve against His own nature. He could've had food anytime He wanted. He could've flexed the power that was gifted to Him by His Father—but He didn't. I tested Him to teach Him that He could stand on His own, that He had the guts to become what He had to. And like Him, I gave you a choice to teach you the one thing you needed to learn."

His words vibrated in my head, filling me with confusion and turmoil. I didn't understand him then. It would be years before I could. He didn't wait for me to acknowledge him. He continued:

"You had to learn that, in life, separation is the greatest teacher. Nothing else will teach you more. You made some bad choices, kiddo. I won't lie to you about that. But they were *your* choices, and they led you exactly where you were supposed to go. You couldn't have made those choices if we hadn't met."

"Then they weren't actually choices, were they?"

"That depends on how you want to look at it. How you *choose* to look at it, even. You see a life wasted in regret and resentment, afraid of your own shadow, running from demons you chose to see. I see a life enabled to its full capacity, tempered with those sour emotions, lifting you up where you need to be. Whether or not you dissect my words, you will still reach the conclusion that you are who you are, for better or worse. You are who you *chose* to be. Where you go from here is up to you."

He turned his back to me and took a couple of steps toward the corner of the building. I watched him go with tears clinging to my eyes. He paused for a moment, cocked his head to the side, and smiled.

"She loved you something fierce, kiddo. Jesus didn't have the luxury of a Granny, but you did. Be thankful for that."

And then he was gone, leaving me standing in the dark, taking deep panic breaths. I leaned back against the brick wall of the funeral home, buried my face in my hands, and cried.

Memories are a funny thing. Sometimes the ones you try to keep afloat in your mind sink into the murk, lost forever in a sea of consciousness; other times, what you try to keep submerged has a habit of popping up to the surface when you least suspect it. I realize now that those things I left behind have come to define certain pieces of me, like vital corners of a jigsaw puzzle. Without them, the frame of a whole picture is lost, and the more integral pieces are harder to place.

Not long after Erica and I were married we returned to Corbin to visit family and found ourselves standing in Granny's dilapidated home. The property was in its final stages of being sold, and my family was there to clean out what was left of Granny's belongings. The old house had fallen into disrepair, its roof caving in, water stains on the plaster and mold growing along the walls.

I stood in the living room, smiling at old memories that hadn't surfaced in years. One piece here, a piece there, all part of a greater whole that defined the man I'd become.

Affixed to the adjacent wall was a framed newspaper cutout. The drawing was something I'd done in Kindergarten, accompanied by a story of two boys going fishing. Somehow, some way, that story ended up in the local paper, becoming my first publication. Staring at it, I suppose I should've known the path I was meant to take, but memories, well, they're a funny thing.

At the far end of the room was Granny's old writing desk. I remember her sitting in her armchair, reading a newspaper while I sat at the desk, pecking away at her old typewriter, its keys occasionally sticking, double-printing letters on the page. I'd typed a story of gibberish, letters without any meaning, tearing the page from the roller and handing it to her with a big stupid grin on my face.

"Do you like it, Granny?"

She smiled. "I do, honey." She handed me another blank piece of paper. "Now write me another one."

I saw this in my head through the transparent haze of a memory tucked away for almost two decades. I walked over to the desk and lifted its rolling cover. The typewriter sat alone, covered in a thin sheet of dust. A piece of paper was stuck in its roller, waiting for me, as if it knew I'd come back some day.

Smiling, I reached out and typed three words: ALL GONE DARK.

The last key stuck, and I closed the desk with a sigh. Turning back, watching my wife walk through the house I grew up in, watching the rest of my family pick its rooms clean of any last remaining artifacts, I reached into the past for something to remind me of what Granny and I once had. Something to reassure me and settle my fears that I'd done the right thing.

I found that something, sitting in a jumble of memories, coated in dust just like the typewriter. Me as a child, barely able to walk, sitting on Granny's knee while she sang a lullaby. She looked down at me, smiling that big heartwarming smile of hers, and told me, "You're my boy, Toddy. I'll always love you and nothing will ever change that."

I closed my eyes and took a breath. I waited, holding that picture in my mind, until everything else—the fear, the doubts, the demons—were silenced and left to drown in the shadows of the past until they, too, had all gone dark.

THE DARKNESS BETWEEN DEAD STARS

Commander Foster was memorialized today. Well, *honorary* commander. A posthumous and somewhat dubious rank, if you ask me. Maxwell Foster was never enlisted in any branch of the military, nor was he actually *in* command of anything since his ship was fully automated. The corporate executives wanted to make his death look good for the cameras and newspapers and blogs, and hey, I can't say I blame them. I'd do the same thing in their position. I suppose that's one of the things they teach you in Public Relations 101: How to Make the Best Out of a Dire Situation.

And my God, Foster's situation was most certainly dire.

How dire depends on who you ask. Offworld Incorporated's PR department already has a stranglehold on most forms of media, and I'm sure enough pockets were padded to effectively stall further inquiries by the White House-appointed Foley Commission. Such collusion between corporate interests and the various branches of government comes as no surprise, really, but in this case, I find it particularly offensive.

It's the flagrant disrespect, I think. Maxwell Foster was a civilian just like you and I. The 'official' story of what happened aboard the

DSS in Foster's final hours is a slap in the face—not only to the public but to his memory, and I'm writing this to present another version of the truth.

After playing my part in jettisoning Mr. Foster off this rock to his untimely demise, I believe that revealing the truth is the absolute least I can do. I realize this in no way absolves me of my sins, but if it at all casts doubt on the lies my former employer is feeding to the masses, then perhaps I can go to my grave with a clearer conscience.

The official story of Maxwell Foster's demise aboard Offworld's first Deep Space Shuttle, the DSS, is one of cold simplicity. A manual override of the ship's automation system ODESSA was triggered and the ship's airlock subsequently disengaged, resulting in an immediate depressurization event that caused Foster's death.

What officials were willing to reveal about this mysterious override was buried in jargon that most citizens can barely grasp, and the ultimate synopsis of the matter boiled down to a simple lapse in judgment. Offworld, Inc. has a contingency plan for just about everything, even with a fully-automated security blanket like the billion-dollar ODESSA system, but when you are millions of kilometers from Earth and you open the door to a vacuum, there isn't much Mission Control can do about it.

Maxwell Foster died twice that day. Once in the vacuum of space and again on the screens of Mission Control twenty minutes later. None of us were prepared for what we saw.

Some of the images captured by the shuttle's onboard cameras were released to the public as part of the Foley Commission's official report. Those are the images you've already seen, the ones plastered across every screen on the planet. We've all seen the blown hatch and the eerie stillness of the aftermath, with pieces of detritus floating forever in the shuttle's sterile spaces. There's the one of his toothbrush hovering out of focus before the camera. And then there's the famous photo of Maxwell's naked hand clutching the side of the airlock portal moments after he was sucked out, presumably holding on in one final attempt at saving himself. The media loved that one.

Then again, the media loved everything about the project, didn't they? "*Offworld, Inc. seeking volunteer for one-way trip to Mars.*" Variations of that headline ran for at least a year along with that disgusting slogan, "Are you Earth's MVP?" Yeah. That's the best our marketing team could do.

I was one of the lucky few appointed to the so-called MVP committee. I helped plan and execute a nationwide hunt for a suitable candidate. In the interest of Offworld's profit margin, we restricted our focus within the country, screening thousands of candidates who all thought they wanted to be Offworld's MVP. Needless to say, our task was a daunting one. After nearly three years of screenings, we narrowed our list of possible candidates down to just three. Maxwell Foster was one of them.

You probably remember the media circus around the 'MVP Three'. That was all part of the plan. Behind closed doors, our superiors told us that part of the program's success hinged on public relations. We were, after all, selecting an ordinary citizen for what amounted to a long-term suicide mission. An average, ordinary, *non-suicidal* citizen. The irony of our task was not lost on us. That little detail proved to be the ultimate crux of the whole program: which one of the candidates would be the least compelled to self-harm?

Imogene Croswell of New Hampshire, age 34, was disqualified on account of her history with substance abuse in her early 20's. She failed to disclose at the onset of our investigation, or else we might have overlooked the matter considering her decade of sobriety. Unfortunately, the prospect of sending a recovered addict into space aboard a ship stocked with a moderate supply of emergency painkillers didn't sit well with my cohorts.

David Ruiz of Arizona, age 29, was disqualified on account of being a registered sex offender. Considering he met all other requirements, my peers argued that he would be an ideal candidate for expulsion from the planet based on his disposition toward children. Once our superiors learned of his record, however, Mr. Ruiz's candidacy was denied.

Maxwell Foster of Arkansas, age 25, was a normal, healthy male of above-average intelligence, with no history of violence, substance abuse, or sexual deviation. His parents were killed in a car accident when he was nineteen. Following their deaths, he learned to live on his own, working in a garage by day and attending trade school at night.

My first impression of him was less than hopeful. His psychiatric evaluation revealed a longstanding guilt over the death of his folks. This sort of result was a huge red flag, even in the face of all his favorable qualities, but compared to the other two—and in the interest of our timetable—our superiors urged us to clear him for duty.

So after three years of screening, testing, and deliberation, Offworld Incorporated finally found their MVP.

In the months following his selection, we subjected Maxwell to every possible degree of training we could muster. Physical training, safety drills, zero gravity acclimation, preparation for atmospheric ascent—he took it all in stride. Maxwell was sharp like that. He could wrap his mind around just about anything you gave him.

We even gave him a crash course on ODESSA's override commands in the event of an emergency. That genius decision was made by Paul Pinsky, Offworld's former CEO, much to the chagrin of pretty much everyone involved in the project.

A lot of emails circulated over that choice, many of which made their way into the Foley Commission's final report on the tragedy, and for good reason. The whole point of the system was its ability to self-correct and negate the need for manual commands. The entire MVP initiative was built around this proprietary tech. Pinsky had effectively given Maxwell Foster the keys.

"It's a fail-safe for our fail-safes," Pinsky wrote in one email. "The odds that Mr. Foster will need to engage a manual override for any reason are a million to one. A billion, even."

Months after the disaster, when the finer details of Maxwell Foster's final days were coming to light, Chief Justice David Foley (the Foley Commission's namesake) subpoenaed Mr. Pinsky to testify before a congressional committee.

Of course, he never made it to that hearing. Paul blew his brains out an hour after he received the subpoena. They're still scraping him off the walls of his office. Poor bastard.

The commission built their entire case around Paul Pinsky's lapse in judgment. I admit it was, in some ways, unfair to paint Mr. Pinsky as the villain in the whole affair, but at the end of the day, someone had to play that part. The public demanded answers to the most fundamental questions related to the tragedy: Why did it happen, and who was to blame?

Pinsky took the spotlight for the latter. The former, however, is something that will be studied, speculated, and puzzled over for decades to come. Data transmitted from ODESSA indicated that there were no anomalies prior to Foster's engagement of the system's manual override. Why, then, did he engage it? And why open the airlock?

Why, indeed.

Here's something they didn't disclose to the public.

About a week before the depressurization event, Maxwell Foster sent a transmission to Mission Control requesting a full scan of the shuttle's systems. His reasoning, he said, was due to a strange knocking heard from outside the hull of the DSS. Mission Control complied with the request, but with the caveat that he get more rest. ODESSA reported all systems were functioning normally.

Two days later, Foster sent another transmission: "Knocking again. Please re-scan. Louder this time." As before, all scans returned with normal results. When this was communicated back to ODESSA, Foster responded with four words: "It has a pattern."

Let that sink in for a moment.

Maxwell Foster was approximately 30 million kilometers from home and roughly halfway into his journey. His trajectory was calculated and plotted by a supercomputer and then re-checked by a team of geniuses. Short of there being an errant chunk of rock floating through the chaos of space—which would've done more to the shuttle than produce a simple tap on its hull—there was absolutely no reason for anything to be knocking on the outside of the ship.

Foster's comment raised more than a few eyebrows. Naturally, everyone thought he was hearing things, that the knocking was perhaps his mind's response to a lack of stimuli, similar to the effect of a sensory deprivation chamber. To be honest, that seemed like as good an explanation as any, but the executives in the company weren't taking any chances. They ordered constant monitoring through all means necessary.

Until that point in the mission, the DSS's onboard cameras were checked only once daily. Foster signed away his right to privacy the moment he accepted his place aboard the shuttle, but the folks in Mission Control still liked to stay out of his hair when possible.

Simply put, watching a man live day to day on a space shuttle is pretty damn boring.

After his troubling messages, privacy was a luxury he could no longer be afforded. Mission Control began monitoring the camera feeds at regular hourly intervals. These were more than still images. I'm talking about full video and audio—yet another fact conveniently omitted from the Foley Commission's final report. If there truly was something knocking on the outside of the ship, we'd hear it.

So we flipped a few switches and started listening.

Most of those recordings were about as banal as you'd expect. We recorded Maxwell talking to himself, singing along (poorly) to the music he'd brought along for the trip. Occasionally, we'd hear him snoring. Mostly, all we heard was the hum of air circulating through the shuttle.

And then…there it was. A pattern of sounds: *Knock. Knock. Knock-knock. Knock. Tap-tap-tap.* On repeat, at various speeds and pitch. One of our engineers spliced together the footage of multiple camera feeds from throughout the shuttle as a way of tracking the sound's progression. The result was a montage of knocks and taps running from outside one end of the shuttle to the other.

I get goosebumps just thinking about that moment. All of us standing there around the computer terminal, listening to this cacophonous rattling of something that simply should not be. And yet it was right there. We could all hear it, and not one of us could offer an explanation for its origins. The team at Offworld had conceived of every scenario imaginable in preparation for the worst—except this one. We were watching from the shore of a vast, impartial ocean, and caught in its riptide was the most innocent sailor of all.

God help us, we cast him off without a lifeboat.

Looking back, I think that's the moment everything began to fall apart. Honest panic spread through the Offworld offices. No one really knew how to deal with this discovery, but despite a general breakdown in communication from executive leadership, Mission Control continued to observe and report on Foster's daily toils.

Maxwell stopped responding to our transmissions, and further downloads from the AV feeds revealed that he wasn't just talking to himself, but responding to something coming from outside the ship. He would pull himself along the railings in the halls of the DSS, floating back and forth along the wall with the anxiety of a distressed animal, pausing every so often to press his ear against the surface. What followed was usually an outburst of some kind, either in reply or in defiance.

"I can't hear you," he'd sometimes say. Other times, he would scream, *"I won't! I can't! Impossible! STOP IT! IT ISN'T TRUE!"*

Our camera feeds revealed that he'd injured himself in those final days. One of the techs noticed dark globules hovering in front of one of the lenses. Subsequent footage revealed Maxwell raking his nails down his arms, carving deep crimson canyons into his flesh. That discovery led to another moment of panic among our ranks—not just over the sight of Maxwell's self-mutilation, but our complete helplessness and inability to stop him from doing so. What could we do but watch this young man tear himself apart?

Those final days followed the same pattern. There wasn't a single audio feed that didn't contain the goddamn noise. The knocking was bad enough, but over time, our recorders began picking up a kind of low, raspy gibberish that none of our engineers could decipher. Together, the sounds formed a maddening song only Maxwell could understand. According to ODESSA's latest data report, Maxwell hadn't slept in 72 hours, and it showed. The sickly, mutilated thing we saw on camera in those last active transmissions was a shadow of the young man I knew.

I wasn't there when ODESSA's transmission revealed the manual override had been triggered. After living at the office for the better part of a week, I'd finally allowed myself a short reprieve, removing myself long enough to get some proper sleep. A lot of good that did me though. I spent the time thinking about Maxwell, about the last conversation I had with him before his departure.

The night before launch, I wandered into the office cafeteria to grab a bite to eat, and I found Maxwell sitting by himself at a corner table. He was staring out the window, toward the launch pad where the DSS and its carrier rocket were being prepped for their big day. Even from that distance, the rocket towered over all creation, a silent testament to man's determined curiosity.

And sitting there, looking up at this pinnacle of modern ingenuity, was one brave soul who'd selflessly volunteered to lead his species toward the stars. After I'd collected a bag of chips from the vending machine, I approached and asked if I could join him.

"Sure," he said, smiling. The kid never failed to muster a smile when he was here. It's a smile that haunts my dreams to this day. We sat in silence for a while, staring out toward the DSS. Finally, Maxwell turned to me and sighed. "Do you think anything will happen?"

"Like what?"

He shrugged. "I don't know. There's a whole lot of empty space up there, and we don't know a whole lot about it."

"That's true," I said. "That's why your voluntary service is so important."

"I guess," Maxwell said, "but what if we're not meant to know it? What if we can't?"

"I suppose we'll never know if we don't try." I put my hand on his shoulder. "You'll be fine, Mr. Foster. You have an entire planet cheering for you."

He smiled and wiped his eyes. I was so caught up in staring at the launch pad that I hadn't noticed he was crying.

"Maybe you're right."

Maxwell rose from his seat and wished me a good evening, but before he could leave, I stopped him with a question of my own: "Why did you really volunteer for this? Off the record, of course."

His answer was almost immediate, spoken with that characteristic smile: "Because I have to know." The conviction with which he uttered that statement gave me chills then. It still does.

That was the last time I ever spoke to him. God, what I wouldn't give to go back there and tell that kid to walk away from the whole thing.

I was asleep for maybe an hour when the call came through. The final AV transmission had just finished downloading when I arrived at the office, and I found my coworkers standing around the terminal in horrified silence.

That image you all know from the Foley Commission's public disclosure, the grainy close-up crop of Maxwell's hand clinging to the edge of the hole torn into the side of the shuttle, was exactly that: a cropped still image taken from the video of the entire ordeal. Out of all the available data, Offworld's PR department chose that image because "it would provide the world with closure." Let me cut through the bullshit: All AV feeds to the DSS were in high-definition. The graininess was an effect added to the cropped image by Offworld's media department prior to submission to the Foley Commission.

Here is what was withheld from the world:

The last transmission begins with Maxwell Foster hovering before ODESSA's master panel. His hair is disheveled, and his face and shirt are caked in dried blood. A pattern on his forehead suggests he tried carving symbols into his skin with his fingernails. His eyes are vacant and swollen. For a moment, he looks up into the camera, almost as if asking permission for what he is about to do. A beat later, his head jerks back, and he digs one blood-caked finger into his ear.

"I told you I would," he mutters before clenching his jaw and shrieking, *"I PROMISED I WOULD!"*

When he removes his finger, fresh dollops of blood blossom outward from his ear in a sickly spiraling pattern. He moves his hands to the master panel below, and from off-camera, we hear him inputting the manual override codes. ODESSA's warning system announces the override is in effect.

At this point, Maxwell looks up into the camera once again and smiles. One of his incisors is missing. A thick globe of blood tries to escape his lips, but he sucks it back into his mouth with a childish slurp. He mouths a goodbye to the camera, offers a cursory wink, and leaves the frame.

When we switch feeds to the camera opposite the airlock portal, Maxwell is hovering before the security panel adjacent to the door. ODESSA announces activation of the airlock and begins a countdown to imminent depressurization.

This is where things stop making sense. After the count of ten, the airlock blows open, revealing the infinite pit of space beyond. From that stygian maw comes the source of the shuttle's impossible knocking. One by one, crawling along the rim of the portal like insects, are hands. Small, bloated hands, their flesh flecked and peeling like wallpaper, all beckoning to Maxwell's floating, agonizing body.

The young man is already suffering from ebullism and hypoxia, struggling against the fate he has wrought for himself, gasping for air that no longer exists. And waiting for him are those impossible hands, tapping and knocking along the rim of the portal.

A total of fifteen seconds elapses following depressurization, during which Maxwell endures one of the most painful deaths imaginable. In the final frames of the recording, the hands reach into the portal, clutch his body, and pull him from the vessel. The infamous 'closure' shot of Maxwell's hand gripping the edge is nothing more than a matter of happenstance as his fingers drag along the portal's rim.

The video looped on repeat for twenty minutes before anyone regained enough composure to stop it.

Most of Offworld's staff resigned that day. I stuck around long enough to see through the commission's inquiry, hoping I wouldn't have to do what I'm doing now. As I mentioned before, congressional pockets were lined with enough blood money to keep my testimony from seeing the light of day. Everything I've said here was stricken from the commission's record.

I'm not so naïve as to believe that what I've revealed to you here won't be met with speculation and conjecture. I'm cognizant of the fact that I will be labeled as a conspiracy theorist. So be it. The A/V footage—all ninety-six hours of it recorded from the first sign of the knocking anomaly—has been uploaded to the deep web for your perusal. It's there if you know where to look. And when you do, I encourage you to watch it. Form your own opinion.

To this day, I still cannot reconcile the events as I witnessed them, nor do I suspect I ever will. I can only speculate. Whenever I look skyward, I find myself contemplating Maxwell's words that night in the cafeteria. Perhaps what Maxwell Foster found waiting up there in the ravenous darkness between all those dead stars were answers to his questions.

What if we aren't meant to know? What if we can't?

HUMAN RESOURCES

From: Alex Newmarth
Sent: October 28, 2014 2:38 AM
To: Elizabeth Cameron; David Miller; Rena Oppegard; Mary Griffith;
CC: Charles Boid
Subject: My resignation—Boid be praised!

To All:

It is with deep regret and sorrow that I must bid you farewell. Effective immediately, I am resigning from my duties as HR manager on account of having just murdered my assistant and misleading others at the company. Additionally, let this email stand as my last will and testament, and as my confession for the sins I have committed against our glorious prophet, Charles Boid.

Three months ago, members of our IT department approached me with evidence of misappropriation of our company resources. Although they could not prove it at the time, signs pointed to one of our senior programmers, Charles Boid (Praise His Glory). They alleged that he was using our company's software and network to build, and I quote, "something evil."

Although improper usage of company resources is a serious

matter, I was taken aback by their claims, and I can honestly say that I have never heard anything like it in my twenty-year career. That being said, I approached the matter with utmost care and professionalism, and acted accordingly despite my ignorance of the greater picture. My intention now is to set the record straight regarding these allegations and sing the praises of the Anointed One who has shown me the truth beyond this veil of flesh and electrons.

My original report contained a number of egregious errors which I intend to rectify for you now, per the instruction of the Anointed One:

• Charles Boid's attitude and work ethic are not "poor" and "questionable" as previously indicated; the Anointed One requires isolation to contemplate the nature and machinations necessary to resurrect He Who Lurks Beyond the Code. In light of this, I find our prophet's actions acceptable, and I was wrong to factor them into my investigation.

• An addendum to the previous point: The account of my assistant, Jessica Beatty, which included allegations of "harassment" and "violent conduct," are hereby stricken from my report. The Anointed One's reaction to Ms. Beaty's interruption of his meditative process should only serve as an example of our prophet's dedication to his cause. Furthermore, Ms. Beatty recanted her statement shortly before transcending beyond this mortal plain. May she find solace and mercy in her ascension as she is judged by He Who Lurks Beyond the Code.

• Mr. Boid's usage of company resources to further his explorations into the electronic abyss by building and testing the gateway known as "zerzeph.net" should not be considered misconduct. By building the website in-house and utilizing the company network to test it, the Anointed One has been able to commune directly with the Old One known as Zer Zephanum, a name not spoken aloud by the tongue of man since the Fourth Reconciliation. Boid's communion will bring about a great revelation for all of humanity once the site is ready for public consumption.

In light of these arguments, I believe we were wrong to terminate his employment from the company, and as my final act as HR manager of ███████████, I recommend his position be reinstated immediately.

Furthermore, I encourage you all to experience the glory that is Mr. Boid's creation, as it was a vital part of my own personal enlightenment. Human words cannot accurately express the glory of the Old One—you must bask in the electrons and let Zer Zephanum commune with your mind. With enough time, you may transcend into that dark abyss beyond the Code and become one with His Majesty. Together, we will be one with divinity and usher forth a new era of existence for all mankind.

As a gesture of my faith in those who lurk beyond the electronic threshold, I will offer this vessel of flesh and bone in accordance with the instructions outlined in the zerzeph.net FAQ: *I want to transcend this existence. What do I do?*

Only believers of the One True Faith may truly transcend, but if your mind is pure and committed to communion with He Who Lurks Beyond the Code, then all you need do is make an offering of your most prized possession: your life. Refer to the Rituals and Incantations section for further details.

After much careful preparation, I am ready to shed this skin and become one with Zer Zephanum, Lurker Beyond the Electronic Threshold, Devourer of Minds, and Defiler of Worlds. Praise be to our prophet, Charles Boid, for showing me the way. May the world follow in his footsteps.

Warm regards,

Alex Newmarth
Manager, Human Resources
███████████████

HOUSE OF
NETTLE AND THORN

"Are you sure this is a good idea?" Jim Auster peered through the window at the old Victorian. "This doesn't even look like a sorority house."

Nick parked the car along the curb and checked the GPS. "This is it, bro. 220 Stine Way. Just like Krystal said."

They were a few miles from campus, tucked away in folds of suburbia that Jim didn't recognize, and while the house itself didn't give him the creeps, the empty neighborhood certainly did. The streetlights illuminated a cul-de-sac devoid of human presence. The other houses sat lifeless and mute, their lights extinguished despite the early hour, with yards crowded by overgrowth and thick ropes of ivy clinging to the outer walls. Jim checked his watch and saw the time was barely eight o'clock. Frowning, he turned back to the sorority house.

"What time did she say the party starts?"

"Sunset," Nick said, trying to downplay his excitement, but Jim knew better. He'd only lived with Nick for a couple of months, and he already knew how to read the guy. Not that there was much to read. In the little time they'd been together, Jim was privy to all sorts of stories about Nick's sexual prowess, recalling his high school conquests and online girlfriends. *The Internet is an untapped resource,* Nick once told him. *There are chicks everywhere looking to get laid! Social media just makes it even easier, bro!*

Some men, Jim decided, were meant to do great things, curing diseases or walking on celestial bodies; Nick Edgleman's contribution to the great human identity would be equal to a crusted stain on a pair of boxer shorts with the reek of Axe body spray.

Jim coiled his fingers on the door handle and sighed. "I was supposed to study with Megan tonight."

They climbed out of the car and stood on the sidewalk. Nick put his hand on Jim's shoulder and gave him a squeeze. "Forget about Megan. It's her loss. Just relax, bro. Be my wingman tonight and I'll introduce you to some of the ladies in my history class. They put Megan to shame."

"Thanks," Jim said, recalling his roommate's complaints about the 'lack of quality vagina' in History 101. "You're a real *bro.*"

But Nick was too caught up in the moment to catch Jim's sarcasm, walking the length of the moss-covered wall that separated the sorority grounds from the sidewalk. Jim followed his roommate to the large wrought-iron gate. He paused when he saw the symbol emblazoned between the black iron bars.

"What sorority is this again?"

Nick scratched his head, staring up at the darkened house. "I don't remember. Sigma-something."

Jim traced his fingers over the symbol. "These don't look Greek. They look like…flowers."

They *were* flowers—three of them, with their blossoms in the center supported by an odd jumble of vines. Entangled in the center of that sinewy mass was the figure of a man on all fours.

A cool October breeze rustled the trees outside the sorority house, scraping limbs against the old Victorian's gray siding and startling Jim away from the effigy on the gate. A slow chill crawled up Jim's spine as he peered up at the home of the Sigma-something sorority.

Nick's phone chirped. He reached into his pocket and thumbed the screen.

"It's her," he said, grinning.

"What'd she say?"

"'Where r u? Party is dope!'"

Jim looked up at the second-floor windows, listening for signs of life. All he heard was the crackle of leaves caught in a breeze, dragging like bodies across the empty suburban street. Sitting in the dorm and pining over the one that got away was starting to look more appealing.

"Some party," Jim mumbled. He looked back at Nick. "Listen, I'm starting to get a bad feeling about this. No one else knows we're here, and this girl is from the Internet could be anybody."

Nick rolled his eyes. "Would you put your tampon back in? Just relax. I've done this before. Besides, would you turn down tits like that?" He held out his phone, revealing a photograph of a naked, pasty-pale woman from the neck down. Jim felt a twinge of jealousy stir in his groin.

"No," he said, his eyes lingering for a little too long on the photo. "No, I don't think I would."

Smug, Nick lowered the phone and began to type out a reply. "That's what I thought. There's hope for you yet, bro."

Jim forced a smile, but deep inside, he was raging against a well-known fact of life: Hot girls always fell for the douchebags. The sting of Megan's rejection was still fresh, and her choice to date one of Nick's fraternity brothers was a shotgun blast to his pride. "I still want to be friends," she'd said.

Of course she just wanted to be friends. Jim was well acquainted with the dreaded 'friend zone'. He'd spent a week wondering what he could have done differently, gorging himself on a diet of fried comfort food while wallowing shamelessly in self-pity. Oh, what it must be like to be on the other side of the fence, to actually be *wanted* by the opposite sex instead of merely acknowledged, tolerated, and passed over.

Nick's suggestion that he stop sulking and get out of the dorm for a while seemed like a good idea at the time. After seeing the bare breasts of Nick's future conquest, Jim wondered why a girl like that would be cruising the university's social network looking for guys, but then again, who was he to question good fortune?

Maybe she saw something in Nick's profile photo, his face painted blue and white to match the university's colors as he flashed a cocky, sideways smile at the camera. Maybe it was the way he always popped up the collars on his shirts. Or maybe it was his listing of 'Hot Bitches' as an interest on his profile that led this Krystal person to send him a private message. Maybe she saw a hint of intellect in those narrowed eyes and arched eyebrows.

And maybe she's just a desperate nympho, Jim mused. *Lucky son of a bitch.*

"All right, I texted her back and asked if we have the right address—"

The porch light switched on, draping the yard in a warm glow as the front door creaked open.

A figure appeared at the threshold. "Nick?"

Nick pushed past to open the gate, crossed the yard, and climbed the porch steps. Jim followed cautiously, running his hands along the porch banister as he ascended. An old, dry vine had wrapped its way along the length of the railing, its leathery surface almost prickly to the touch.

"Are you Krystal?"

Jim rolled his eyes. Of course she was; her profile said as much. He paused behind his roommate, taking in the sights while they introduced themselves. She was taller than he expected, but evenly proportioned, her emerald green dress clinging to her body in all the right places. Her hair was pulled up in an assortment of curls, accented with a trio of purple flowers tucked behind her ear. Jim was immediately drawn to her cleavage—not because of the ample real estate but because of the glimmer of light off the flower-shaped amulet wedged in the canyon between her boobs.

"I'm so happy you could make it!"

Krystal stepped forward and wrapped her arms around Nick. She kissed his cheek and whispered something in his ear with a soft, coquettish giggle. Then her eyes met Jim's, and her playful demeanor vanished.

"Who's this?"

Grinning, Nick turned back and put his hand on Jim's shoulder. "This is my buddy, Jim. His girlfriend just broke up with him, and he's feeling a little lonely." That was a lie, of course. He and Megan hadn't actually gone that far in their relationship. In fact, 'relationship' was a loose term in this sense. Jim's cheeks flushed. "Thought maybe we'd introduce him to some of your friends."

Nick winked at him, but Jim was too focused on their host to notice his roommate's gesture. He stared at the caricature of a woman standing before them, not quite entranced by her beauty but by the *façade* of her beauty. Jim squinted, trying to determine if her face was real or just a mask.

Krystal was gorgeous, borderline perfect in the eyes of a horny nineteen-year-old, but something about the way she was staring at him, and the way she recoiled when she saw him, made him uneasy.

There was a flicker in her eyes, a glint of hatred he hadn't accounted for, and within a moment of meeting this girl, Jim wanted nothing more than to turn on his heels and run away like a scared child.

"So whaddya say, babe? Can my bro join the party?"

Krystal flashed a liar's smile, her lips extending ear to ear while giving Jim a once-over. The flicker in her eyes was there for just a moment longer before vanishing behind that smiling façade.

"Of course," she said. "I'm sure we can find someone to keep him company while we party."

"Listen, I don't want to impose." He could take a hint—he certainly wasn't welcome—and come to think of it, he wasn't exactly sure he wanted to be here anyway. Not now. He looked at Nick and shrugged. "Give me your keys. Just text me and I'll come pick you up."

"No way, bro." He looked back at Krystal, who was tangling her fingers in her amulet's silver chain. "She said it's no problem. Right, babe?"

Krystal flashed that smile of hers before staring at Jim. The heat on his face intensified as a cold snake coiled around the middle of his spine. The phantom serpent tightened, hardening his guts into stone, and he wanted to protest again, but the words just weren't there.

"No," Krystal said, "it's no problem." She gave him another once-over before taking Nick's hand. "Come. Let's party."

The foyer gave way to a large sitting room on the left replete with candelabras on the end tables, a staircase to their right, and a hallway straight ahead. Jim had never set foot in the sorority houses on campus, but he'd been in his share of fraternities, and they were all one safety inspection away from being condemned. He expected sororities to be tidy, but not *this* tidy. No, this house was immaculate and far more elegant than he'd expected—even for a sorority that operated off campus.

A gold chandelier hung above the foyer. Glass sconces garnished with red roses lined the soft green walls, leading a path of light down a hallway beside the staircase like a trail of golden crumbs. A purple velvet curtain separated the foyer from the hallway, muffling the vibrant tones of classical music playing from elsewhere in the house, its notes flitting through the air like butterflies. The room was thick with a ripe, sweet smell that Jim couldn't quite place.

"Wow," Nick said, craning his neck up to the chandelier. "Nice digs."

"Thank you," Krystal said, "it's been in our mother's family since the last reconciliation, a reward for a bountiful harvest."

Last reconciliation, Jim wondered. *Bountiful harvest? What the hell is she talking about?* He let the couple wander a few steps away, edging close to the door. Krystal excused herself for a moment, promising to return after she told her sisters about her 'boyfriend'. Once she disappeared behind the velvet curtain, Nick turned to him with his hand held up in the air, grinning like an idiot. Jim stared at him, frowning.

"Oh come on, bro. Don't leave me hanging."

"I don't think I should be here," Jim whispered. "Did you see the way she looked at me? And what's this shit about reconciliations and harvests?"

Nick reached out and pushed Jim back against the door. "I came to have a good time, and that's what I'm gonna do. You go be a little whiny bitch for all I care, but don't fuck this up for me. Maybe getting laid will do you some good, bro. That way you'll stop being so uptight and get over that bitch who dumped you."

Jim clenched his teeth. He pushed Nick back and held out his hand. "Leave Megan out of this," he growled. "And I'll stay out of your business but only if you give me your keys."

"You're not drinking?"

"No. And if you know what's good for you, you won't either."

"What, you think I'm gonna get roofied?" Footsteps echoed down the hall. Nick dropped his keys in Jim's hand and playfully slapped his cheek. "You can't rape the willing, bro."

Krystal emerged from the hallway and held out a plastic cup. "Follow me. I'll introduce you to my sisters."

Nick took the cup and followed, looking over his shoulder to mouth the word 'sisters' to Jim. The hallway stretched the entire length of the house, and the deeper they went, the more Jim felt like an outsider. Was it the way Krystal glared at him? Was it the house? A strangely familiar scent filled the air, and he was about to say something when he saw the grin on Nick's face. *Just stop it*, he told himself. *Try to relax and have a good time. It's just a party.*

"There's the kitchen," Krystal said, pointing to their right. Jim stuck his head over the threshold, observing a pair of women standing around the island in front of the sink. A dark green liquid rippled within a punch bowl. The women—both brunettes, thin and pale and dressed in snug, emerald gowns—offered Nick the same rehearsed smile as Krystal before focusing on Jim's presence.

The first brunette ladled some of the green punch into a plastic cup and offered it to Jim. She didn't smile.

"Drink? It's rich. Loosens the soil. Good for the roots."

"No thanks," Jim said, shrinking back into the hall with Nick and Krystal. "Maybe later."

"—And here is the study."

Jim turned to the room opposite the kitchen and stuck his head in the doorway. Other guys—some of them barely college age from the awkward look of them—were paired off with Krystal's sorority sisters, drinks in hand, laughing and chatting. Two sofas lined the opposite walls and were occupied with couples, their limbs entwined, heads pressed together and sucking face.

"This looks like my kind of place!"

Nick turned to Krystal and grinned as he lowered his hand to the small of her back. She ran her fingers through Nick's hair and leaned forward to whisper something in his ear. When she was finished, she flicked her tongue lightly against his earlobe.

"Is this my date?"

A new, kinder voice lilted from across the room as they entered the study. A thin girl with raven black hair seemingly floated across the room, her green dress whispering against the wooden floor. She wore a smirk on her face and a purple flower tucked in her hair, and within moments of taking her in, Jim forgot about Megan and studying.

"Jim," Krystal said, "this is Cora."

He stuck out his hand to shake, but she twisted her way into his arms before he could react. She caressed the back of his head, cradling him for a kiss. Her lips were wet and warm, and her tongue slipped into his mouth just an instant, almost so quick he later wondered if it had actually happened. Her skin smelled of honeysuckle and summertime, but the taste her tongue left in his mouth was almost metallic, gritty. He was struck with a brief sense of euphoria, his head suddenly ten pounds heavier.

Cora pulled away from him and smiled. "Nice to meet ya, handsome."

"Uh, hi." He realized his hand was wrapped around her waist, her hip pressed up against his stomach, and the sudden heat between his legs could only mean one thing. He dry-swallowed, waiting for the embarrassment to set in, but if Cora felt his erection, she made no sign. This mysterious girl had managed to fill his mind with her own form of light, and for a while, his thoughts of Megan were reduced to fading shadows, vanquished to forgotten corners.

"Sweet." Nick raised his hand again. "You gonna leave me hanging this time, bro?"

Stunned, his mind lost among a series of dark waves lapping against his skull, Jim didn't leave his roommate hanging this time.

"Maybe you'll have something in common," Krystal remarked just before tugging on Nick's arm. "Come with me. I want to show you something."

Nick flashed a sideways smile at his roommate. "I'll see you later, bro."

Jim watched them leave the room and disappear into the dim hallway. He turned back to his date. "So…did you grow up around here?"

She ran her fingers through the back of his hair, sending chills marching all the way down to his groin. "You could say that," she said. "Most of us grew up here, but some are transplants from the old country. Some of us are hybrids."

The orchestral music swelled to a crescendo as the couples on the sofa explored each other with ravenous desperation, their hands and lips venturing into forbidden territories. Wide-eyed, Jim watched as one of Cora's sisters lifted up her skirt and forced her date's face between her legs. She closed her eyes and cooed.

Beside them, one of the sorority girls pulled away from her date—his eyes were narrow slits, one corner of his lips turned up in a half-cocked grin, cheeks flushed—and kept eye contact as she lowered herself to the floor and slid her hands down the front of his pants.

Jim stared in awe. *Holy shit. Is this really happening?*

"Let's give them some privacy," Cora whispered. "Want to see the house?"

He didn't have a chance to respond before she took him by the hand and pulled him from the study. She led him through the house, wandering from room to room, seemingly at ease and at other times incredibly giddy as she gave him the tour.

Jim didn't care. His head was still reeling from all he'd seen. These girls were unlike the others he'd dated, and that fact simultaneously terrified and excited him. The red flags of alarm still flew in the back of his mind, but the more he listened to Cora's voice, the less he cared. He thought she was beautiful and the realest girl he'd seen all evening, lightyears beyond the likes of Megan Whitfield and far less fake than Nick's conquest.

Cora's syllables seeped into his bloodstream and brain like a fine gin, and by the time they reached the sitting room, he was drunk on her words and captivated by every breath.

"—and this is our wonderful mother, Iris."

He followed her gaze to the portrait over the fireplace. The painting depicted a large, blossoming flower, its purple petals interwoven with a series of prickly needles protruding from within while a number of vines faded into the earth.

Jim stepped closer, inspecting the painting's finer details. Several dark hands were trapped in the vines, their fingers clawing at the roots, trying to free themselves from their prison. Small, gray tendrils were threaded between the fingers, pulling them back down into the earth.

He remembered the insignia on the gate and turned back to Cora. She smiled with pride, and although Jim found her warmth disarming, he also found her ease with the macabre scene equally unsettling.

"So…Nick mentioned you're part of a sorority, but he couldn't remember the name. What Greek organization is this?"

"We are the House of Nettle and Thorn, true daughters of Demeter."

Jim paused for a moment, waiting for her expression to crack and reveal the big joke, but her smile never faltered, her eyes never narrowing to betray a con. "Right," he said, forcing a smile. "That sounds like a great organization."

"It truly is," Cora went on. "Our seeds are scattered across the world, but here, our roots run deepest. So they have since the last reconciliation, and so they shall until the next."

Jim kept smiling while idly checking his watch, wondering where the hell Nick ran off to. *You know where he went*, Jim scolded himself. *He's probably upstairs somewhere, suffocating himself between Krystal's enormous tits.*

Cora laced her fingers with his. "Would you like to see our garden? It's in the backyard."

She looked up at him with dark violet eyes and a smile that made his stomach flutter. Crazy never looked so beautiful, and it smelled like the sweetest of flowers.

Flowers. Yes, that's what he couldn't place earlier in the hallway, the floral smell of a greenhouse—or funeral home.

That familiar cold serpent coiled tighter around his gut, but he couldn't place why. His senses were dulled and his mind clouded by the experience. This mysterious girl both excited and terrified him. Finally, after chasing Megan for more than half a semester, he'd found a girl who was willing to show him the attention he craved, the attention he deserved. A girl who wanted *him* for a change.

He forgot about Megan and the uncertainty swelling up in his chest, giving himself over to this beautiful woman and letting her lead him by the hand down the hallway, through the kitchen, and out the back door.

The cold night air took his breath away. He hadn't realized how warm it was inside the house. Cora let go of his hand and floated down the steps to the patio; at the edge was a large flowerbed that stretched the entire length of the backyard. Jim knew little of horticulture, but he could spot a rose anywhere, and she was dancing between the rows, her body moving in time with the muffled tune coming from within. He took a seat on the steps, watching her odd dance and wondering if this night could get any stranger.

Cora danced halfway across the garden before pirouetting between two rows of flowers. She fanned her fingers across the leaves and petals, communing with the flora as she made her way back to the patio. When she returned to him, her dress was dampened by the evening dew and stained with fresh soil, but she didn't seem to care. Her eyes glistened in the moonlight, and when she fixed her gaze upon him, Jim found he could not look away.

"Do you like me, Jim?" Her lips parted into an innocent smile. She walked over to the edge of the flowerbed, lifted her soiled dress, and stepped out of her slippers. She curled her toes in the dark earth.

Confused, eager, frightened, intrigued—these were but a taste of emotions that set his heart afire. He'd had so many false starts with Megan, so many promising nights that ended in disappointment and masturbation, that when the opportunity finally presented itself, he found he didn't know how to react.

"Yes," he whispered, his mouth suddenly dry. Even the tip of his tongue throbbed, aching to taste her skin.

"I like you," she said, kneeling before him, her eyes never leaving his while her hands worked independently, first unclasping his belt before unzipping his jeans. She held his gaze a moment longer, her mouth upturned in a playful smirk, her lips full and glistening. "I *want* you."

Cora took hold of him, and he almost came right there. He bit his lip to hold back the wave, groaning as he throbbed in her hand. The last thing he saw before losing himself in a blizzard of mental static was the clarity of her gaze and the shimmer of violet in her eyes.

She closed her mouth around him, lapping her tongue against the underside of his shaft before taking him deeper into her throat. Jim felt the pleasure of her full lips for only a moment before the pain shot through him like a bullet, white hot and searing, every nerve standing at attention and screeching in agony.

Needles. Thousands of tiny, hot needles jabbed into his sensitive flesh. Cora moaned softly as he struggled to push her away, mistaking his discomfort for pleasure, and the more he resisted, the deeper she sucked him into her throat.

Tears filled his eyes as he writhed in agony, squirming to free himself from the vise of her mouth, and in a moment of desperation, he did the only thing he could: He gripped a handful of her hair and yanked. She moaned once more, tightening her grip and sending a new wave of blinding pain shooting into his gut. The pressure spread through his groin and down his thighs. Splotches of color danced before his eyes, and a single, calm thought occurred to him as the darkness came to claim him: *She's going to swallow me alive.*

The absurdity was what saved him. He blinked away tears, closed his fingers around the flower in her hair, and tugged.

Cora cried out in pain, shooting backward in surprise and releasing his bloody member. Jim rolled onto his side, his hands drawn instinctively to his crotch, curled up as if that might hold back the burning and throbbing.

"Why would you do that?" she cried, cradling the flower in her hair. He looked over at her through a wall of tears. The purple blossom hung limp to one side. He'd cracked the stem in two.

"Why would you do *this?*" he rasped, lifting one leg to examine his wounds. He was flaccid and bloody and bruised. Dark beads of scarlet oozed from a thousand pin-pricks in his pruning flesh.

Cora climbed to her feet, and when he looked up at her, his blood went cold. Pale green veins bulged beneath her forehead and cheeks, accented by two thick streams of green tears oozing from her eyes. She cradled her head, nursing the flower as if it were attached—

Oh God.

The painting over the fireplace flashed before him, sending his heart down into the pit of his gut where it continued its frantic pace. The green drinks (*good for the roots*), the floral smell, even the gritty, metallic taste of Cora's tongue that he now realized was dirt—the pieces were there, jabbing into his brain, completing a grotesque portrait of horror that made his heart plunge.

Jim met her stare. "What the fuck *are* you?"

Cora's face screwed up as she began to sob. She looked away, her tears dripping into the earth. Small tendrils snaked out of the dirt and blossomed around the droplets, drinking in her sadness. She turned back to the stalks of foliage in the garden with her face buried in her hands, her cries echoing into the night. Jim wanted to feel bad, but the sharp, prickling pain in his groin told him he shouldn't.

"Y-You didn't have to hurt me," she stammered. "We could be part of something greater forever. You could join our harvest, be part of our next reconciliation."

She turned back to him as a clump of tendrils rose from the soil. They curled up her legs and around her waist, blossoming into full, purple flowers.

Jim scrambled to pull up his pants and fasten his belt.

"Where are you going?" she asked. Jim wanted to respond, but his words failed him. His mind raced with more urgent matters. He hoped his wounds were superficial, but even that wouldn't rule out a hospital visit—never mind how the hell he was going to explain this to a doctor. As soon as he found Nick, he'd—

His stomach lurched. Where the hell was Nick?

"Please don't leave me," Cora cried, but Jim didn't listen. He scrambled back across the patio, leaving his date rooted in the garden.

"We haven't seen him. Have a drink." The brunette with violet eyes offered him a plastic cup full of green liquid.

Jim waved her away, frowning. "He was just here half an hour ago. With your friend Krystal."

"Oh." Violet Eyes gave him a vacant look before downing her own cup of the green punch. "Maybe he left."

He reached into his pocket for Nick's keys. They jangled against his fingers. "No, he's still here."

Violet Eyes shrugged. "I don't know what to tell you."

No, he thought, *I guess you don't.*

"I think I like you," Violet Eyes said. "Have you been claimed?" Her cheeks darkened, glaring up at him with a mischievous smile.

Jim glimpsed faint green lines sprouting out from her eyes. He offered her a weak smile in return as he edged his way out of the room, wincing with every step as the prickling, burning pain shot through his groin. *Nick first*, he thought, *and then the hospital.*

Jim avoided the study, wandering instead down the hall toward the staircase.

"Nick?" His voice echoed in the empty foyer. A grandfather clock ticked idly from the sitting room. Jim stood at the bottom step and called up into the dark. "Nick? Hello?"

Silence from above. He waited, and when Nick didn't respond, he turned for the door.

A low, abrasive hum gave him a start, forcing the hairs on his neck to stand at attention.

"What the hell?"

The short hum paused before starting up again. Jim stepped away from the staircase and toward the hallway. A cabinet sat in the corner recess where the hall met the foyer, its surface adorned with a number of trinkets, including a collection of shiny silver baubles. As he drew near to the source of the hum, he realized it wasn't a hum at all, but a rough vibration. Something was vibrating in short, regular bursts.

He pulled open the cabinet drawer.

There were at least two dozen phones in the drawer of varying sizes and ages, the oldest of which was a huge Motorola the size of a brick. There were others, including several dead smartphones, some scuffed, some engraved, and some with rubber cases. One case with blue and white trim caught his eye. He flipped it over and found the initials N.E. imprinted on the back.

That cold, uneasy feeling rose up once again in his gut, forcing the pain of his groin out of his mind for just a few precious seconds as he held Nick's phone in his hand.

"You wouldn't leave without this," Jim whispered. He turned on the phone and read the display. Two missed calls, one of which was from less than a minute ago.

Jim chewed his lip and tried to ignore the pounding in his chest as he thumbed through the menus. In some ways, he felt ashamed to be invading his friend's privacy, but the situation, he decided, necessitated drastic action. He opened the social media app and navigated to his roommate's direct messages, scrolling through a number of conversations until he found what he was looking for: Krystal Demeter.

He scrolled past a number of nude images she'd sent Nick, as well as several perverse chats until reaching the end of their chat history—and the beginning of their conversation. Krystal was the one to initiate contact, casting her line across that great expanse of the Internet in the hopes that someone would bite—and bite they did:

Hey I saw u at school and I think ur cute. Want 2 B Friends?

Jim sighed, frowning at his roommate's stupidity. The conversation went downhill from there. Defeated, Jim put the phone in his pocket.

He was about to turn away when something else caught his attention: the other phones.

Most of them wouldn't turn on, their batteries long dead and corroded, but there was one that flickered to life. There were over a hundred missed calls and even more unopened text messages.

He wasn't sure what led him to open up the phone's social app. Curiosity, maybe, or perhaps it was the evening's turn of events lending credence to all the personal alarms firing within his mind.

Maybe it was almost having his penis ripped off by a mutant plant-girl, or maybe it had to do with the drawer full of abandoned cell phones. Either way, Jim's curiosity got the better of him, and when he flipped through the private messages, his blood stopped cold in his veins:

Hey I saw u at school and I think ur cute. Want 2 B Friends?

No, he thought. *Please no.* He thumbed down through the messages, pausing on the same dimly lit photo of Krystal's naked breasts. Shaking, he pulled Nick's phone from his pocket and compared the messages. His heart sank. They were identical except for the time stamps. The other phone's messages were dated almost a year ago.

A loud shriek startled him so badly he dropped both phones. They clattered on the floor, and he waited foolishly like a rodent caught in the open, waiting for one of the sisters to find him rifling through their things.

Except these phones didn't belong to them. They belonged to the dozens of other young men who'd fallen prey to…whatever the hell they were. An uncomfortable sting rose up in Jim's groin, and he pressed his hand there to hold back the pain. Something squished in his pants, and he knew if he didn't find Nick soon, he could forget about ever getting laid.

Another scream filled the hallway, followed by another. Jim's heart surged, thumping in his chest to the beat of what he thought was the 'Blue Danube' waltz. Adrenaline took hold of him, and against his better judgment—

What the fuck are you doing? Get the hell out of there! Take Nick's car and go get the cops!

—he pushed aside the heavy curtain and walked softly down the hallway.

"Take their seed, sisters. Take it all."

Violet Eyes stood at the study's threshold and clapped her hands softly as more screams overpowered the classical waltz. A lump manifested in Jim's throat, filling his airway like a ball of cotton. Violet Eyes smiled at him as he approached before turning her attention back to her sisters.

Jim thought he was ready for what lay beyond the threshold. He was wrong.

The men in the room were entangled in a series of vines protruding from the arms of the sisters, thick ropy tendrils squirming and digging their way into their victims' exposed flesh. One of the guys turned toward him and moaned in agony, his arms twisted at impossible angles while his date took him relentlessly in her mouth. His eyes rolled up into his head as his cheeks sank inward, his body cavity imploding at the will of his attacker. A moment later, the bro with the half-cocked smile collapsed into himself like a deflated sex doll.

Violet Eyes turned to Jim, smiling proudly. "They learn so fast," she said. "This harvest will be the best yet!"

Jim tried to speak, but words failed him. His mouth was suddenly dry, and any attempt to find his voice was met with a dull ache shooting through his groin. The other girls were sucking their guests dry, and for a moment, all that raced through Jim's mind was that it could've been him.

Violet Eyes traced her fingers along his arm. She smiled and licked her lips. "My name's Holly, by the way."

"He's mine, Holly." Cora shuffled into the hallway, the hem of her dress caked in soil and her cheeks streaked with an atlas of green tears. The broken stalk of her flower hung limp to one side. She avoided Jim's gaze, focusing her stare on Holly. "Krystal paired us."

"But I haven't claimed anyone tonight—"

Cora struck her with the back of her hand. The slap echoed down the hall but did nothing to interrupt the deathly orgy in the adjacent room.

"He's *mine*," Cora growled. "Now leave us be."

Holly stepped back, speechless and nursing her cheek. She retreated through the kitchen, and just before she exited to the garden, Jim saw a hint of dark green ooze dribbling down her chin. He looked back at Cora. He wasn't sure if he wanted to kiss her or run away.

"Where's Nick?"

Cora sighed. She took his hand and rubbed her thumb across his fingers. "He's with Krystal. He was special to her, just as you are special to me. Our special ones are taken to the basement to meet Mother Iris. Come."

"In the basement? I don't understand. Why—"

Her lips pressed against his, and for an instant, he forgot about the pain coursing down his thighs and the fear racing through his mind. For that moment, there was only Jim and Cora, a quiet center of the universe separate from the pain and confusion of the world. Her tongue darted into his mouth, accompanied by the metallic taste of soil, and Jim wanted to pull away—but he didn't.

A sickening warmth overcame him in that moment, filling his head with desire and displacing thoughts of Megan and Nick. A single thought swam through the empty spaces of his mind: *This is what it's like to be wanted.* He opened his eyes and lost himself in the subtle glow of Cora's violet gaze.

Their lips parted, and Jim felt himself lean forward for more.

He wanted more. He *needed* to taste her one more time, but she wouldn't let him. Cora looked away and squeezed his hand. "I'm sorry we couldn't spend more time together, Jim. Come with me." He tried to kiss her again, but she held him back. "I insist," she said.

Jim tried to lean in once more but paused when he saw they had an audience. The other girls from the study watched from the doorway, their cheeks swollen with light green veins, their violet eyes glowing in the dim light.

"Harvest him, sister. Complete the reconciliation."

Cora closed her eyes. Green tears spilled down her cheeks. "I know, sisters. I know." She tugged at his hand. "Come, Jim. It's time you met our mother."

Cora led the way down the basement stairs. The walls were aged and cracked, and a thick musty smell of soil permeated the air. Jim hesitated in the doorway as he stared down into the dim abyss, his heart rapping so hard against his chest that he had trouble catching his breath. Part of him wanted to find a way out of this. There was a voice somewhere in the back of his mind, screaming like a frightened child, begging for him to find Nick and—

Forget Nick, whispered a voice. It was soft and soothing yet spoke with authority. *Come to me, child. Let me look at your beautiful face.*

Jim pivoted, turning back to the kitchen where the other sorority sisters watched. They looked less human now. More green veins rose to the surface of their porcelain skin, their violet eyes bulged, and small gray tendrils snaked and flirted around their arms and necks. They stared at him with rabid urgency. One of them even licked her lips.

"Go on," she said.

"Meet our mother," said another.

"Jim, come with me."

He turned back and looked down the stairwell. Cora stood at the landing, peering up with her hand held out to him. The tears had aged her face, filling in every crack and crevasse, giving her cheeks a pale green complexion. He remembered Krystal's face when she met them at the doorway: a façade of beauty.

He felt hands trace the back of his neck and shoulders; he felt the hot, soiled breath of the others at his ears, their flirtatious voices whispering, "Go, sweetie. Go."

Drunk on their words, he took Cora's hand, and they went down the last set of steps together. Another large, velvet curtain hung from the basement ceiling, cordoning off the rest of the room from the stairs.

"Mother Iris," Cora announced, "we've come to pay you a visit. I have a special one for you. The last of tonight's harvest to complete the reconciliation."

She drew back the curtain, revealing a large space illuminated with bright UV lights and a large, bulbous *thing* planted in its center.

The world Jim thought he knew was already shaken that night, its foundations cracked by almost having his penis ripped off by a mutant plant-woman. What he saw waiting for him just beyond the threshold of that room finished the job, sending his concept of reality teetering into an endless, blackened void.

Until that moment, Jim Auster hadn't considered the possibility that Nick might have suffered a similar fate as those unfortunate young men just one floor above. He didn't know what he expected to do when he found Nick. Persuade him to leave? Had he been so naïve as to think that would actually work?

Nick was dead, of course. Jim could tell from the way his roommate's deflated limbs were sticking out of the creature's maw. The only identifiable part of him was the tribal tattoo on his twitching, bloody arm. Nick's other limbs were folded side by side in a sick display of human origami, his remains soaked in a viscous, green fluid secreted from the jaws of the monster that claimed him.

Standing at the threshold, staring at what he presumed was Mother Iris, Jim Auster heard her sweet voice in his mind, urging him to let go. *Let it happen*, she cooed. *Just let it happen. I want you to be one with us, child. Complete our harvest.*

A wall holding back the last of his sanity crumbled to dust. The sensation was slight, subtle, as the rest of his sanity seeped away through the cracks. He suddenly felt very small and very young, like a child having wandered across the borders of a dense, dark forest. Here, he was lost among a tangle of underbrush, and the sweetest voice was calling his name, calling him home.

The dark green bulb that had devoured Nick's last remains was bisected down the middle; it split in half for just a moment, revealing seemingly endless rows of sharp thorns, their amber color tainted with a hint of scarlet. Surrounding the bulb were large, vibrant petals that fluttered erratically, filling the room with an anxious rustling noise that made his ears itch. To either side of the flowery mass was a human leg bent at the knee, the flesh a fractured pattern of dark green veins, the muscles bulging and convulsing in time with the rustling petals. Jim's mind finally caught up to his senses, and he realized he wasn't looking at two disembodied legs. No, the legs and the flower-bulb thing were connected to the same mass.

His stomach lurched as realization struck, and he opened his mouth to scream, but no words came to him. Instead, his mind shrieked for him: *She's giving birth to that thing.*

Mother Iris lay on her back, legs spread and exposed to the room, but she wasn't giving birth to the creature protruding from her vagina. The flower was a part of her, used to satiate her divine hunger for centuries, feasting on the blood and bones of other hapless men drawn into her trap, their sweat and lust and semen a delicacy to her taste buds.

Krystal appeared from behind the writhing creature. She was nude, her body pockmarked with leafy wounds oozing that same viscous green fluid. Her breasts peeled back, blooming into patches of swirling vines and small, violet flowers. A thick, green tendril coiled out from behind Mother Iris and wrapped around Krystal's legs, inching its way up her body with the ease of a python. A small, green nozzle at the tip of the vine latched onto the purple flower in Krystal's hair, enveloping the petals in its trunk and fusing to her head.

A second green tentacle lurched out of the flickering shadows and beckoned. Cora stepped away from him and walked willingly across the room. She bowed her head, welcoming the elephant-like trunk as it wrapped around her thin body, wrinkling her dress. There was an audible *shurp* sound as the tendril latched onto her like a leech.

Both girls went limp as the appendages lifted them off their feet, twirling them in the air like dolls. Their eyes drained of color, transforming into the milky-white of cataracts, and their mouths flapped open and shut as Mother Iris tested their muscles. They were a part of her now, and when Mother Iris spoke, she did so through their vocal cords.

"Come to me, child. Let us have a look at you."

Jim wanted to run, but a voice from within suggested the impossible, the insane: *Why not stay?* His feet were unwilling to move, and for each moment he stared into the many eyes of this monstrosity, the desire to remain intensified, building to a slow crescendo with each successive heartbeat. He forgot about the prickling pain in his groin—that was just a flaw of the flesh, and what good would that be to him if he could become part of something divine?

The bulb curled open and excreted one of Nick's loafers. The damp shoe was covered in gelatinous ooze. It plopped on the ground before Mother Iris. Jim stared at that shoe, a part of him horrified while another part coveted Nick's place within the goddess.

"Take me," he muttered. A chill ran through his body, and he lowered his gaze, for he was unworthy. Everything he held dear and hoped for until that moment—school, family, losing his virginity, the girl he thought he wanted—now seemed so trivial. He was but a grain of sand at the edge of a vast ocean, and Mother Iris was a sailor of those strange, wondrous waters.

"Take me with you," he said. His hands trembled.

Mother Iris considered his proposal, her tendrils swaying in the air, carrying Cora and Krystal like marionettes.

"Do you seek our glory?"

Jim fell to his knees. He wiped tears from his eyes and bowed his head. "I want to be with you, Mother. Please take me with you."

The crack in his mind splintered further, separating his heart from all manner of logic. The reasonable part of him, that screaming young man tucked away in the shadows of his mind, grew distant, shrinking away as he became blinded by the glory of Demeter's daughter.

The bulb split wide open and flared its prickly thorns. A long, slender vine protruded from the center of the leafy maw and inched its way across the floor toward him. He closed his eyes and relinquished himself to Mother Iris. The tendril curled around his wrist and began to pull. Inch by inch, Jim Auster was dragged to his fate, a destination to which he would have gone willingly.

Within a moment, he would be a part of something greater. He would never again feel rejection or sorrow. There was only the warm bliss of acceptance, his mind lost forever amidst the nettles and thorns, his flesh devoured sweetly within the belly of a living goddess.

WHEN KAREN MET HER MOUNTAIN

-1-

Karen Singleton's daddy once told her, "Honey, sometimes things just happen and there's nothin' to be done about it." That was thirty years ago, when she was little enough to sit on his knee. "When there's a mountain in your way, you either climb over it, or find a way around it. There ain't no in-between."

Walking through the Arizona desert along Route 93, her favorite Sunday dress stained a dark shade of ruby, Karen finally realized her daddy was right all those years ago. Squinting, raising one hand to shield her eyes from the rising sun, Karen kept on walking down that dusty stretch of highway. Her feet ached. She looked down at bare toes caked in sand and blood, wondering when she'd lost her shoes.

Sometimes things just happen.

Karen cracked a smile and began to laugh in quick, hoarse bursts. Her voice sounded like a dying mule, the thought of which made her laugh even more. She clutched the hatchet and wiped the chipped blade with the hem of her dress. Daddy once told her a dull blade wouldn't cut anything, but he was wrong about that.

Daddy wasn't perfect. He couldn't be right all the time.

-2-

"**Y**our father never much cared for me, anyway."

Karen opened her eyes to a dusty brown expanse of desert sage and tumbleweeds slipping by in a blur. Her face's reflection in the dirty window depicted a tired woman, a mourning woman. Dr. Martin Singleton hadn't stopped talking since they'd left her daddy's funeral, and after the day she'd had, all she wanted was to go someplace quiet. Someplace far away from here, from the deserts of her youth and the complacency of middle age.

"Are you even listening to me?"

Karen tilted her head away from the window and nodded. She closed her eyes, swallowed a pool of saliva on the back of her tongue, and patted his knee. Martin glanced at her, frowning.

"Your therapist says it's best you talk about these things, Karen. So you don't, you know…"

Relapse. He didn't say it, but then again he didn't have to. She knew all too well, but that didn't change the fact that she didn't want to talk about her daddy's funeral.

She hadn't spoken to her daddy all that much in the last years of his life, a fact she regretted as each mile quickly slipped away, lost to the desert behind them. Daddy was a hard man to live with; his dedication to the church had driven her away, first to college and then into the arms of an atheist, but she still loved the old man. He provided for her, cared for her, loved her in his own way. In hindsight, Karen supposed that was why she'd been drawn to Martin in the first place: he reminded her of her father, in some ways.

Martin was right, though—her daddy never did care for him much.

Any boy who walks away from God's glory is trouble. You watch yourself, honey. I'll never forgive him if he breaks your heart.

Karen smiled. Even her daddy, Pastor Marlon Ellis, could be blinded sometimes. Martin's devotion never faltered, not after her miscarriage, not even after the accident that followed. Daddy was wrong about Martin, and Karen's heart ached when she realized she'd never be able to tell him that.

Martin leaned back against the headrest and sighed. "Karen, you need to talk to me eventually. You can't keep these things bottled up inside."

"I'm fine," she said. The terse response was almost mechanical, an instinctual reaction driven by necessity. Martin was right, but for now she just wanted to remain inside her own head. Confronting her sadness always ended in tragedy.

Karen turned back to the window, watching the emptiness of Route 93 flow past in a sandy blur. Her husband frowned, shook his head, and turned on the radio. Static rose and fell in waves, crashing against a DJ talking about upcoming events somewhere else in civilization, and a moment later Hank Williams began to sing "Weary Blues From Waitin'."

Now we're talkin', her daddy said. He loved Hank Williams.

She leaned her head against the window and closed her eyes, remembering the way her daddy used to sing this song to himself whenever it played on the radio. She could almost see him sitting on the edge of the bed, humming the tune while pulling on his black dress shoes.

Karen followed that memory down into the darkness of her mind as the hum of the engine lulled her to sleep—

"What the hell?"

Karen shot forward and cried out when the seatbelt dug into her shoulder. The world swam for a moment as an ache worked its way down to the base of her neck, and when she opened her eyes she saw they had come to a full stop in the middle of the highway.

Martin gripped the steering wheel. Karen followed his gaze through the windshield.

A white, rust-spotted pickup truck sat on its side between the highway and hillside. A carpet of shattered glass spread out from the wreckage, and a woman lay a few feet away in the middle of the road with her back to them. A few strands of her dirty blonde hair fluttered in a low breeze.

"Oh, Jesus." Martin shifted the SUV into park and was about to climb out of the car, but Karen put her hand on his knee and shook her head. "I have to, Karen. She's hurt."

And then he was out the door, jogging across the gap toward the woman in the road. Karen watched her husband, trying to swallow the uncomfortable lump slowly rising in her throat.

Somethin' ain't right, honey. A pickup doesn't just fall onto its side. You need two to tango. Where's the other car?

She leaned forward and looked at the road. No skid marks or other tire tracks. All the shards of glass were off to the side, sprinkled along the edge of the truck. There were no pools of gas or oil, and although the thought made her stomach twist into itself, there wasn't any blood, either.

Karen's shaking fingers found the latch and opened the door. She stepped out into the dry Arizona heat and struggled to find her voice. *Don't go there*, she wanted to cry out. *Get away from her, Martin.* But her words failed her, and Karen stood frozen to the highway as shapes emerged from behind the overturned truck.

Martin knelt beside the woman with his fingers on her neck. He looked back when Karen closed the SUV door.

"She's alive," he said, climbing to his feet. "Grab my cell and call 911."

Martin was still watching her, his face a mixture of grim

determination and puzzlement, wondering why his wife wasn't doing as he'd asked. He was so perplexed by Karen's immobility he didn't hear the approaching footsteps.

He didn't notice the young woman with the dirty blonde hair roll onto her back. He didn't see her toothless smile and her gums riddled with blackened, bloody holes; he didn't see the rusty blade in her hand.

"Thy will be done," the woman said, jamming the knife through the center of Martin's loafer.

In her mind, Karen made a mad dash across the road toward her husband, sprinting as fast as her heels would carry her. She tore the blade from her husband's foot and slashed the blonde bitch across her face, spreading that toothless grin even wider by a few bloody inches. She saw herself turn to the figures advancing toward them from beyond the pickup truck; she saw herself fending them off with the blade, protecting the man she loved, the man who had nurtured her through the aftermath of her accident. She wouldn't let them hurt him anymore than they had, and oh, they would pay dearly for doing so.

Except that wasn't right.

Confused, Karen blinked and found she was back inside herself, snapped out of her trance and into a reality punctuated by the agonized shrieks of her wounded husband and the gleeful laughter of a crazy woman lying in the road.

Five masked men in dusty black robes emerged from behind the pickup truck and approached the pair on the highway. One man broke away from the group and turned toward her, crossing the distance with quick, able steps. His mask was blood red and depicted a pained expression, with one side of its cheek drawn downward in agony. Jagged cutouts framed two crazed eyes that glimmered in the late afternoon sun—and they were boring a hole right through her.

The other men fell upon Martin while the blonde crowing bitch climbed to her feet. She danced around them, singing in her cackling manner, *"Thy will be done! Thy will be done! The time is at hand! Thy will be done, oh Lord!"*

Karen saw one of them cup a dirty rag around Martin's mouth while the others held him down. Her husband stopped kicking a moment later, his body suddenly limp. She heard one of the men groan as he braced against Martin's dead weight.

You'd best get movin', honey.

Karen's daddy didn't have to tell her twice. She reached for the passenger door and yanked it open.

"Now where're you goin', little lamb?"

She was halfway across the passenger seat when hands fell upon her ankle, and she kicked instinctively, holding that image of her husband's limp body in the forefront of her mind. She had to get to the driver's seat, get Martin's cell phone, and call for help—like she should've done when he'd asked her. God, if she hadn't been so slow and so stupid. She reached for the console. The cell phone was just a few inches more—

"Easy there, little girl." The masked man laughed as he tugged her leg. She kicked again, and her shoes flew off. "You might be needin' those. The sand won't be too kind on your teeny toes."

Martin's phone shrank away as the masked man pulled her from the vehicle. She fell in a heap on the road. Her attacker pulled off his mask, revealing a grinning face pockmarked with enough acne scars to rival the moon. *No wonder he wears a mask*, her daddy said, and Karen had to bite her cheeks to keep from laughing.

Her captor produced a dirty rag of his own and looked down at her with his crazy blue eyes.

"Sorry, little lamb. We only need one, but the Lord will welcome you with open arms, I'm sure of it."

Karen raised her hand to strike, but he caught her arm. A sudden heat flushed her cheeks when she realized what held his attention. He squeezed her wrist as he twisted it around to face him, sending a sharp pain racing down the length of her arm. This time when Karen bit her cheeks, it was to keep from crying out.

"Maybe I spoke too soon," he muttered, tracing a finger along the length of her scar. "The Lord don't take kindly to suicides, little lamb."

Embarrassed and seething with rage, Karen gave one last effort to free herself. She raised her leg and tried to kick him in the groin just like her daddy had always told her to do, but she was too slow; the robed man stepped aside and yanked on her wrist, pulling her away from the SUV. He fell upon her and drove one knee into her gut, knocking the air from her lungs.

"Enough of this," he growled. "You sleep now."

He pressed the rag against her mouth. The fabric stank with a pungent chemical odor that made her throat and nostrils burn, and when she tried to fight him off Karen found her arms and legs simply would not cooperate. The world swam, and the darkness behind her eyes looked so inviting—but she didn't want to go there, not now. She still had to save Martin from those other men and she had to make that blonde woman stop laughing, but everything felt better with her eyes closed, and how would she do anything with her eyes closed?

The robed man spoke from somewhere far away as she slipped further into herself, away from the dry desert air and into a cold void. His echoing words made her shiver:

"Let it happen, little lamb. Just let it happen. You'll be with the Lord soon, and He will welcome you with open arms."

A dark hole opened in the world and Karen sank into its bottomless depths.

-SESSION #1-

"*Do you understand why you're here, Karen?*"

Dr. Tanner leaned forward and smiled. A strand of curly brown hair spilled from her forehead, and she brushed it away, tucking it behind her ear. Karen stared through the doctor, lost in her own mind and clutched by a cold grip that sent shivers through her soul.

"Karen?"

The doctor wouldn't leave. She knew this, knew she'd brought this all on herself, and that was just fine because she deserved everything that came to her.

Karen focused on Dr. Tanner's smiling face. "I'm here because I deserve to be."

Dr. Tanner glanced down for a moment, scribbling something on her notepad. "And why is that?"

"Because I'm not a fit woman. I'm not a fit mother."

Dr. Tanner set down her pen. "Karen, that isn't true. I think you're a fit woman, and I think you'd be a good mother. I'm sure your husband would agree with me." She picked up her pen and scribbled a brief note, paused, and then met Karen's vacant gaze. "But that isn't why we're here, is it?"

Karen stepped outside her mind for a moment. She saw herself reaching forward, plucking the pen from Tanner's hand, and jabbing the felt tip into the doctor's eye. Enough cat and mouse head games, Doctor. You know why I'm here and what I've done. You know I deserve to be, so cut the bullshit and get on with it.

Those words were venom on her tongue, but she was pulled back inside her head before they could be spat at the doctor. She swallowed and grimaced from the taste of bile at the back of her throat.

"I hurt myself," Karen whispered. "I hurt myself because I'm not a fit mother." She ran her fingers across the bandages on her wrists, tugging absently at the edges. The stitches were beginning to itch. "After I lost

the baby I couldn't look at myself anymore, and I couldn't bear to look at Martin, either. I don't deserve the happiness of being a mother, and I don't deserve the happiness of being Martin's wife because I can't bring him happiness. I see that now. I understand it. And if I'm not fit to have those things, what is the point?" She was crying now but the words still came, blubbering and tripping over themselves in a saline mess. "So I ran a hot bath, took Martin's straight razor, said a prayer to God for His understanding, and cut a gash straight down my wrist like this."

Karen dragged a finger down the bandage of one wrist, and then the other. She shook her head, shrugged, and cocked a smile at the doctor.

"I did it because I'm a coward. That's what you want to hear, isn't it? You want to know why? Well, that's why, Doctor Tanner. I did it because I felt something growing inside me, and then it died. I did it because I couldn't face my husband after it all happened because he was so excited we were having a baby. He used to lie awake with me at night, holding me in his arms and talking about what we might name that baby, talking about which room to convert to a nursery, what colors to paint the walls, contemplating what sort of person that tiny life might grow up to be—and now he doesn't. He doesn't hold me anymore because I don't deserve to be held. Because I'm filth. Because I'm shit. Are you getting all this? I can slow down if it helps you."

Dr. Tanner lowered the pen and leaned back in her seat, trying to keep her composure. Karen's outburst had set her on edge. "No," she said, forcing the faintest of smiles. "Please. This is good. Continue."

Karen closed her eyes, waiting for the maelstrom of thoughts to settle in her head, and out of that roiling dark spoke her daddy's voice: You never were a climber, honey. Always a runner.

She smirked, snorting back the mucus in her nose. Dr. Tanner tilted her head and gave Karen a quizzical look.

"What's funny?"

"My daddy," Karen mused, picking at the skin at the corner of her mouth. *"He used to ask me, 'Karen, what'll you do when you meet your mountain?' And I used to tell him, 'Daddy, I'll just go around it if I have to.'"*

Dr. Tanner leaned forward, offering a perfunctory smile. "What do you think he meant by that?"

But Karen ignored her question. She met Dr. Tanner's inquisitive gaze with an intense stare that chilled the doctor's heart. "He also used to tell me that suicides burn." Karen smiled as tears spilled down her cheeks. "Suicides burn."

-3-

She stirred, moaning softly as her head swam. Her nostrils still burned with that chemical smell. What was the name for it? Chlorophyll? No, that wasn't it.

Chloroform, honey. Her daddy always knew the answer.

Karen cracked her eyes and peered at the world through thin, blurry slits. Her bare feet pressed against the warm vinyl of the door, and her dress was bunched up to her thighs. The late afternoon sun hung low, streaming through the glass, and baking her bare skin. Her fingers twitched to life, moving to pull her dress back down—

Don't, honey. The bad man dosed you, but not good enough, and he didn't have the common sense to tie you up. He thinks you're still asleep.

Karen tapped her fingertips against the pad of her thumb.

Not yet, sweetheart. You'd best keep yourself a secret for now. Play possum for a while. I'll let you know when it's time to bite.

She did as her daddy suggested, tilting her head to watch the bad man in the black robe steer them off the highway. Stones tumbled and clattered against the undercarriage, the suspension crying out in protest against the rough terrain, and she remembered Martin had scheduled a service appointment for next week.

Martin.

Her heart shot into her throat, and she almost sat up in earnest, ready to dig her nails into the face of her attacker. *No, Daddy* whispered, *just wait.* She took a deep breath and let the air turn to churning fire in her lungs; her head swam when she exhaled, shooting patches of black and white across her vision. She forgot about the scarred man behind the wheel, turning within herself to find a shattered image of Martin lurking in the shadows. The last she'd seen him, that laughing bitch had jammed a knife through his foot. He was screaming—God, she could still hear him—and then she'd failed to get help, watching as that group of masked men fell upon him. Had they killed him?

Daddy's voice echoed in that darkened chamber: *You won't find out if you don't get yourself out of here, honey. Focus.*

Karen held her tongue, narrowing her eyes, glaring at the pockmarked cheek of her abductor. She dug her nails into the vinyl seat.

Minutes crawled by as the bad man drove her deeper into the desert. She was lost in her thoughts and trying to figure out a way to escape when the SUV began to sputter and cough before slowing to a halt.

Her abductor turned and looked down at her.

"All right, little lamb. Out of gas with just a few inches to spare. The Lord does provide!"

Karen peered up at him through squinted eyes, wondering if he could see her watching him. Her heart rapped against her chest, thudding so hard her whole body vibrated with its fury. He climbed out of the SUV and slammed the door.

Now, Daddy?

Not yet, honey.

Footsteps crunched over stones, tracing a path around the vehicle, and Karen followed them with her mind while doing her best to remain a mannequin.

The back door opened. A warm breeze met her face. The bad man's hands gripped her arms. He pulled her from the backseat and dropped her in the hot sand.

"Don't you go gettin' excited on me now. You be a good little sinner. Be a good lamb."

He knelt beside her and ran his fingertip across the top of her exposed thigh. Her skin burned at his touch and she wanted to tear away that strip of flesh, erasing every trace of his existence from her body. Only one man was allowed to touch her. Only one. And if he was dead she would make them suffer.

The bad man traced his other hand along her naked wrist, rubbing the pink scar that ran across a network of veins and halfway down her arm.

"Such a shame." The scarred man chewed his lower lip and shook his head. "You would've birthed good young."

He cupped her thigh and slowly moved his hand north toward sacred ground. A series of chills crept along her stomach and she bit the insides of her cheeks to keep from screaming. She felt dirty, her skin covered in a grimy film that wouldn't come clean no matter how hard she scrubbed.

"Maybe," he began, "maybe just a taste, Herman."

Herman. She almost laughed aloud, more out of hysteria than hilarity, but the comedy of Herman the Scarred Man was immediately lost as he lowered his head. His tongue left a trail of saliva along her inner thigh.

Karen watched this vile creature desecrate her body from outside herself.

What about now, Daddy?

Now, honey. Now you can bite, little possum.

Her fingers searched the scorching sands and fell upon a rock the size of a baseball. Herman was almost to her panty line when she sat up and struck him. He cried out in shock as a bloody tooth landed on her dress.

"Thhhh," he sputtered, his wounded lips failing him as he tried to formulate words. Karen pulled back and struck him again. The rock split his temple with a sickening crack.

Herman sprawled backward and clipped his head against the door of the SUV. His eyes went cloudy for a few seconds before he steadied himself. He reached forward and pulled himself toward a patch of sagebrush.

"Help!" With a mouth full of blood, his cry sounded more like "hup." He spat a dark stream into the sand as he crawled into the scrub. Karen climbed to her feet and watched him beckon to something out on the horizon. "Help me, brothers!"

Karen squinted against the sun. The shadow of a rocky butte about a mile away shielded a group of RVs baking under the early evening sun.

"Martin," she whispered.

Her legs propelled her forward. She fell upon Herman, digging her knee into the small of his back. He squealed in agony, shooting thick, scarlet streaks across the sand.

"Where is he?'

Herman sobbed, blubbering something about penitence. She reached around his skull, found the soft meat of his eye, and punctured that gelatinous orb with her thumb. Warm liquid oozed outward as she separated her nail from his skull.

"Don't make me ask again."

"A sacrifice," Herman cried. "Our Lord demands sacrifice, so the Children of Melchizedek give Him the blood of the damned."

Karen clutched his robe and pulled the collar against his throat.

"*Why not me?*" she screamed, her voice scratching at her throat, a guttural cry that echoed from her toes. "Am I not damned?"

"Only men—"

She stood, braced her bare foot against his shoulder, and flipped him onto his back. Blood gushed from his wounded eye, and a dark stream trickled out the side of his mouth. Her mind became a red haze while a million accusations raced through her, the words like lashes on her naked skin.

Martin was pure. He was a good man who cared for her, loved her, saw her through that terrible time. Now he was caught up in this madness, judged for sins he hadn't committed.

Am I not damned?

The question raced through her mind as she gripped the rock.

"Am I not damned?"

She raised the stone. Herman turned his head and closed his good eye.

"*AM I NOT DAMNED?*"

The stone connected with his face with a sickening crack, leaving a dent in his skull. Karen was too caught up in her rage to notice he was dead before she hit him a third time. She cracked the stone against his skull twenty times more until his face collapsed into a bowl of cerebral jelly. When she was finished, she sat back against the SUV and stared out toward the grouping of RVs on the horizon.

Martin was out there. Damned or not, she had to save him—just as he had saved her.

-SESSION #7-

D r. Tanner took a seat across from her and smiled. "You seem to be doing well. Better spirits?"

"Much better," Karen said. "It's nice to be home again."

"Good. That's good." Dr. Tanner reached for her notepad and pen. Karen watched the other woman's movements, feeling her blood pressure increase, noticing a subtle throb at the base of her skull.

"How long will we have to do this?"

Dr. Tanner wrote something across the page. "I'm sorry?"

"Our sessions," Karen said, forcing a smile. "How—how much longer before I can stop visiting?"

"Well, Karen, that depends on you, and that's why we're meeting still."

"But you discharged me—"

"I discharged you because I believe you're no longer a threat to yourself." Dr. Tanner waited a beat, observing her patient with a cautious eye. "Was I wrong?"

Karen deflated, shrinking back in her seat. She averted her eyes to the window. "No, doctor. You're not wrong. Let's just get on with it. I still have some shopping to do. Martin asked me to cook tonight…"

"And how is your relationship?"

"Our relationship?" Karen blinked. "I don't understand what that has to do with anything."

"In the past, you mentioned feelings of worthlessness. That you felt you didn't deserve your husband's love." The doctor flipped through her notes. "Last month you told me you two weren't speaking much."

Karen closed her eyes and bit her lip to hold back the slow throbbing in her skull. She spoke slowly, evenly, each syllable cleaving the air one slice at a time: "I find it difficult to face him when I am smothered by my shame."

"How do you think your husband feels about your silence?"

"I want to talk to him, I really do, but anytime I look at him I see the look on his face when he found me that night. I was supposed to be gone by the time he got home, but his shift ended early. I was so weak I couldn't get up to lock the bathroom door. He wasn't supposed to see me until I'd drifted away, and the shame of facing him…" Karen looked away. She wiped a tear from her eye. *"I love Martin with all my heart, Dr. Tanner. I'd do anything for him. Some days I just don't understand why he bothers to love someone like me. I betrayed him just like my mother did my daddy."*

Dr. Tanner frowned. *"Tell me about your mother."*

Karen wiped her nose and shifted uncomfortably in her seat. *"Not much to tell, really. My daddy was a preacher when I was younger and my mother resented the time he spent with the church. Claimed he loved God more than her. So she left him and sued for divorce. Daddy loved her too much to put up a fight. It broke his heart, but he let her go because he wanted her to be happy. That's the only time I ever saw him cry."*

"And the night your husband found you—"

Karen nodded sheepishly. *"He cried like a baby."* She ran her fingers through her hair and stopped when she realized her hands were shaking. *"I saw Daddy in Martin's face that night, and I'll never forgive myself for hurting him like that. Why aren't we speaking much? That's my answer, Dr. Tanner. It's just my way of going around the mountain. Climbing to face myself is more than I can bear right now. Always has been."*

-4-

Karen wiped the dead man's blood from Martin's cell phone and dialed 911. The call failed a moment later, and she tried once more before shutting off the phone to conserve the battery. She would need it once she found Martin—provided she could get a signal.

Next, she searched the dead man, but he had nothing of use to her except for a pair of sandals two sizes too big. They might be awkward, but they would keep her feet safe from the scorching sands. She slipped them on and turned back to the SUV. Herman must have driven them a good distance into the desert to have run out of gas. When she looked toward the horizon, she saw nothing but desert and sky.

She sat on the passenger seat, her legs dangling through the open door, nursing water from Martin's Aquafina bottle as she took in her surroundings. Other cars and trucks were scattered across the area, long abandoned and left to bake in the unrelenting sun. *We aren't the first*, she thought, surveying the dumping grounds. Herman's words echoed in her head: *Only the men.* Where did that leave her? Was this Golgotha of lost cars and wayward travelers meant to be her final resting place?

Karen glanced over at the dead man. A metallic smell rose from the body as flies swarmed around his battered skull. Now she would never know.

She watched as the sun fell behind the rocky butte and a long, oppressive shadow crawled across the valley. Night would soon follow. Time to move.

Her thirst slaked, Karen used the remaining drops to cleanse her hands of Herman's dried brain matter. She tucked the cell phone into her bra, clutched the stone—it had served her well so far—and set off across the desert toward the encampment.

Most men would have felt apprehension or fear in those moments, creeping across the shadowy waste toward potential death, but Karen felt neither of these emotions. She was driven by a singular purpose, an urgent desire to find her husband and seek retribution against those who took him—especially that laughing blonde bitch from the highway. Especially her.

Keep a clear head, her daddy whispered.

"But I do," she said, smiling to herself. "I do."

Night fell before she reached the first RV. A slick coating of sweat clung to her exposed skin, working in conjunction with the cool air to produce a bone-deep chill that would not cease. She shivered in the dark, hidden in the shadow of that motor home behemoth. There were voices within, clattering, footsteps, and then a door slammed.

One of the robed men wandered around the side of the RV before she had a chance to react. He stopped at the edge, hiked his robe, and began to piss against the side.

"Goddamn Herman," he groaned. "Dimwit cocksucker could get lost puttin' on his underwear."

Karen froze, her heart shuddering something fierce, quaking her entire torso. He hadn't seen her. The adrenaline was exquisite, and the stone in her hand felt weightless.

The cultist's prick was still in his hand when she struck him, practicing the same maneuver on him as she had on Herman, quickly fracturing his skull before he could alert the others. He collapsed in a heap, the open wound hemorrhaging blood at an alarming rate. Karen stepped back after her attack and marveled at how quickly the dark matter oozed out of his head. If she had the time, she might have entertained watching him bleed out just to see how fast it would happen, but she had to save Martin first. Maybe on the way back. Maybe.

Something caught her eye. The hatchet was tucked into a loop of a belt made from a length of golden brown rope. She pulled it from the makeshift holster, examined its dull blade, and dropped the trusty stone in favor of something less awkward.

A dull blade won't cut anything, honey.

"We'll see, Daddy."

Hatchet in hand, Karen crept to the end of the RV and peered around the corner. The mobile homes were parked in a semi-circle and illuminated by a series of tiki torches. Party lights colored red, white, and blue were strung from RV to RV, flickering in and out of life as a generator hummed from somewhere out of sight. In the center of the half-circle was a makeshift idol, a bizarre construction of junkyard parts assembled into the effigy of a creature with hubcaps for breasts and two pieces of bent rebar for horns. Its face was the same mask worn by Martin's attackers, giving the creature that same dimwitted, slack-jawed appearance.

The idol stood eight feet high with burning torches in each of its elongated arms, making for a sinister, contrived appearance. Karen thought it looked like the worst piece of modern art she'd ever seen.

"Michael?"

Another loud bang filled the night as the screen door slammed home. Karen tightened her grip on the hatchet and readied herself. She stepped out of Herman's clunky sandals and curled her toes in the warm sand.

"Shit, boy, where'd you go? It's almost time to go pay our respects."

The robed man wandered into the gap between RVs. His mask sat upon the top of his head, its fastening string cutting divots into the sides of his bushy beard. Karen waited for him to turn away—he did so, calling out yet again—and stepped into the open. He heard her footsteps and turned back around—

"Michael, we ain't got time—"

The hatchet blade sank into his skull with a single crack; a moment later his body went limp, collapsing into a heap between the mobile homes. His left leg twitched rapidly.

Karen leaned over, planted her foot against his chest, and pulled the hatchet out of his skull. The blade came away covered in the dead man's gore and chips of bloody bone. She was busy examining the blade when another door creaked open.

"What the fuck? Ezra, it's that bitch from the road! She killed Joseph!"

Two men emerged from the RV across the clearing. One of them held a rifle in his hands. Karen froze, her mind racing. Should she run? She'd be no good to Martin if they shot her.

Ezra raised the rifle. "You got lost in the wrong neighborhood, darlin'." He glanced at his partner. "Aaron, go fetch your sister. The Lord's sent a lamb to us. We're 'bout to have us some fun before the sacrifice."

Aaron turned to his partner. "Me? Why me?"

"'Cause I got the gun, dummy."

Karen listened to their exchange, the glimmer of fear pushed from her blood by the onset of adrenaline. She stepped outside of herself for a moment, allowing her body to work its magic while she watched, a cheering spectator to her own private film. Karen watched as she ran forward, her muscles pumping and propelling her toward the first man, Aaron.

Rage took over, filling her lungs with fire and boiling her blood. For a brief moment, watching her body close the gap, Karen saw not a woman but a demon from the dark bowels of Hell, a red-skinned creature with hate in its eyes and the taste of blood on its tongue. That vile thing sprinted forward and leapt onto Aaron like an animal.

He screamed as she sank her teeth into his throat. The poor man never had a chance: he twisted and turned in place, trying to shake this seething, raging thing from him, but the harder he shook the tighter she clenched her jaw.

Karen's mouth filled with Aaron's blood as she tore out a chunk of his neck. A dark stream spurted into the night, anointing her head in a warm arterial spray. Aaron panicked, his shrieks weakening into desperate gurgles, and he thrashed from side to side in one last effort to dislodge the gnashing bitch. When he spun on his heels, Karen saw the other man over Aaron's shoulder and pushed away from her victim.

She fell flat on her back with a jolt as the rifle fire punched her ears and blew a hole through the back of Aaron's head. Bits of hair, bone, and brain cascaded across the sand beside her as Aaron's body collapsed in a gory, smoking heap.

"Aaron? Oh God, Aaron?"

The gunshot's echo snapped Karen back into herself, suddenly aware of the low vibration coursing over her skin in waves. The coppery taste of Aaron's blood in her mouth twisted her stomach, but now was not the time to be squeamish. Karen climbed to her feet and spat blood. She clutched the hatchet and met Ezra's terrified stare.

"You stay back, you godless cunt." His shaking hands struggled to chamber the next round, but Karen was faster. She closed the gap in two strides just as Ezra shouldered the rifle and buried the hatchet blade between his eyes. Ezra's eyes rolled back into his head as he sank to his knees. The hunting rifle clattered to the earth.

Karen tugged the blade from her victim's face, her chest rising and falling in heavy convulsions, one labored breath of fire after another. The taste of blood lingered on her tongue and she spat again, her spittle pooling in the open gash between Ezra's eyes.

You've got a hell of a bite, little possum.

"Goddamn right, Daddy."

Movement from the corner of her eye. She looked up to see the blonde woman step out of a nearby RV. Karen was already moving before the blonde bitch saw her, the raw pads of her feet slapping all the way across the clearing.

Blondie turned and had but a moment to react, her chipped nails clawing to open the screen door as this bloody creature raced past their burning idol toward her.

"You get back from me, demon!"

Karen didn't listen. The same fire that drove her to kill the others filled out her lungs, taking her blood to boil, fuming out her mouth and nostrils like a dragon. Maybe she *was* a demon.

"Am I not damned?"

Blondie paused, her wrinkled cheeks sagging as she tried to understand the question, but Karen's question was merely rhetorical. She already knew the answer.

"*BROTHERS!*" Blondie screamed. "*AARON! MICHAEL! EZRA?*" She choked back tears, shrinking against the screen door. "Joseph? Herman?"

"All dead, honey."

Karen grabbed a fistful of Blondie's hair and yanked her off the short steps, dragging her back to the center of the half-circle where the bodies of her accomplices lay still and bleeding. Blondie collapsed over Aaron's body, her hand sinking in the mushy exit wound that was his face. She screamed, teetering backward and landing flat on her ass.

"What did you—Why didja do this?"

Karen knelt beside Aaron's body and stuck her hand into the bloody hole of his skull. Blondie turned her head and vomited. She retched until there was nothing left to expel, her chest convulsing into a hoarse coughing fit.

"Look at me," Karen said. Blondie did as she was commanded, looking up at the demon through teary eyes.

Holding the blonde woman's gaze, Karen raised her hand and smeared Aaron's blood down her face. "Where is my husband, you blonde bitch?"

-SESSION #15-

Dr. Tanner shifted in her seat, clicking her pen against her nails. Karen had never seen her so nervous before, but she liked the idea. Tanner had always come across to her as one of those holier-than-thou types, getting off on other people's misery, and to see her so jittery was almost empowering.

"Something wrong?"

The doctor looked up from her pad of paper and offered a light smile. "Just collecting my thoughts for our session. How are you doing?"

"I feel better," Karen said. She smiled wide, an expression that made her doctor shrink back in her seat. "I feel more like myself."

"And…and how are things with your husband? Have they improved?"

"Martin is great. I love him so much. He's the best thing to happen to me, and I'm so grateful that he was there for me through all my troubles. Without him, I would be dead by now."

"Yes, Martin…" Dr. Tanner trailed off. She clicked her pen against the pad of paper. "Karen, I spoke with your husband last week. He said he found you crying in the shower the night your father died, and when he tried to get you out, you growled at him like an animal."

Karen ignored the comment. "Martin has been so supportive. He's driving me back to my hometown this weekend for the funeral—"

"Your husband also told me about an incident a couple of weeks ago at a restaurant. Do you remember?"

"I remember," Karen said, her expression drooping as she clenched her fingers around the edge of her blouse. "I remember the way that waitress looked at him. The way she flirted with him. He's mine, and I told her as much."

"Karen, you threw your glass of water at her. Martin says you've stopped taking your medication, that you still won't talk to him, and when you do, it's one- or two-word responses. He's frustrated and…" Dr. Tanner

paused, composing herself. She cleared her throat. "Karen, I'm going to refer you to another specialist. I don't think we can maintain this relationship any longer."

Fine by me, *Karen thought, but held her tongue. Her mind turned back to Martin. How sweet he was to offer to drive her back home to see her daddy laid to rest. Martin never got along with her daddy all that well, but in the end, Martin was still there for her. Thinking about him, and how supportive he was, filled her to heart to its brim.*

A chirp filled the office, startling Dr. Tanner from her seat. She walked across the room to her desk and picked up her cell phone.

"I'm sorry," she said.

"Take your time," Karen said. "Do you need to take that?"

Dr. Tanner smiled, blushing like a teenager just for a moment before remembering her place. She returned to where Karen sat and extended her hand to shake.

"Best of luck to you, Karen."

But Karen was too busy staring off into space, fantasizing about her husband, the man she loved, her hero and savior. They had been through so much, but now there was a light at the end of their tunnel. She would do everything she could to make him happy—or die trying.

"Best of luck to us," she whispered.

-5-

Blondie screamed as the fire blistered her skin, melting the flesh into a waxen glob while Karen held the torch to her face. She stood with one foot pressed against Blondie's chest, holding the toothless woman at bay, watching the blonde bitch squirm and squeal in agony. Karen smiled and counted off the seconds.

One one-thousand. Two one-thousand. Three—

"HE'S AT THE ALTAR!"

Karen raised the torch but kept her foot in place. Blondie's face was bubbling and red, her eyes swollen shut, a clear fluid dribbling down from her eyelids. Karen shifted her weight, easing her heel into the soft curve of Blondie's throat.

"Where is the altar?"

"Up the p-path," Blondie sobbed. "Along the ridge. P-Please just luh-let g-go."

Karen looked up at the opening of the circle and noticed two burning tiki torches stuck in the ground near the butte wall. Their flames cast dancing shadows along the rock.

She curled her toes and pressed her weight against Blondie's throat, crushing the woman's larynx and giggling at the labored, wheezing sound gurgling from that toothless mouth. Karen waited until she stopped struggling before lowering the torch and setting Blondie's curls alight.

"Thy will be done," Karen said. She smiled up at the flaming effigy of their silent tin god. "Here's another lamb for you."

Karen's heart slowed to an even pace as she passed a rusty red pickup truck. She looked inside, eager to find a set of keys, but they were absent. *One of them must have the keys*, she thought. *I'll look on the way back.*

She wandered through the dark toward the torches. The fire in her lungs abated and the adrenaline drained from her system, leaving her limbs feeling weak and filled with jelly. *Martin*, she thought, *I'm coming. Just hang on, honey. Almost there.*

An endless pattern of stars stretched overhead, twinkling back at her, congratulating her on reaching her destination. She marveled at the view, wondering if her daddy was one of those stars winking at her.

You know it, sweetie.

Karen smiled. She loved her daddy so much. Now he was an angel by the side of the Lord.

A sandy trail rose alongside the incline of the butte, marked by the pair of torches she'd seen from afar. Her muscles ached and her feet cried out with each step, but she didn't dare stop now. Martin was waiting for her at the top. Her mind flashed back to the blonde bitch jamming that blade through his foot. He would need medical attention.

She pulled the cell phone from her bra and powered on the device. She held it up to the display of stars, praying for a cellular signal from one of those twinkling angels. The screen lit up: NO SERVICE.

Frowning, Karen continued her ascent up the path to the top of the ridge, following a trail of sand and burning torches every few hundred feet. She leaned against the rock wall for a moment to catch her breath and steady herself. Her hands were shaking again, and her throat was scratchy, dry.

The cell phone vibrated, startling her so badly she almost dropped it. She fumbled with the device, its bright screen stinging her eyes, and a moment later she found her focus, reading the jumble of letters across the display.

There were several missed calls, three unread text messages, and two unread emails. Karen tapped the screen.

At first, the message didn't make sense. She had to read it a few times before understanding dawned on her, and when that epiphany finally eclipsed her mind, she felt the strength give out of her legs. Karen sank to the dirt path, struggling against the urge to cry, her throat clogged with cotton.

When can I see you again?

She scrolled down through the list of unread messages, all from the same sender.

Are you home yet?
Did the crazy bitch lose her mind at the funeral?

Karen moved on to Martin's replies. They were dated as recently as yesterday.

I can't stop thinking about you, Meredith.
What you did last week, my God, your lips were like heaven.

Tears wrapped her eyes. This was wrong. This was impossible. He wouldn't. Martin loved her. He was there for her when she needed him. He saved her from herself, stood by her even after losing their baby. Why would he do this?

The phone chimed. Another email. Karen opened Martin's inbox and died a little bit more. The email was from M. Tanner:

"Have you made it back yet? You're not answering your phone and I'm getting worried. You were supposed to be back hours ago. I miss you. Call me when you can."

Karen scrolled down to the other messages from M. Tanner. They went back for weeks, beginning innocently enough: Martin first emailing to ask how the sessions were going, from one doctor to another, you see. Later the emails became more personal, more playful. A flirtatious comment here, a proposition there, all the while pivoting around a rather large elephant in the room: Karen's sanity.

"I'm worried about you being alone with her, Martin. Her depersonalization isn't improving, and I'm concerned that there's a deeper psychosis we haven't seen yet. I'm afraid that when she snaps again it won't be with suicidal tendencies."

Martin replied: "I know that, but I'm stuck for now. We talked about this, Meredith. I'm scared to leave her. Scared of what she might do to herself or what she might do to me."

Meredith again: "Do you still love her? You can be honest with me, Martin."

And Martin: "I care about her, but I don't love her anymore. I can't after what she put me through. I need something real, something stable. I need you."

Karen pressed the power button, leaned back against the rocky wall, and began to cry. Her sobs were long and loud, pulled up from the deepest recesses of her soul, beginning in hoarse, guttural fits and rising into quick animal shrieks. A coyote returned her cry, its ghostly howl echoing from somewhere below the ridge.

She waited there until morning, sobbing in dry uncontrollable fits until the heat of the rising sun became unbearable. Her throat was swollen from dehydration, and her muscles ached as she climbed to her feet. A pit opened in her stomach and growled with disapproval.

Martin was near, but the thought of facing him terrified her.

Get on with it, possum. He broke your heart after all, but that ain't no reason to lay down and die.

No, it wasn't. Karen pushed away from the rock wall, stepping out of the shadow of the ridge and continued her ascent toward the summit.

Blondie hadn't lied: the altar was at the flattened top of the butte, erected some twenty feet from the edge. A series of stones circled a dusty old refrigerator positioned to serve as a bed of sacrifice. Martin lay sprawled across its surface, his arms and legs tied at uncomfortable angles over the edges, each extremity pointed outward like a perverted form of the Vitruvian man.

At another time, Karen might have rushed to the side of her

husband, showering him with kisses, working to untie his restraints, but not this morning. Not now. Not after shedding her humanity and spilling blood in his name. His heart belonged to another now.

Vultures circled overhead, casting brief shadows that flickered over her unconscious husband. Soon they would descend when he was not quite dead, ready to pluck the softer meats from his skull and relishing their sweet flavor. A part of Karen wanted to watch that happen, but she was not yet so removed from herself as to allow such inaction. No, she needed to say goodbye to Martin once and for all.

He stirred as she approached. His lips were chapped and his forehead blistering from sunburn. A puddle of blood had dried beneath his wounded foot, the loafer forever stained a rich shade of scarlet.

"Martin?"

He turned his head, groaning as the muscles popped in protest. He squinted through sun-blasted eyes. "Karen? That you, honey?"

Honey. She let the word roll off her like a bead of sweat, taking a seat at the foot of the hollow refrigerator. A soft breeze lifted up around them, stirring sand among the stones. She closed her eyes, relishing the air on her burned shoulders.

"Karen, you've got to get me out of here. Untie me so—" He strained to get a look at her. "My God, honey, you're covered in blood. What the hell happened? What—"

"When I was young," she began, "Daddy used to tell me the story about the binding of Isaac by his father Abraham. See, God commanded Abraham to sacrifice his son at the top of a mountain. He loved his son, but he loved and feared God even more. But an angel intervened, Martin. An angel intervened and saved Isaac from his father's blade. And you know what Abraham did?" She waited, watching the vultures circle overhead. Martin was too weak, too awestruck to respond, and she went on when he didn't answer. "He sacrificed a ram instead because he still owed God something for His mercy."

"Karen, this isn't funny," he croaked. "Untie me so we can get the fuck out of here!"

She turned and glared over her shoulder. He froze at the sight of her. Blood was smeared down her forehead and cheeks, dried and caked in the cracks of her skin like red powder makeup, and her hair was matted to her face.

"Do you think an angel will intervene, Martin? Do you think God will forgive your adultery?" She lifted the hatchet and traced one bloody edge along the side of Martin's leg. "I'm feeling a bit like Abraham right now, and there's not a ram in sight."

Martin's cell phone rang. Karen looked at the device vibrating in her hand and smirked. Dr. Meredith Tanner's name lit up the screen, along with a picture of her dark brown curls and bubbly baby cheeks. She glared at her husband and answered the call.

"Hello, Dr. Tanner. My husband is right here and you can talk to him for as long as you want. Until the battery dies, anyway. He said your lips were like heaven and I find that fitting because you're his angel today." Karen put the phone on speaker and placed it beside her husband. Meredith's frantic voice filled the air.

"Martin? Martin? What's happened? What's wrong?"

"Karen, I'm sorry," Martin croaked. Tears streamed down the side of his face. "Just let me go and we can sort this out. I didn't mean to hurt you. I was going to tell you, I swear."

Karen turned back toward the horizon, watching the morning sun begin its arc across the sky.

"I love you, Martin, but you're in God's hands now. Maybe your angel will save you."

She turned back toward the trail, kicking up sand as she plodded down the path, her husband's scratchy shrieks and Meredith Tanner's distorted cellular cries a form of intermingling poetry all their own.

-6-

Karen wandered back to the encampment and dug through pockets of the dead. Ezra had the keys, and she took them back to the red pickup. A sorrowful, twangy tune filled her ears as she started the pickup. She smiled.

Hank Williams. Daddy's favorite.

She drove until the truck ran out of gas just outside of Prescott, and rather than stew in her own thoughts she decided she would walk until someone found her or until her mind baked in her skull. Either way was fine with her.

Parched, her skin burning from the late morning sun, Karen walked down that empty highway, her favorite Sunday dress stained with the blood of the damned. Squinting upward to the sun, her daddy spoke up once more in her head:

Remember what I used to ask you when you were little? What would you do when you met your mountain?

Karen Singleton cracked a dry smile as she walked along the desert and away from sanity.

"I'll climb over it if I have to, Daddy." Her words were empty, lifeless, but her heart smoldered with a quiet rage that had only begun to burn. "I'll climb over it if I have to."

THE HARBINGER

"This town reeks."

Grimacing, Felix Proust lifted his suitcase and slammed the car door. He'd passed a sign for a pig farm a few miles back. The stench of the farm's crop wafted over the motel parking lot, thickening the air. Felix's stomach tumbled over itself and he swallowed hard to fight the bile lingering at the back of his throat.

His cell phone made a knock-knock sound from within his pocket. He reached for it and ran his thumb across the screen. There was a text from his editor, which read "Let me know when you arrive."

Felix responded, "Just made it."

A few seconds later: "Good. Everything okay?"

"Fine. Tired. Really could use a drink."

A flight delay had left him stranded in the airport for two hours. Years ago he would've gone straight to the lounge for a drink, but over half a decade of sobriety kept him grounded, focused. He wanted the drink, but he wanted his job even more.

The phone knocked again. "Very funny. How is Doll Town?"

"It smells like pig shit, Larry. Thanks for asking."

Amused with himself, Felix shoved the phone into his pocket and made his way to the motel's office. A large, hand-carved sign over the door read "DALTON R&R MOTEL—WHERE REST AND RELAXATION MEET!" He gave it a quick glance before opening the door.

An old man with thick glasses and a ratty blue flannel shirt sat behind the counter, hunched to one side and watching a portable television. A long, silver antenna protruded from the side. *Christ,* Felix thought, *didn't realize they still made those things.* The sound was garbled, and the screen flickered erratically. The elderly clerk slammed his fist on the top of the TV.

"Damn thing," he spat. Felix shuffled his weight from one foot to the other, waiting for the old man to acknowledge him. A sign on the counter read "Please ring bell for assistance," and Felix did so carefully, punctuating his annoyance one ring at a time.

Ding. Ding. Ding.

The clerk turned around with a big grin on his face, moving almost mechanically, as though he'd rehearsed this a thousand times. Based on his apparent age, Felix suspected this wasn't too far from the truth.

"Good afternoon!"

"Hi," Felix said. "I'd like a room."

"Well, friend, I reckon you've come to the right place." The old man leaned down, reaching for something beneath the counter. Felix caught sight of his nametag—JERRY—and smirked. *Jerry, an eccentric good old boy working down at the Dalton R&R. I'll have to mention him in the article.*

Jerry pulled out a large brown book and flipped it open. The motel register was worn and dusty, and the last entry was dated almost a year prior.

"Looks like I'm the first visitor in quite a while," Felix said. "How do you keep this place up and running?"

Jerry smiled. "You're ahead of the tourist season. The folks come from far and wide to see those dolls. You might say Miss Maggie keeps this place runnin' all year 'round."

"Miss Maggie Eloquence," Felix said, signing the register. "She's actually why I'm here."

The old man tilted his chin, squinting over the edge of his glasses. "That so?"

Felix smiled. "I work for *Toys in the Attic*. I'm here to interview her for an article."

"I see…" The old man turned the register and read his visitor's scrawl. "Mr. Proust. I'll go fetch your room key."

"You don't want my credit card?"

Jerry smiled, shaking his head. "No, Mr. Proust. We still do things the old-fashioned way down here in Dalton. Besides, you look like you're good for it."

He gave Felix a quick wink before turning away from the counter and hobbling into the back office. Felix eyed the old man, noting his suspenders and feeble gait. He wondered how long Jerry had worked at the motel. *Probably all his life*, he thought. *Not much else to do in this Podunk town.*

Felix leaned against the counter, taking in the *mise en scène* as Larry would say. A pair of potted plants stood on an end table, accompanied by a folding chair and a water cooler missing its jug. Yellowing floral wallpaper was complimented by dusty photographs of the town's heyday, documenting a history of hard labor. The largest photograph showed a group of tired men in dirty overalls and hardhats standing in front of a mine entrance.

Felix had done his homework before booking his flight to

Charleston. The small town of Dalton was built by the mining company's owner, Ezra Dalton. Maggie Eloquence was Ezra Dalton's daughter and sole heir to the family fortune—or what was left of it. His research had stopped at a long list of liquidated properties and bad investments.

When the coal mine dried up in the 1970s, so did most of the Dalton fortune—until Maggie opened Dalton Dollworks, that is. Felix followed the trail of photographs to the far end of the room where a large color print of the Dollworks factory hung in the center of the wall, a shrine to the last artery keeping the town alive.

Felix almost didn't see the child when he turned back around. The kid was standing in the corner, obscured by the edge of the motel counter and the waxy leaves of a potted plant. He glimpsed black hair and a tiny arm drawn up against the wall. Confused, he pulled away from the counter and turned the corner to get a better look.

What the hell?

The little boy stood in the corner, his arms drawn up against the wall, face buried in his hands as though hiding away from the world. Felix stood frozen in place, unsure of what to say. The air in the room was suddenly thick with the stench of shit. He felt the miasma pressing against his face like a warm pillow, its smell invading his nasal passages, burning away at his nerves. His eyes watered, and he feared he might throw up his breakfast.

"I see you've found Noah." Jerry walked past him, twirling a key ring around his index finger. He leaned down next to the boy. "Cat got your tongue? No need to be shy, now. He's a guest!"

Noah said nothing.

"Sir," Felix began, swallowing back the taste of bile. He held out his hand for the key. "I can find my way to the room—"

"Nonsense." Jerry reached down, grabbed the kid by the back of his collar, and turned the boy around. "This is why you came, isn't it?"

The doll's arms fell away, revealing a pale, emotionless face and black eyes. Relief slipped over Felix like a warm blanket, but even that wasn't enough to mask the hideous stench. He wondered how the old man seemed to mind it, but figured that after years of living so close to the pig farms, the acrid aroma had burned away most of his sense of smell.

A tag hung from the doll's sleeve, adorned with the logo for Miss Maggie's company, Dalton Dollworks. Jerry reached down and flipped over the tag, revealing the name "Noah" written in rich, black calligraphy.

"Miss Maggie gave him to me herself. As a gift."

Felix couldn't take his eyes off the figure. The doll's face was smooth, almost pale with a hint of rosy hue, but lacked the typical luster found with most dolls. That was Miss Maggie's trademark secret. No one but her staff knew how the dolls were made, or so the story went.

"Do you have kids, Mr. Proust?"

Felix met Jerry's gaze and offered a weak smile. "Uh, no. Kids aren't my thing. My ex…" He trailed off, biting back his words while his cheeks flushed. No matter where he went, Helen haunted him now even more than when they were still married. A familiar thirst rose from the back of his throat, and he tried to swallow it down. Thoughts of his ex-wife always brought on an urge to drink.

Realizing his silence, Felix reached out and shook Noah's hand. His white, chiseled fingers were surprisingly warm.

"Charming. Lots of personality, too."

"No two are the same," Jerry said, his eyes enormous and bulging behind his thick glass lenses. He stood the doll back in the corner.

"They say Miss Maggie tailors them herself out of her dreams. And Noah, well, she made him just for me after I lost my son some years ago. She even named the doll after him, God bless her soul." The old man held up the key and wandered over to the office door. "You never know, Mr. Proust. Dalton has a way of changing a man's mind. Maybe Miss Maggie will make a doll just for you."

Jerry opened the door and held it for his guest. Felix looked back, ruminating on the old innkeeper's words. Noah the Doll stood in the corner, staring out into empty space with those pitch black eyes. *I sure as hell hope not*, Felix thought.

Dalton, West Virginia spread out below the motel, nestled in a short valley at the foot of the Appalachian Mountains, alight with the afternoon sun. Felix Proust's first impression of the small burg was that the town looked ancient, and in that respect, he was right. A single road snaked its way down the hill and connected to Dalton's Main Street.

I'm going to give Larry hell for sending me to this shitty town. Felix came to a stop sign at the corner of Main and First. The local drugstore stood to his right, its picture window sparse and adorned with aged, yellowing signs. The fluorescent lights inside went out, and a moment later an old man emerged. A young, brown-haired boy followed after him.

The child gave Felix a piercing scowl while the old man locked up for the night. When he was finished, the store owner took the boy's hand and led him around the corner. The child craned his head around, continuing to glare in Felix's direction until he fell out of view.

A chill crept across Felix's shoulders just as the sun passed behind a patch of clouds. For a moment he felt like the last man alive on earth, shivering alone in the dark. He shook his head and moved on.

He saw everything Dalton had to offer within the span of ten minutes, creeping along from one block to the next, passing a closed post office, an empty Dalton IGA supermarket, a clothing store displaying the latest fashions right out of the 1970s, and Dalton's town hall. At the last corner stood a place called Meyer's Diner, and it was the only business on Main Street that seemed to be teeming with life.

Felix sat at the stop sign and looked through the picture window at the patrons within. Every booth was occupied by families— possibly every family the town had left—one man, woman, and child to a table. They sat solemnly, eyes averted downward, eating their meals with joyless discipline. Even the waitress who brought their meals looked tired, lifeless.

A little girl sitting across from her parents in a window booth looked up from her plate, turning almost mechanically toward Felix. She had bright red curls that spilled over her shoulders, accented by a red and white polka-dotted bow atop her head. When their eyes met, Felix felt something give way within his mind. That feeling wasn't quite fear, but a distinct mixture of sorrow and urgency. Sorrow for the way she was living, for the fact that her odds of leaving this town were slim to none; urgency for the scorn and contempt beaming back to him from those dark eyes. They weren't the eyes of a child.

He felt that familiar chill tip-toe across the back of his neck and onward to his shoulders. The little girl wasn't the only one staring now. One by one, the other children looked up from their meals, all dark-eyed and frowning, beaming their hatred toward him. *I've entered the Village of the Damned*, he thought, before easing off the brake and making a left. The GPS chimed, announcing his destination was two miles away. Felix stepped on the gas.

"And to your left is the head assembly line."

Felix followed Sheila's finger and peered through the Plexiglas window, watching as pale, dismembered doll heads rolled their way down a conveyor belt. The previous highlight of the tour had been the section of the process in which arms and legs were affixed to torsos with machine precision. He'd toured numerous factories during his years writing for *Toys in the Attic*, and there was a universal constant at work in all of them: they put together toy parts. Usually, when toy makers stranded him on a factory tour, they'd either forgotten their appointment, or they just didn't give a shit.

He checked his watch and frowned. He'd been at the factory for almost two hours—the first of which was spent in the front lobby— and Miss Maggie Eloquence had yet to make an appearance. His story was supposed to be about Miss Maggie, not her manufacturing process, and based on what he'd seen so far, he suspected his article would not be very flattering.

Old Jerry at the Dalton R&R piped up in his head: *They say Miss Maggie tailors them herself, out of her dreams.* Watching the expressionless doll heads roll their way down the conveyor, Felix decided the old innkeeper hadn't bothered to take a tour himself. *I still have to hand it to Miss Maggie,* he thought. *She knows how far a little mystique will take her product. Speaking of which…*

Felix raised his hand, interrupting his elderly tour guide. Her wrinkled lips pursed into a frown.

"Yes, young man?"

"Sheila, this is all incredibly interesting, really, but I was wondering when I would get to sit down with Maggie Eloquence?"

"No one meets with Miss Maggie."

He forced a smile. "Her publicist assured me I would be able to interview Ms. Dalton. It's why I'm here in the first place."

"No one meets with Miss Maggie," she repeated, her eyes narrowing into thin slits. "If there's a problem with the tour, young man, I might suggest you speak with management."

Felix chewed his lower lip for a moment, sizing up the icy old crone while his cheeks flushed with heat. Larry spoke up between his raging thoughts, reminding him to keep his cool. *Kill 'em with kindness*, Larry quipped.

"No," Felix said through clenched teeth, "there's no problem, ma'am. I was wondering, though, if you might show me to the gift shop. I think I've seen enough of the assembly line for my article, and I'd like to purchase one of these nice dolls for my daughter."

Sheila shrugged her shoulders as if to say "Suit yourself," and pushed past him into the next observation room. He followed her along a series of corridors that ran parallel to the assembly line, and by the time they reached the exit to the gift shop, completed dolls were rolling down the conveyor belt. He paused for a moment, watching their androgynous faces regard him with blank, accusing stares. That unsettling feeling crept into the pit of his gut once more, treading a line between fear and anxiety, and he jumped when the old woman called after him.

"Coming," he said, all too eager to turn away from the Plexiglas window and the black eyes watching him from beyond.

The gift shop was a menagerie of Dalton's primary export. Hundreds of dolls sat upon shelves numbering five high all the way to the ceiling, their hands positioned over their eyes, forming their signature "pouting" look. More of them stood along the wall, pointed away from any patron brave enough to enter, frozen forever in a permanent expression of sorrow and apology.

Felix noticed the smell immediately. *Pig shit*, he thought. The room was so rank with that sour stench that his eyes watered. He wiped his tears on his sleeve. If the old woman noticed, she made no mention of the odor, nor did she apologize for it. Felix thought of inquiring about it but didn't want to be rude. The last thing he needed was word getting back to Larry about his manners. And besides, weren't the Dalton Pig Farms the source of the town's secondary export?

"Another customer, Sheila?"

An elderly man stood behind the counter, watching them with a big grin. The old woman pointed to him. "Craig will set you right up. He'll help you pick something out for your daughter."

Felix wiped his eyes and nodded, smiling. "Been a real pleasure, Sheila."

She offered a grunt in return before doubling back through the factory exit.

"Don't mind her," Craig said. "Dana's our usual tour guide, but she's off today. Sheila's not used to being around young folks like yourself."

"Young folks, huh?" Felix leaned against the counter. "That's kind of you to say. I must be wearing forty rather well."

"Forty, eh? I remember those days. That was a good age, that 'un. I remember back when…" Craig rambled on, shuffling his feet in anticipation as he waxed nostalgic. Felix was a hundred miles away, piecing together the article he would write, slamming the Dalton Dollworks for the smell in their factory. The article was supposed to be about the history of the dolls in the owner's own words—a character piece, really—but all he had to go on now was a factory tour, a crotchety old tour guide, and a room reeking of shit.

"Aww, listen to me ramble on. I'm sorry, mister. You need a doll for your daughter, right?"

Felix blinked, torn away from his angry reverie. He shot the old man a confused glance for a moment before remembering his lie. He turned, staring at the dolls in their simple clothes. He didn't have a daughter but supposed that if he did, she'd want something girly. There were plenty of those dolls to go around—the pale figures were arranged girl-boy-girl all the way around the room, their faces turned away, dressed in simple country clothes. The girls had red bows tied up in their hair, and the boys wore denim overalls with red rags sticking out of their back pockets.

"I'll take that one," Felix said, pointing to the blonde doll with the blue polka-dotted dress. He reached into his pocket for his cell phone but stopped when he felt a hand upon his shoulder.

"Each doll's special," Craig said. "They choose their owner, not the other way around. You don't get a second chance." He was still smiling, but the sound of his voice was cold. Felix was sure he was just imagining it, though—after all, he was worked up over the lack of an interview. Maybe he was just projecting his anger upon this old man.

"Sure," Felix said, smiling. "I'm sure my little Jenny will just love this one. Blue's her favorite color, you know."

Craig nodded. "As you wish, mister. If you give me just a few minutes, I'll go get you a box and some wrapping paper. We'll make it super-special for your girl."

"Sounds like a plan, my man."

Felix held his smile and waited until Craig had disappeared into the back room before lifting his cell phone to his ear. He chewed his lower lip, listening to the rings chirp one after the other and exhaled when Larry's voicemail picked up. When the recording beeped, Felix discovered he was so angry his hands were shaking.

"Larry, it's me. This whole trip was a waste of time. Not only did she stand me up, but these dolls—" He paused, looking over his shoulder for Craig. The old man was still in the back room rummaging for wrapping paper. "—these dolls are fucking *ugly* little things. They smell, too. Anyway, I'm going to see if I can dig up something else before I head back to the airport. Call me when you can."

He ended the call, shoved the phone back into his pocket, and was about to turn back toward the counter when something caught his eye. One of the dolls—a boy with curly brown hair—sat on the third shelf with his legs dangling in the air. He stared at Felix, expressionless, unblinking, his black eyes glaring downward in a gaze of silent accusation. For a moment Felix was frozen in place, his knees weak and feet cemented by a sudden fear that this child—no, this doll—had heard what he'd said. Hadn't it turned around to watch him? Weren't they all turned away from him just a moment ago?

Preposterous, he thought. *The doll's just above the doorway. It had to be sitting like that when I walked in and I just didn't notice it. Relax.*

Craig placed a small box and a tube of red wrapping paper on the counter. He took the doll with the blue polka-dotted dress from the shelf and put her in the box. Felix thought she looked like a child in a casket, ready to be lowered into the ground. His morbidity ushered a chill across the threshold of his shoulders. That chill crept all the way down to his toes, and by the time he was ready to pay, he found he could hardly steady his hands.

"One more thing," Craig said, his smile faltering for a moment. He stared at Felix, holding his gaze with an alarming intensity. "Miss Maggie crafts her dolls a special way. Sometimes, if you talk to 'em, I swear by God they'll listen to ya. And maybe if you're lucky, maybe they'll talk back."

Felix offered a faint smile. "If I'm lucky?"

"Oh yes," Craig said, his eyes welling up with tears. His jaw quivered slightly for a moment before steadying itself. "You might say all of Dalton's lucky, mister. Maybe you will be, too."

Felix thanked the old man, tucked the wrapped box underneath one arm, and offered the gift shop a cursory glance before making his way for the door. He was about to push his way out into the lobby when the hairs stood up on the back of his neck.

Can't be, he thought.

He turned back once more. An entire row of dolls was turned to face him, watching his exit with their empty, black eyes. Felix blinked, shook his head, and made his way out of the building with long, fast strides. He didn't look back.

"What do you *mean* she canceled?" The phone's tiny speaker sizzled with Larry's agitation. Felix started the car and threw up his hands, immediately feeling foolish for doing so. His only audience was the doll, and she was wrapped up in a box with a big white bow.

"She didn't just cancel, Larry. She didn't show at all."

"Well didn't you ask to see her?"

Felix scoffed. "Of *course* I asked to see her. Apparently, no one sees Her Majesty. Ever."

"Bullshit," the phone hissed. Cellular reception really was shoddy out here in the mountains. "That doesn't make any goddamn sense, Felix. *They* called *us*, remember?"

He did. Maggie Dalton's publicist had called three weeks ago, raving about an article he'd written on the recent trend of "Time Out" dolls. Felix offered to schedule a phone interview, but the publicist wouldn't have it. "Miss Maggie only interviews face to face, and she wants *you*, Mr. Proust. She wants you."

And yet here he was, traveling on Maggie Dalton's dime with nothing to show for it—except for an overpriced doll and a lot of wasted time.

Larry seethed through the phone's speaker, and Felix knew better than to chime in at this point. After working with Larry for more than ten years, Felix knew that once his editor got going, nothing would stop him until he ran out of steam.

Larry was putting a lot on the line by sending Felix down here. Falling off the wagon had done more than ease the pain of divorce; it had nearly destroyed his career, and Felix had struggled to regain his editor's trust ever since. Felix knew this was his chance to redeem himself, to prove he could be trusted again. When the assignment landed in his lap, he couldn't turn it down—even if it meant traveling to Hog Shit, West Virginia.

"Larry," Felix cut in. "Look, I'm getting a lot of static here. I'll poke around town, see what I can stir up from the locals. Maybe I can still get a scoop on Maggie Eloquence. One way or another I'll get you an interview. I won't let you down."

"You do that," Larry said. Felix could see the veins popping out of his editor's forehead even from 700 miles away. "Text me when you have something."

"Will do," Felix said, and ended the call. He buckled his seatbelt, looked over at the wrapped box in the passenger seat, and shook his head. "Not a word, little girl. Not a word."

Meyer's Diner seemed like the best place to start—if for no other reason than his growling stomach. He'd skipped lunch in favor of getting ahead of Charleston traffic, and after getting worked up over at the Dollworks factory, he was feeling particularly famished. He parked along the curb in front of the diner and went inside.

A blonde waitress leaned against the far end of the counter, chatting with the cook while an older man sat in a middle booth, spooning soup into his disaster of a beard. A jukebox stood to his right, but it wasn't plugged in, and the quiet murmurs of the diner staff carried across the tiled floor. Felix took a step across the threshold and paused.

A trio of dolls—two boys and one girl—occupied the nearest booth, positioned with their elbows on the table. They sat glaring at one another, expressionless, their dark eyes exuding a chilling nothingness that made Felix's skin crawl. While he watched them with cautious curiosity, that familiar stench found his nostrils. The odor of pig shit wafted over the diner's otherwise appealing aroma, smothering the scent of burning grease and frying oil.

"Howdy."

Felix turned away from the dolls. The cook approached the near side of the counter, wiping his hands on a dirty rag.

"Hi there," Felix said, displacing a wad of cotton from his throat. His voice sounded oddly weak, distant. "Not very busy today, huh?"

"No, sir. Have a seat. Diane here will take your order."

The blonde waitress gave him a wink. Felix nodded to her in return, taking a seat one booth away from the diner's single bearded patron. A new aroma met his nose, underscoring the pig smell and stirring up unpleasant memories.

He'd spent time with his fair share of winos back in the day. This was after his divorce and imminent DUI, after proclaiming that his ex-wife may have taken his money but not his balls, goddammit. One crash and Breathalyzer later, Felix found himself serving probation for a first offense, working in a soup kitchen to fulfill his mandatory community service hours. There were plenty of drunks milling down the line with their hands out, paper plates ready for whatever was on the menu that day—and they always reeked of malt liquor. The smell made his mouth water.

Felix made eye contact with the old man in the next booth, offering a gentle nod to greet him, but the bearded fellow stared through him.

"What can I getcha, hon?"

The waitress walked over and stood beside the table with a notepad in her hand. Felix smiled up at her while trying to find his appetite. His hunger was down in his stomach somewhere, buried beneath the town's stink and the lingering scent of booze, the latter of which tickled the back of his tongue something fierce. His mouth watered.

"What do you recommend?"

"I can have Maynard whip up one of his famous Dollface Burgers. Comes with a side of Doll Fingers and a pop. How's that sound?"

Dollface Burgers and Doll Fingers. Appetizing.

"Uh, sure. Sounds great."

"Comin' right up, hon." Diane plucked his ticket from the pad and stepped away from the table. A few moments later Felix heard the hiss of the grill, and his appetite returned with a fury all its own, pig stench be damned. He turned his attention to the picture window beside the booth, staring out into the looming shadows brought on by a late afternoon sun.

The window looked out onto an empty side street. No cars or trucks. No people, either. Just the shadows and an occasional clump of dry leaves caught in a breeze. He'd grown up in a small town like this, spending his early days dreaming of ways to make his escape to the big city. Back then the streets usually cleared out after business hours, everyone gone home to their families or other errands. That was over thirty years ago. These days, even his hometown was crowded at all hours, bustling with a population of just fifteen thousand people.

He looked at his phone, noting the time was barely six o'clock. Dalton should've been alive and kicking at this hour, and the fact that it wasn't made him feel very uneasy.

Enough of that, he told himself. *Most of the businesses in this place have dried up. You saw that on your way in. All that's left is this little dive, the R&R out by the highway, and the Dollworks.* He sniffed, grimacing at a whiff of the underlying stench of the place. Even the scent of grilled meat couldn't overpower it. There was still the Dalton Pig Farm. He couldn't forget that place, and there was no telling what other little Mom & Pop shops were scattered about the town, places he hadn't seen from Main Street. There had to be more here for people to make a living. Why else would they stick around?

His editor's voice piped up again, chiding him: *Stop scaring yourself, Felix. This is just a Podunk town out in the sticks. The people are weird and the town smells like shit—what else is new?*

Movement caught his eye, tearing him from his reverie. The old man rose from his booth and dropped a few singles on the table.

He caught Felix's gaze and nodded, then quickly looked over his shoulder. Felix followed, noting that the waitress was occupied at the cash register, and Maynard was still preparing his meal.

"Mister," the old man whispered. He took a step, leaning over Felix's table. The smell of liquor surrounded him like a cloud. "You need to git."

A cold nail drove itself into his gut, pinning him to his seat, and that familiar lump of cotton returned to his throat. "What?"

The old man's eyes widened, straining to make his words clear. "Git *out* of here, boy. Before they pick you."

"Sir, I don't—"

The drunk took his wrist and squeezed. "Eat yer food and meet me round the corner. Don't do nothin' stupid, neither, or else they'll be on to us. I'll be waitin'. Tell ya what you need to know so's you can tell everyone else."

"Henry, what'd I tell you about pesterin' our customers?"

Diane leaned over the counter, one finger held out in a scolding manner like a school teacher, and Henry recoiled as if he'd been shot. Chin down, he offered Felix a brief wink before turning around to face her.

"I's just makin' po-lite conversation, Diane. I ain't done nothin' to bother this nice man. Ain't that right, bubba?"

Felix straightened up in his seat and flashed the waitress a smile. "He ain't done nothin', ma'am."

His sarcastic slip into their accent went unnoticed. Diane's scolding expression softened a little, but not enough to put the old drunk at ease. She stared at them a second more before turning back to the register, prompting Henry to turn back around. Felix, however, still had a perfect view of the waitress, and he could see she was watching from the corner of her eye. The way she tucked her hair behind her ear was another tell that set off an alarm in his mind. *What the hell is going on here?*

Felix leaned forward and looked up at Henry. "After my meal. Around the corner."

Henry said nothing, only nodded in agreement as he retreated to exit the diner. As soon as he was out of the building, Diane brought over a tray of food and set it down on the table. Felix offered her a smile and thanked her.

"No problem, hon. Say, don't you mind that old drunk. He ain't done nothin' but heckle everybody—especially tourists like yourself."

"He wasn't bothering me," Felix said. "But I appreciate your concern."

Diane smiled. She was missing a few of her lower teeth. "You just let me know if there's anything else I can do for ya, hon."

Felix thanked her again and waited for her to return to the counter before digging into his food. Even then he couldn't get the old man's worried face out of his head or those words out of his mind. *Tell ya what you need to know so's you can tell everyone else.* He'd promised Larry an interview one way or another, but from the sound of things, something bigger had just fallen into his lap.

"**O**ver here, boy."

Felix almost missed him. Henry leaned against a dusty wall of the adjacent building. Shadows clung to him like a cloak in the failing daylight, and Felix nearly jumped out of his shoes when the old man beckoned to him.

"Swig?" Henry held out a small bottle, sloshing the pale amber liquid within. "Ya might need it before I'm done tellin' what I got to tell ya."

"No thanks," Felix said, although he was certainly tempted by the offer. His mouth watered a little. "I quit a long time ago."

"Suit yerself," Henry said, tipping back the bottle. He finished it off in four hard gulps. "I heard fallin' off the wagon is too goddamn easy, so I never bothered climbin' on it."

Felix stepped back and pressed himself against the opposite wall. He watched the old man, wondering if his warning to "git" out of town earlier was just the ramblings of a liquor-soaked mind, but the urgency in Henry's voice—combined with the way that waitress had been watching them—tickled the right nerves in the back of his head. He was a journalist, after all. Or used to be. These days he wondered about that.

A breeze picked up around them, filling his nose with that foul pig smell. He grimaced.

Henry scratched his beard and sniffed the air. "You git used to it, that stink. Wasn't always like that, though. Dalton used to be a great town, but it ain't been the same since they shut down the mine."

Felix nodded. "You could say that about any coal mining town. What makes this shit hole any different?"

The old drunk crouched against the wall, sighing as his knees popped. He lowered his head, chin to chest, and spoke barely above a whisper. "They found somethin' down in that mine. You won't find nothin' about that in no newspaper, no sir. They'll tell ya the coal vein dried up, but that ain't the truth. I should know, bubba. I was down there when they found it."

"What do you mean?" Felix stepped forward and knelt beside him. "What did you find down there?"

Henry looked up at him and wiped tears from his eyes. Booze or not, Felix knew that desperate look. He'd seen it in the mirror before, in the days following his discovery of Helen's lies. What the old man said next sent a chill racing all the way up his spine.

"Pure evil," Henry sobbed. That icy feeling sank its teeth into the back of Felix's neck and wouldn't let go. "We found the devil down in that hole, and damned if we didn't bring him right back up the shaft with us." He wiped his nose on his sleeve. "Three of us broke into that room down at the bottom of the mine—me and Tommy Wilkins and Jarvis Hennigan, all of us were there, saw the room all laid out like an altar with that little stone figure in the middle."

"Stone figure?"

"Yessir," Henry snorted, "in the shape of a baby, with two nuggets of coal for eyes and smellin' like Satan's asshole. We'd never seen nothin' like it. Maggie's daddy Zachary Dalton even come down to the mine that day to see what we'd found, and he took it home for his daughter and…and…"

Henry's blubbering got in the way of his words, devolving into a series of hard, drawn out sobs. Felix stared at the crying man, allowing his words to sink in while the silence of the town crept between them like a looming shadow. A light breeze swept down the alleyway, lifting the scent of liquor to new heights above that ever-present pig stench, and his mouth watered some more. *He's drunk*, Felix thought. *I'm wasting my time with the town drunk.*

He knew what the drink could do to a man, and the longer he sat watching Henry cry, the more he saw a reflection of himself. How long had he been sober now? Five years? Six? Time didn't matter anymore in that respect; he was dry and planned on staying that way. He swallowed back the saliva accumulating in his mouth and climbed to his feet.

"Mister, I appreciate you taking the time to talk with me, but I'm a journalist, not a novelist. I think maybe you've had too much of the old rotgut—"

Henry lashed out, gripping Felix's ankle. "Now you lissen 'ere, city boy. Mayhap I like to drink, but I know'd what I saw that day. That thing we found swallered this town, sucked the life right out of it." He met Felix's annoyed gaze and frowned. "It used Miss Maggie, used her like a puppet. It took our kids just like it took her soul. Replaced 'em with those infernal dolls. There ain't been no kids in this town since they dug up that demon in the mine. It's been leechin' from us ever since. Ain't you wondered why everyone's so old here, boy?"

"This is insane. You're drunk, old man. If you know what's best for you, find an AA meeting and stick with it."

Felix kicked away Henry's hand and started for his car. Henry rose to his feet and struggled to keep his balance. He braced one hand against the wall to steady himself.

"If ya don't believe me, boy, you get in that fancy car of yers and drive out to First Baptist on Maple. Take a peek inside and then tell me if I'm just a poor-ass drunkard." Henry's warning broke up into a fit of laughter. "You go right ahead, young'un. You'll see, and then you can go drive back to the city and write with yer fancy words. Write about how old drunk Henry Watson was right. Go on, city boy. *You go on and git!*"

Felix picked up his pace, exiting the alley as fast as he could. The old man was obviously crazy, his voice cracking as it switched between laughs and cries. A stone idol down in the mine? Some buried evil that had enveloped the town and taken the children? Felix scoffed. If it weren't for the old man's ignorant speech, Felix might have figured Henry had just read too many books.

Except the old bastard probably can't read. Not well, anyway.

He unlocked the rental car, climbed in, and started the engine. He was on the verge of doing a U-turn in the street and hauling ass back to the Dalton R&R when movement caught his eye. He looked over to his right, toward the large picture window of the diner. Sitting at the nearest booth were those same three dolls as before, their faces pressed against the glass, dark eyes staring with a kind of cold anxiety.

"That's not right," he whispered, remembering how they were just an hour before when he'd first walked in. He saw them clearly in his head, sitting with their elbows on the table in secret, conspiring poses. They could have been young children whispering to one another if not for their pale skin and dark eyes.

And yet there they were with their heads turned, staring in accusation while he sat in the car, trembling.

"The old man's crazy," he said aloud, listening for some reassurance in his voice, but the light tremble of his words suggested otherwise. He had seen actual children since his arrival, hadn't he? What about the old man and the little boy coming out of the drugstore? What about the children sitting with their families at the diner earlier that afternoon? They were kids, weren't they?

Of course they were, he thought, remembering the way they had moved on their own, staring at him with—

A cold hand curled its fingers around his gut and squeezed as Henry Watson's voice echoed in his skull: *Two nuggets of coal for eyes.*

"What are you doing, Felix?" Helen's words were out of his mouth before he could stop them. Even in his own voice, he could hear her tired disdain and frustration, and if he concentrated hard enough, he could see her standing in the doorway of their bedroom, the drying tears on her cheeks preserved forever in memory.

"What I have to," he whispered, snapping himself from that reverie.

Felix Proust sucked in his breath and put the car in gear, cursing his promise to Larry. He drove two blocks, flipped on his turn signal, and turned onto Maple Street.

First Baptist sat at the top of a small hill removed from the rest of the town. The small building stood like an aging sentinel, its days of jubilation and brimstone long silenced by an apparent catastrophe the magnitude of which Felix could only imagine. And imagine he did, his mind working overtime with the old drunk's taunts and warnings. He had to hand it to the guy: Henry sure knew how to pique a man's curiosity.

The church's windows were boarded up with thin, rotting sheets of plywood that bore scars of the elements. Even the steeple leaned to one side as though drooping in defeat. The late afternoon sun sank behind the mountains, casting the hillside in a thick shadow, and a stiff breeze rustled the tall grass along the sidewalk.

Felix held out his cell phone, illuminating the concrete steps as he walked toward the church's double-doors. He stopped when he saw the entrance barred with a series of two-by-fours, each corner nailed to the door frame. Written across the center board was a single word in what might have been a child's scrawl: HERETICS.

"That's inviting," he muttered, almost chuckling to himself. The nagging question of *Why* kept nipping at the back of his mind. Why would someone do this? Why board up the only church in town? Why had the people of Dalton lost their faith?

Helen's voice piped up in his head: *Plenty of reasons, but so far all you've got to go on are the words of a drunk. Ironic, isn't it?*

"Fuck off, Helen." Felix sniffed to clear his nose, but when he did he caught a whiff of something foul in the air. This wasn't just the smell of pig shit—he was getting used to that, believe it or not—but something far more rank. Something vile. And whatever it was, it wafted from beyond those doors.

Heretics, he thought. *What would a town of religious zealots do to heretics?*

His imagination ran rampant with possibilities, leading him back to college days spent learning about the Spanish Inquisition, but he forced those thoughts from his mind. *Keep your focus*, he told himself. *You owe Larry one.* But he didn't just owe Larry one; he owed Larry several. The AA meetings gave him a lot of perspective, and his debt of gratitude to Larry Malone was just one of many things which Felix now saw with perfect clarity. This was more than just an assignment; this was a debt to be paid.

So put your big boy pants on, he heard Larry say, *and go get that story.*

Felix sniffed the air again, ignoring the reeking miasma surrounding First Baptist. He approached the door and pulled at one of the boards with hope that it was rotted through, but he had no such luck. The two-by-four resisted his force, seeming to mock him with its childish scrawl.

He held out his cell phone, illuminating his way through the tall grass around the side of the building. The windows were also nailed shut, but at the far end he spied an opening. One of the slats had rotted through, hanging limp like a dead limb. Felix reached out, pressing his fingers into the wood, and frowned when they sank into the pulp. He wondered how long the church had been closed.

Felix reached through the opening, braced his elbow against the window pane and his hand against the board, and gave a single, forceful push. The rotted beam gave little resistance, easing its way free of the nails holding it in place before snapping in two. The pulpy remains collapsed inward.

The stench from within hit him like a sucker punch, twisting his churning guts inside out until he was ready to vomit, but all that came was a single dry heave. He spat, wiped his mouth, and clutched his tie against his nose to hold back the stink. Shaking, Felix lifted up his cell phone and peered inside.

A number of emotions went through his mind in the span of seconds which followed, each more unsettling than the last, seemingly emptying his soul with each lingering moment until there was nothing left but the hollowed husk of a frightened man.

His eyes were playing tricks on him. Surely those shapes piled up on the floor weren't what he thought they were. No, they couldn't be. They *shouldn't* be. Perhaps it was the poor lighting. Yes, that had to be the cause of his confusion—the dim glow of his cell phone combined with the moonlight filtering through the cracks of the boarded windows were making those shapes on the floor look like the remains of children.

An oppressive heat rose up in his chest, and he realized he'd been holding his breath. He exhaled, unable to look away from the pile of things that were most certainly *not* children but also unable to reconcile what that monstrous amalgamation of shapes might otherwise be. He panned the light over a mound that reached as high as the ceiling, refusing to believe those bones belonged to children, some of them merely infants, little bundles of putrescent joy that were branded as heretics by Miss Maggie's coal-eyed stone idol.

It used Miss Maggie, used her like a puppet. It took our kids just like it took her soul.

Felix finally recoiled from the window, and this time his dinner shot up from his stomach. He doubled over, retching until there was nothing in his guts left to give, and he teetered backward away from the defiled tomb that was Dalton's First Baptist.

He staggered back to his car in a daze, feeling as though all he'd seen in that one-room church had somehow sucked away his last ounce of energy. His stomach ached, but his heart hurt worse. He felt as though someone had punched a hole through his chest and ripped that vital muscle right out of him. How could anyone do that to all those children?

His hands were shaking so badly that he had a hard time putting the key in the ignition.

"Get a grip on yourself," he said, staring into the rearview. He slicked his hair back and wiped his mouth. "You made it through the DTs, you can make it through this."

He steadied his hand and started the car. *Act casual,* he thought. *Just get back to the motel, get your things, and get the hell out of here.*

But as he turned off Maple and back onto Main, Felix found that he had a hard time driving the speed limit.

"Larry, goddammit." Felix pressed the phone to his ear and slammed the door to his room. Larry's voicemail message played back in his ear. The beep chimed, signaling his time to speak, but he found his words were blocked by the lump in his throat. He hung up, chewing his lower lip while frantically searching the stale motel room. His suitcase sat open on the bed, and some of his clothes lay in a pile beside it.

Those familiar fingers curled around his gut once again. He stared at the pile of clothing while his fingers fumbled with the phone. He dialed Larry again. Three rings. Four. *Pick up, Larry. Don't do this to me now.*

Heart pounding, Felix walked to the edge of the bed with the phone to his ear and began shoving his clothes back into his suitcase. He tore off his tie and tossed it into the suitcase as well, zipping everything up with his free hand while the call went to voicemail.

Beep.

"Larry," Felix began, cradling the phone against his ear with his shoulder. He struggled to wrap the zipper all the way around the suitcase. "This is going to sound really batshit, but I'm pulling the plug on this article. I'm checking out and getting back on the highway to Charleston, and I'm going to call the cops when I do. Something's really wrong here, man. There's a church in town full of—"

Three short, quick knocks rapped at the door. Felix paused as the blood in his veins went ice cold. He lowered his voice.

"Look, I'm sorry, I know you trusted me on this but I need you to understand I am not okay here. Something is wrong with this place, and if I don't leave, I'm afraid something is going to happen to me. Call me back when you get this."

He ended the call and set the phone on the nightstand, watching the door rattle as the knocks continued, growing heavier with each beat.

"Mr. Proust?"

Felix closed his eyes as the adrenaline left him feeling lightheaded. He shook his head, embarrassed by his skittishness, and cleared his throat.

"Yeah, Jerry?"

"Everything okay in there?"

He walked over and opened the door. The short old man peered up at him from behind a pair of thick glasses, his lower lip tucked inward. The expression gave his whole face a concave look.

"I saw ya run by the office in a hurry and the way you slammed the door plum shook the whole building."

Felix made himself smile. "Sorry, Jerry. I'm just in a hurry. I'll be checking out tonight."

"Is that so? Huh. Ain't that a shame. Yes sir, that's a damn shame."

"Yeah," Felix said. He stepped back a few feet and lifted the suitcase from the bed, extending the handle so he could pull it along its wheels. "Say, did housekeeping come around while I was gone?"

"Housekeeping?" Jerry seemed puzzled, his eyes huge like an owl behind those thick goggles. "No, sir. This time of year we don't keep no housekeepers on staff. Too slow for that. Why, there somethin' wrong?"

"No," Felix sighed, shaking his head. "Some of my things were moved around. Maybe it's just my imagination. It's been a long day."

"Say, maybe Noah lit into your room while you was gone. I keep tellin' him not to do that, but he won't listen to me none."

In another time, Felix might have laughed at the old man, taking his comment as a lighthearted joke. Tonight, however, he found the thought of that pale, dark-eyed thing sifting through his clothes not only terrifying but repulsive. His mind flashed back to the mound of bodies inside the church, prompting his guts to roll and tumble once again.

"You sure you ain't okay, Mr. Proust? Yer lookin' awfully peaked."

Felix forced his smile as he shuffled out of the room and closed the door behind him. "I'm just tired, Jerry. Here's your key. I'm going to go put this in my car and then I'll be right back to pay you."

"Sure thing, Mr. Proust."

Jerry followed him as far as the front office before disappearing inside. Felix took a breath and rolled his suitcase over to his rental car. *Keep calm*, he kept telling himself. *Act casual. Nothing is wrong.* He was so caught up in the act of behaving normally that he didn't notice the subtle chime coming from the inside of the car. He was too wrapped up in his own thoughts, walking himself through what was bound to be an incredibly awkward conversation with the state police. *Yes, officer, you heard me correctly. There's a pile of dead children inside the local church. How did I know to look? The town drunk told me so. This was after he told me about the strange idol they found down in the mine back in the 1970s. Oh, and did I mention I'm a recovering alcoholic?*

He closed the trunk and paused. The chime finally caught his attention. He'd left the keys in the ignition, expecting his departure to be swift. Perhaps he hadn't closed his door all the way? He walked around to the driver's side and tugged at the handle. The door didn't budge.

A cold spike tickled the back of his neck, working its way all the way down to the small of his back. The car's dome light was on, illuminating the interior, casting a dim sheen across the shreds of wrapping paper in the front seat. The gift for his imaginary daughter lay on its side, the top popped open and the bright red wrapping paper torn to pieces.

A series of images came rushing back to him, flashing from the dolls in the gift shop to the dolls back in Meyer's Diner and Henry's red, swollen eyes. He remembered the children eating with their parents and the way that little girl had stared at him with cold, unflinching hatred. He thought of the dead children in the church. Pieces of the puzzle were beginning to form in his mind, completing an image of impossible, soul-crushing horror.

Now he understood. Now, watching as the scattered bits of wrapping paper trembled in the soft evening breeze, Felix realized with unsettling clarity just what Henry had been trying to tell him.

He needed to try Larry again. Larry would know what to do. He always did. He'd helped Felix find his way to AA, and now he could help save him from this demonic town. He reached for his phone—and his heart sank.

His phone wasn't in his pocket. It was back in his room, sitting on the nightstand.

"Shit."

He trudged back toward the building, the tension in his neck and shoulders building with every passing moment. He glanced through the window of the front office, expecting to see Jerry waiting for him at the counter, but the old fellow wasn't there. *Good*, he thought. He was beyond polite conversation now, and he imagined himself throwing a wad of money on the counter before hopping into his car and speeding all the way back to the highway.

Felix turned the corner and froze. A short, blonde girl in a blue polka-dotted dress stood against the door to his room, her hands held up over her eyes, pouting quietly in the corner of the jamb. Bits of wrapping paper clung to her hair. He held his breath, waiting for the doll to move. A slow ache slipped behind his forehead, pulsing to the beat of his trembling heart. He exhaled slowly, keeping his eyes locked on the back of the doll's head while he tip-toed closer toward the door.

The figure didn't move, and the rational part of his mind chided him, screaming for him to just open the damn door, get the phone, and get the fuck out of town. He waited another beat and the doll didn't move. Finally, he rolled his eyes, reached over the little figure, and opened the door.

The blonde doll tipped forward, falling face-first onto the brown shag carpet. Felix let out a short laugh, more from relief than surprise, and stepped over the doll.

Two things happened in short succession when he crossed the threshold and retrieved his phone. The first was a noise coming from within the small coat closet adjacent to the bathroom. At first, Felix didn't notice the sound, nor did he recognize what it was.

Between the persistent ache hammering away in his head and his preoccupation with finding his phone, his senses were overloaded to the point of numbness. He didn't realize until it was too late that the noise was, in fact, the stifled laughter of a young boy.

The second was his phone ringing, startling him so badly that he dropped the device. It fell onto the floor, its bright screen facing up and displaying an incoming call from LARRY MALONE. Felix bent to retrieve it, and that's when the closet door swung open.

Noah smiled at him, his plastic brow loosening somehow, wrinkling like a piece of flesh. His coal-black eyes almost shimmered in the yellow lamplight. A series of loose stitches held his mouth in place, and a dark brown liquid seeped through the mesh, dribbling down his chin.

The smell spurred Felix to move. Until that stench hit his nostrils, he was lost in those black eyes, his knees glued to the floor by the dread hardening his veins. The stink of pig shit—and the sight of the foul liquid dribbling out of the boy's mouth—fired his nerves into overdrive. He snatched up the phone and shot to his feet.

Noah giggled, but the sound that came from his tiny frame wasn't the voice of a child; it was the shrill squeal of swine, underscored by a guttural roar that made Felix's arms tingle with gooseflesh.

"*Outsider*," a voice growled, but it wasn't the boy who spoke. A sharp pain stabbed into the back of Felix's calf, forcing him to cry out, swinging his leg forward. The girl with the blue polka-dotted dress fell forward, rolled over, and laughed at him. He teetered backward, working to put as much space between himself and those infernal creatures as possible.

Noah had other plans, however. He vaulted onto the bed, ran three steps, and launched himself at Felix. The plastic child's fingers had separated from their singular mold, flaring outward like claws. They pierced Felix's shirt and sank into his flesh.

Adrenaline dulled his senses, barring the immediate shock of pain. Felix reached up, gripped the back of Noah's shirt, and yanked him away, sending a trail of blood splattering across the bed. More of that dark, viscous liquid dribbled from the boy's mouth as Felix held him in the air, his stomach tumbling from the agonizing stench filling the room.

"No wonder everything smells," he said, watching with a sick sort of wonder as the doll-child kicked and scrambled to free itself from his grasp. "You're all full of pig shit."

He looked over at the little girl climbing up the edge of the bed and laughed at how absurd this all was. *Talking dolls*, he thought. *Angry, shit-spewing dolls with claws.* Absurd though it was, his present situation hadn't improved. He still needed to get the hell out of there, and despite the adrenaline rush, he found that he was trembling.

"*Outsider*," Noah growled. He took a swipe at Felix's face, slashing the tip of his captor's nose. The sting made Felix's eyes water.

"I think I've had just about enough of you," Felix snarled. He squeezed Noah's neck, slammed him to the floor, and brought the heel of his foot down on the back of the doll's head. There was a low cracking sound, followed by a heavy squish. The sides of the doll's head exploded outward as Felix's loafer sank into a mess of hair, wrinkled plastic, and pig shit. He caught a whiff of the excrement and fought a rising urge to vomit.

Felix lifted his foot from Noah's remains and reeled backward. He braced himself against the door frame, gasping for fresh air in a moment of respite from the insanity.

"I've got to get out of here," he muttered, shooting a sideways glance at the girl in the polka-dotted dress. She stood at the edge of the bed, peering down at her ruined accomplice. Felix wasn't about to stick around and ask her what she thought of the mess.

He slid along the wall, put one foot through the doorway, and was about to make a hasty exit for his car when a wooden baseball bat collided with his temple. Stars exploded with brilliant color before his eyes as the impact sent him reeling. The cell phone flew from his hands and met the pavement with a sharp crack.

Felix saw the world through a watery filter for a few seconds before his legs gave out and everything went dark. Jerry stood over him, lifting the cracked Louisville Slugger over his shoulder. He looked down at Felix and spat.

"That's for tryin' to leave without payin'."

"I can't do this anymore, Felix. I won't be badgered and I won't be bullied. It's over."

Helen's shrill voice rose from nowhere, echoing off the chambers of his empty mind. Felix opened his eyes and watched as a series of low, gray clouds floated by. A sign reading DALTON DOLLWORKS trailed after them, followed by a group of streetlights glowing yellow phosphorous across a black sea of emptiness.

He was floating on his back, bobbing along with the dark waves. A door slammed from somewhere far away, the sound carrying across the sea with a heavy wind.

"Helen, open the door."

His own voice sounded strange to him. He was distant, arrogant, unsullied by the burden of that shoulder-riding baboon called Alcoholism. More streetlights trailed, followed by another sign reading DALTON PIG FARMS: THIS EXIT.

"No, Felix. It's always about what you want. Goddammit, I don't want what you want."

The night sky swirled with a jumble of fractured images, and through them he saw himself aged ten years younger, heartbroken and alone, diving into a brown bottle for the first time. He saw those long nights of depression and remorse racing by in an agonizing montage.

He saw Helen standing in the doorway of their bedroom, arms crossed at her chest, her chin quivering and her eyes barely holding back tears that would most surely come when they were ready. *This isn't right*, he thought. *This happened before.*

And it had. She'd come home early in a huff, frantically tearing through the drawers in their apartment bathroom, muttering things to herself like "*It has to be here*" and "*Where did I put them?*" What she was looking for was long gone, however, and Felix knew this because he'd found the pills that morning on the nightstand. They weren't just any pills, either; they were Pills. He didn't have anything against contraception, but he did have something against his wife lying to him.

"*I flushed them.*"

The look on her face told him it was over even before she said it herself. She'd never wanted children—and still didn't, for all he knew—and he should've known better when, after trying for years to convince her otherwise, she finally acquiesced. He should've known better when their months of trying to conceive bore no fruit.

"*When you were out of town last year, I went to a clinic and had an abortion.*"

Was she just saying that to hurt him? Or was there some truth in her words? She glared at him, measuring his reaction, and he found he could do nothing but step back and sit down on the bed. Oh, how he'd wanted to strangle her then, but the mixture of confusion, heartache, and betrayal racing through him at that moment prevented him from doing anything.

"I used to think you'd grow out of it," she said, *"but I knew in my heart you never would. It's your eyes, Felix. The way your eyes light up whenever you see a baby on the street, the way there's always a spring in your step, I knew you'd never back down from being a father. And maybe you will—but not easily, and not with me. I can't—I won't do it to myself."*

Floating there, watching his younger self be torn apart by Helen's cold words, Felix returned to something he'd known ever since he went dry just a few years back: It just wasn't meant to be. Sure, he'd fought that axiom, going as far as the bottom of a bottle to escape it, but in the end, the epiphany remained waiting for him, steadfast in its resolve.

Overhead, the stars blossomed into the pallid faces of Dalton's youth, peering down at him with mesh mouths and coal-black eyes while the squeals of swine filled the air. He was transfixed by the sight, unable to move while the black waters lapped against his bloated face, and when the pale, clawed hands rose from the waves to claim him, he offered no resistance.

Felix sank back into murk, dragged down to the bottom once more by the hands of unborn children.

Something wet pressed against his cheek. Felix waited for the fog in his head to clear before opening his eyes, only to find he was staring into the mud-covered snout of a pig. The creature shrank back, startled by his cry of surprise, squealing as it scrambled over to a short wooden fence.

His head throbbed, and warm blood trickled down his right temple from the wound. A series of snorts and squeals rose from behind, calling to mind an image of a street sign he'd seen in his dream, except now that he thought about it, he supposed he hadn't been entirely unconscious. He could've done without seeing Helen's cold face once again, though. He could always do without that.

Felix turned and realized he was staring up at the dusty rafters of a tall ceiling. Bare yellow bulbs hung along the center beam, casting a dim glow over the room. When he tried to move he found that neither his arms nor legs would cooperate. He craned his neck to get a better look and winced when something dry and coarse dug into his throat. Pulling on his arms or legs made the cord tighter. *Of course they would hog-tie me*, he thought.

He relaxed his head and rested against a mound of muddy hay. The musty smell made his nostrils itch. He closed his eyes, wondering how the hell he was going to get out of this mess.

A large brown hog with a pale spot on its side wandered over to the fence and stuck its snout between the slats. Felix opened his eyes and stared at the beast, grimacing at the stink of its breath and the frothy spittle dribbling from its open snout.

"Bessie likes you."

A woman's voice echoed across the room, followed by the appearance of a blurry shape that floated into the background behind the hog. Felix strained his neck, trying to catch a glimpse of the woman, but she was too far to his right.

The visitor cleared her throat. "Mr. Martin? Mr. Brody?"

Felix lifted his head and watched as two middle-aged men hopped the fence. One of them had a knife in his hand. Felix's natural instinct was to shrink back, recoil from the blade as much as he could, but his restraints prevented such movement. Defeated, Felix closed his eyes and waited for the sharp jab that would end his life.

The tension left his restraints.

"On yer feet, boy. Don't they teach ya respect in the big city?"

One of the men—Brody or Martin, he wasn't sure it even mattered—gave his leg a swift kick, and the sharp pain spurred Felix to move. He climbed to his feet, rubbing at his neck, and wondering if the rope had left a mark.

A young brunette smiled at him from beyond the gate. She wore a black silk robe that shimmered even in the dim lighting.

"I'm sorry for the hassle, Felix. May I call you that?"

"Sure. What should I call you?"

The young lady smiled. "My name's Maggie Eloquence Dalton. I'm sorry for the… poor hospitality." She motioned to the wound on his head. Felix raised a finger to it and discovered a huge knot had erupted near his temple. "I couldn't let you leave without giving you what you came for."

He stared at her, realizing for the first time that he'd never actually seen a picture of Miss Maggie before. Despite his research and the years of press coverage, no one had published a photograph of the Dalton Dollworks CEO. The woman who stood before him couldn't be her. Maggie Eloquence was in her seventies. This tall, slender brunette wasn't a day over 30, easy.

Felix forced a smile. "I think I've had enough of the games, lady. No more bullshit."

One of the men shoved him. He keeled over into the dirt.

"Mind yer manners, ya little shit."

"Brody." Maggie's voice went cold. Felix looked up at her, then back at the two men. They shrank back to the end of the stall, grouped with the other hogs. "Felix, I must apologize. We got off on the wrong foot."

Felix stood. "Assuming you are the real Maggie Eloquence Dalton, lady, you've got a hell of a lot to answer for."

Maggie smiled, offering him a short nod before opening the gate.

"I s'pose I do, Felix. S'pose I do. Will you walk with me? It's been a long time since I've had a gentleman come callin' for me, and it's a beautiful night out. We do have so much to talk about, after all."

She hooked her arm with his and gave him a gentle tug. Felix let her lead him, realizing he didn't really have a choice.

They strolled outside, down a row between two large, fenced-off areas. Hundreds of hogs rooted through the mud, snorting and squealing, going about their own pig affairs. The stench of excrement was palpable here, but after a day subjected to that smell, Felix barely noticed. He was too caught up in the mystery of the woman in the black robe, trying to work out everything that had happened.

"Are you going to tell me who you really are? Or why you tried to kill me?"

"Kill you?" Maggie laughed earnestly, clinging to him as they left the barn. Her warmth stirred something inside him, something that had been dormant for far too long. A wave of heat flushed through him. "Bless your heart, darlin'. Why would I ever do a thing like that? And I already told you who I am, Felix."

He shook his head. "That doesn't make sense. By my research, Maggie Dalton should be an old woman."

She let go of him, took a step backward, and separated her robe. Underneath was the pale body of a supermodel: agonizingly thin, but perfectly tone, with breasts that hadn't yet learned the aging effects of gravity, and hips that hadn't known childbirth. Maggie put her hands on her hips as Felix gaped. She smiled.

"Do I look like an old woman to you?"

Felix wanted to speak but found he couldn't. He was too stunned, too enamored by her beauty to focus on anything else other than his own lust. He finally made himself look away, embarrassed that the bulge growing in his pants would give away his desires—not that she would mind. Maggie Dalton hadn't struck him as the type who would be put off by something like that.

"N-No, ma'am." Felix strained to avert his eyes, but they just kept wandering back over to that beautiful, pale body shimmering in the moonlight—

"I am seventy-two years old."

Those words broke his trance. He met her gaze, relieved to see that she was closing her robe.

"How is that possible?"

She sidled up to him and hooked her arm with this once again. "The Buried One has made many things possible for me, Felix. It saved my daddy's empire when it was failing. It let me keep my good looks as I aged. And it gave me all the children I would ever want. Isn't that right, kids?"

A strange skittering noise rose up around them, and where at first there had been nothing but pigs and shadows, there now stood tiny figures with white emotionless faces and dark, empty eyes. Felix stopped, frozen by a seeping fear that dribbled into his veins. Maggie sensed his tension and gave his arm a squeeze.

"They won't hurt you, Felix. These are my children. We forgive you for what you did to Noah, don't we?" The dolls said nothing. They stared at him with their empty disdain. "My children are Dalton's sentinels, Felix. When Henry told you about the church, when you tried to leave, they thought you would bring harm to Dalton. Please understand, most outsiders have been… *unkind* to us in the past." She paused, gesturing to the army of hateful dolls watching from the shadows. "But we know better, don't we, children? He is the one we've waited for."

"You were waiting for me?"

"Oh yes," she grinned, "I've been waiting for you for a while, Felix Proust. That's why I asked for you specifically. The Buried One told me you would come, and He has never lied. Not when He promised to keep me young. Not when He promised to keep me wealthy, or when He promised to let Dalton prosper. And now you have come to me, my love."

His head swam with alarm and confusion, but that warm smile and touch of her right breast pressed against his side kept his feet moving. He opened his mouth to speak, but she put her finger to his lips. She smelled of lavender—the first pleasant thing he'd smelled since arriving in Dalton.

"No more words," she said. "Let me show you something."

She led him across the row toward the next barn. The lights were already on, and there were screams coming from within, followed by a low series of gurgles. Men and women cheered. They strolled through the doorway and into a congregation.

There were hundreds of people gathered within, hands raised to the ceiling in unison, their attention directed at a platform off to the far right. Felix stood on his toes to get a better look.

A man and two dolls stood on the platform; beyond them stood a pair of beams affixed in a T-shape, with what appeared to be a system of pulleys affixed to both ends. A rope was threaded through the device, and the end on the left shook violently.

"*Traitor,*" the townspeople chanted. "*Traitor. Traitor. Traitor.*"

He thought back to the desecrated church. A chill crawled its way across his neck. *What would a town of religious zealots do to heretics?*

"Maggie," he began, trying to swallow back the dread rising from his gut, "what are they doing?"

"He wasn't supposed to tell you about the church. You weren't supposed to know until you were ready. He tried to taint your purity, to turn you against us."

The rope stopped shaking. The man on the platform pulled on the other end, wrenching the rope through the pulleys, and acting as a counter-weight. Felix watched with mounting distress as that familiar pit opened in his gut, threatening to swallow him whole. He already knew what was on the other end of that rope before they pulled him up, and when Felix saw the old drunk, he almost vomited on Maggie's black robe.

Henry hung limp from the end of the rope like a drowned worm. Pig shit and offal clung to him in patches, dripping off him like drain water. The crowd cheered, erupting into their violent chant once again.

Maggie squeezed his hand. "Come. We're almost ready."

"Ready for what?"

She smiled. "Our consummation."

"**O**ur…wait, what?"

But Maggie said nothing, merely pulling at his hand in reply. One by one, members of the congregation turned to face them, smiling gleefully while tears rolled down their cheeks. Felix glanced across the sea of faces, realizing their flesh was wrinkled, sagging, and liver-spotted. *The children were murdered*, he thought, swallowing back the sour taste of bile.

The townspeople of Dalton separated, forming a path toward a candlelit circle in the center of the barn. Dazed, his head still pounding from the attack earlier that evening, Felix felt his legs move of their own accord, following the black-robed woman toward the circle.

"The Buried One gave us so many gifts, Felix."

"You killed…you murdered all those children."

Maggie tightened her grip on his hand as her pace quickened. Felix shuffled his feet behind her, struggling to keep up. The world swam around him, throbbing to the tune of an indecipherable mantra whispering in his head.

"They were parasites, draining this town of its life. Heretics of the one true faith. The Buried One helped me see this, and then I shared that vision with the rest of Dalton. Together we sacrificed those awful things and left their bodies to rot at the pulpit of a false idol."

"But they were just children."

Maggie turned and placed her hand on his cheek. Tears rolled away from her eyes, leaving streaks across her porcelain face. "So sweet in your ignorance. You've so much to learn." She took his hand and lifted it into the air. "My flock! Our harbinger has come!"

The crowd exploded with cheers. Some of them openly wept, their hands clasped to their chests, sobbing prayers that Felix could not hear.

"I don't understand," Felix groaned. The cheering, chanting, sobbing, and now that damned voice whispering in his head—he could hardly think straight anymore. And then there was Maggie's pale, smiling face. She put her hands on his cheeks and kissed him. The world fell away for a moment, leaving just the two of them standing in a circle of candles, the volume turned way down except for his beating heart and her soothing, southern voice.

"My dolls are my children, Felix. *Dalton's* children. Behind their eyes are lifetimes of suffering, nightmares, broken hearts, and unimaginable cruelty. The Buried One showed me that all of these ugly little things can be taken away and hidden behind empty faces, used to give life to perfect children who will never talk back or speak out of turn, children who will embody the sins of their fathers. These children—*our* children, Felix—will purge this world of its heretics and bring about a new age. And you, my love, will be their harbinger."

Felix blinked away his tears. The world came back into focus. They stood inside the circle of candles, just to the left of a wooden pedestal upon which sat a small figure carved out of stone. He staggered toward it and took in its features. Maggie's "Buried One" was of simple workmanship, its features carved to portray a fetal child in effigy, complete with an umbilical cord wrapped around its curled legs. Two lumps of coal were affixed to its grinning face, and when Felix looked into them, his mind was filled with that same lurid, whispering chant.

Harbinger, it told him. *You are chosen.*

"I am chosen," he repeated, holding his gaze with the idol.

"You *are* chosen," Maggie said. "The Buried One told me you would come. You will be our harbinger of a new dawn."

Somewhere in the back of his mind, Felix heard himself screaming, but his body would not react. His body and its motions belonged to that grinning idol on the pedestal. He had become detached from himself, watching as a spectator would from the sidelines, and after struggling with all his strength he found he could not break free of that mental prison, nor could he look away.

Maggie peeled back the black robe, letting it fall to her feet like a silk cocoon. She ran her hand through his hair and kissed him once again. She traced her lips across the side of his face and ran her tongue across the tip of his earlobe.

"Consummate with me," she whispered. "Let me take away your heartbreak, your pain, and the demons haunting your soul. Let me give you the child you always wanted, Felix. Let me give you what Helen wouldn't."

Felix gave in to his desire, letting his hand slide up the length of her thigh while his lips returned her kiss, ignorant of the leering crowd around them. Maggie pulled away from him, smiling as she knelt down on the bed of her black robe. There she reclined backward and spread herself for him. Felix smiled softly, stripped off his clothes, and joined her. The sounds of their coupling were masked only by the sudden squeals of swine.

"Spill your seed," she told him. Her eyes had darkened over, and her nails dug into his back. "Fill me."

And so he did, arching his body as he thrust into her one final time, giving the last of himself over to Dalton's matriarch. Exhausted, his head lost in a cloud, Felix collapsed beside her, listening to the thrum of his heart. A new chant had risen from within their audience. They clapped their hands in praise, reaching an almost hymn-like quality as some of them sang *"Harbinger, Harbinger, Harbinger!"*

Maggie her finger across his cheek. "Thank you, my love. I must give our child life now. But you may rest. brushed Your task is just beginning."

Confused, Felix rolled onto his back and watched as she approached the pedestal. She knelt before the stone idol and bowed her head.

"Accept this offering, my Lord. Accept this, my flesh and my blood. Bear this fruit so that our child may spread your word."

An old woman emerged from the crowd with a bundle in her arms. She placed it at the foot of the shrine, bowing her head in reverence before returning to her place among the masses. Maggie unwrapped the bundle, revealing the open body of a plastic doll, its chest peeled back like a cadaver. Felix crawled forward but recoiled when he saw what was inside.

The manure was fresh. Straws of hay clung to it, and a slow tendril of steam rose from the pile's center.

What happened next drove Felix to the brink of insanity; perhaps, in some ways, what he saw may have even driven him over into that unending abyss.

Maggie squatted over the open doll, ran her hands across her belly and down between her thighs, murmuring words that Felix didn't understand. Her eyes had gone black, mirroring the idol's own lumps of coal, and when she raised her head he saw that she was not Maggie anymore. Not really. She gnashed her teeth at him and flicked her tongue like a beast while a steady stream of darkened blood poured out of her into the empty corpse of the doll.

"This is impossible," Felix whispered, his mind reeling from the shock of what he was seeing. Maggie's beast-like demeanor became more erratic, thrashing her arms and flicking her tongue to the air as more of her dripped into the doll. She cocked her head and leered at Felix, grinning with clenched teeth.

"*Harbinger,*" the thing that was Maggie said, "*your will is now mine.*"

The world swam before him as the idol's words spoke through Maggie, and he tried his best to focus and regain his strength, but his limbs were heavy. *Your will is now mine.* Those words repeated in his head in a mantra he could not escape.

His mind was filled with images of the church. He saw its pews overturned and piled with the rotting bodies of Dalton's former youth, sacrifices made to Maggie Dalton's buried god. He saw a town devouring itself as brave parents were cut down by their neighbors for trying to defend their kids. A shrill chorus of screaming children filled his ears, accompanied by the commanding whispers of the stone idol.

Purge, the Buried One said. *Purge the heretics. Cleanse this world for my return.*

"Let it happen," Maggie whispered, smiling as her eyes returned to normal. "You're going to be a daddy."

He looked down and saw the doll's hand begin to twitch. That was the moment that sent Felix Proust spiraling over the abyss, shrieking in maddening horror as the world he knew fell away from him in a single, agonizing gasp.

Felix stared out the window of the limousine, watching as the morning sun rose from between the mountains, spilling light over the streets of Dalton. Sleep tugged at his eyelids, but every time he closed his eyes he found the rigid, glaring face of the Buried One staring back at him. Fragments of the previous night remained embedded in his mind like shards of broken glass, leaving scars that would never fully heal.

There were a few moments he tried to open the door during their drive back from the pig farms. He wanted to fling himself from the car, but his hands would not cooperate. *Your will is now mine,* the Buried One whispered, asserting its dominance with an almost gleeful tone. Even death would not come without its say-so.

The limousine parked beside his rental car at the Dalton R&R. Maggie nuzzled her head against his shoulder like a feline.

"You will do fine, Felix. I know you're nervous, but I have faith in you. We all do."

She leaned up and kissed his cheek. The driver climbed out and opened his door. Felix squinted at the piercing light of the sun.

"Felix?"

He turned, staring into Miss Maggie's tired bedroom eyes and wondering absently what nightmares waited behind the mask she wore. One day, he supposed, he would find out. But not today.

Today he had another task at hand.

"Yes, Miss Maggie?"

"Take care of our child."

"As you wish, Miss Maggie."

They were words spoken by his voice, but they weren't his own. If he'd had any control over his faculties, he would've screamed at the top of his lungs, but the Buried One wouldn't allow that.

She reached across the seat and handed him the fruit of their union: a simple, girly doll with brownish-blonde curls and a peppermint-striped dress. The doll stared at him, unblinking, uncaring.

"Spread our will," Maggie said, smiling. "Come back to me when you are finished. We will birth a new world together."

Felix felt himself nod, his muscles pulled by phantom strings, and then turned toward his car. The doll was rank with the stench of excrement but he couldn't smell it anymore. Like the rest of the town, he'd grown used to that smell, ignorant of its meaning.

He glanced toward the limousine once before climbing into the rental car. Maggie reached out the open window and blew him a kiss just before the limousine pulled away in a cloud of dust. Felix was alone again with their child. He tossed the empty box into the parking lot and buckled the doll into her seat.

Felix Proust sat there for a few minutes with his hands on the steering wheel, trying everything in his power to open the door and run for his life, but the Buried One would not let him. He was its slave now, its harbinger. He would do as it bade him, taking the doll back to civilization where he would spread its gospel.

He glanced down at the doll, noticing for the first time the simple, brown nametag stuck to its hand. Written in sharp, black calligraphy was a single name that made his last ounce of hope sink to the bottom of that shrouded pit within: HELEN.

A flood of tears escaped him. Felix sobbed in quick, uncontrollable convulsions as he started the car.

Helen the Doll reached over and placed her hand on his arm.

"*Daddy*," she said.

AFTERWORD: FIELD ON FIRE

I went on a book tour back in 2023, my first in eleven years, in support of my latest collection, *Cold, Black & Infinite: Stories of the Horrific & Strange* (hereafter referred to as "CBI" for brevity's sake). Dubbed "The Summer of Dread," I traveled extensively through New England and as far south as Kentucky, appearing at indie bookstores, corporate bookstores, and conferences where I met many fans and made new ones. My biggest takeaway from the experience was this: No one knew that CBI wasn't my first collection.

That honor belongs to this big, blue baby you're holding in your hands. You could say this book crawled so CBI could walk, but I think that would be understating its importance in the scope of my career which, if I'm counting right, is 19 years long as I write this. When I appeared on Neil McRobert's *Talking Scared* podcast in 2024, we discussed said career, and the eras in which it's divided. *Ugly Little Things* is the capstone to my first "era," if you will, a period of time spanning from 2006 to 2017 when this book was first published.

It's easy to say it was the beginning of something grand, now with the privilege of hindsight, but at the time I feared it would've been the end. I got my start in self-publishing, first with an extremely limited chapbook, then my first published novel, *A Life Transparent*, and finally, with its sequel, *The Liminal Man*. When the sequel tanked and didn't take off as I'd hoped, I fell into a rut with the third novel, wondering if it was worth the time and expense of production, questioning if my words had any worth at all. There were bigger issues at play—mainly, depression—driving this destructive reflection, but I was too lost in the weeds to see the whole field, and would be for some years to come. That field was fallow, dry, utterly dead.

Sometime in 2013, my friend and fellow author Anthony J. Rapino—who wrote the absolutely stunning *Soundtrack to the End of the World*, and later, *Greetings from Moon Hill*—recommended me for what would become my first anthology publication. I have to admit I was reluctant—I hadn't written short form in many years and wondered if I still could—but I gave it a shot because I didn't want my friend to look bad on my account. The result is a story you've probably read by now: "Radio Free Nowhere." It was, technically speaking, the first "ugly little thing," a title I gave all my short fiction that followed.

That anthology is long out of print by this point—*Exquisite Death*, for the completionists out there—but my inclusion marked a change for me in many ways: personally, professionally, and creatively. It was a much-needed spark offering a brief glimpse of something hidden in the dark.

Through Tony and *Exquisite Death*, I met Mercedes M. Yardley—whose *Little Dead Red* remains one of the more harrowing pieces of fiction I've ever read—who also wrote the foreword for this collection, and who remains a dear friend to this day. I learned a lot about the business from her—querying, feedback, which publishers to avoid, which publishers to pursue, and so on. She saw something in me and my work, and included me in the bigger conversation when I was a nobody in the genre, something I've never thanked her for until now. It gave me hope.

Four of the stories in this collection were initially released as single stories on Kindle, each one part of a series called "Ugly Little Things," and they were surprisingly successful. So successful, in fact, that I compiled them into a limited hardcover edition along with older material and self-published the release through my company, Precipice Books. The book was released as the first volume in a series of planned collections, inspired by Barker's *Books of Blood* which began as a series of paperbacks.

I kept writing, kept chasing that spark, and over time, accumulated a number of short stories and publishing credits to my name. And then, sometime in 2016, I decided to pitch the collection to a relatively new indie publisher that was building a solid reputation. Crystal Lake seemed like a good home for my ugly little things. I made my pitch, and some months later, I received my first book contract.

A two-book deal—one for this collection, and one for a novella about a doomed prog rock band. *The Final Reconciliation* released in February 2017 to much acclaim, which led to being signed by my first agent, and in May of that year, I finally felt confident enough in my work to tackle a project I'd been thinking about for a decade: *Devil's Creek*. Then, in September, this collection was released.

The rest is history, I guess. The spark caught fire, set the whole goddamn field ablaze, and it's been burning bright ever since.

But something happened after *Devil's Creek's* release in 2020. The book was massive, bigger than I'd ever imagined in word count and in reception—so big that it overshadowed everything else in my bibliography. I went from being a short story writer to a "novelist" overnight. My earlier novels, books one and two of the *Monochrome*

Trilogy, and this collection were largely forgotten by the public. Only *The Final Reconciliation* escaped obscurity, likely because it's closely linked to the Southland Mythos I first established in *Devil's Creek*.

Thing is, I didn't realize this until much later on that tour in 2023. Which leads us to now, folks, and the book you hold in your hands. The field is still burning and shows no sign of dying out, but the ignition spark began here in these pages. These stories saved my life, taught me how to navigate a hostile industry, and led to lifelong friendships.

Mainly, though, they reminded me that I'm a writer and a storyteller, and revealed something about myself that I didn't know before: I am a field on fire, and I am burning bright.

Thanks for reading.

Todd Keisling
Womelsdorf, Pennsylvania
March 12, 2025

STORY NOTES

Here is a book of lies, full of ugly little truths, filled to the brim with someone's deepest, darkest secrets. These stories began with the idea of taking all those nasty things that live inside us, transporting them to vessels of their own, and giving them life. You've seen their stitched faces and pallid smiles. You've stared into their empty, black eyes.

But what dark magic makes them walk and dance? What unholy ritual birthed these horrible monsters?

Let's find out. First, you need to make an incision *here*, and then another one *here*. Insert your fingers. Now, slowly, gently, pull them apart.

That's it. Now look at your work.

Look at what wonderful things have come spilling out…

"A Man in Your Garden" was conceived in early 2016 as a writing exercise to get me back into the groove of writing on a regular basis. I'd spent most of the previous year dividing my time between real life endeavors (like buying my first house) and solving the perpetual riddle of my third novel, so I was in need of a break. What better way to ease back into things than with an experiment in second-person perspective?

I had a dream in which I saw someone standing in my back yard late at night. In my dream, I was terrified, even though this anonymous figure didn't do anything. The next day, while daydreaming of ways to escape my day job, I scribbled the opening line on a blue Post-It note. The rest fell into place relatively quickly, something which does not usually happen with my first drafts.

No, I don't have a pergola in my backyard, and I don't own a hatchet. Not yet, anyway.

I began work on "Show Me Where the Waters Fill your Grave" in the fall of 2016. It's the most recent story and the last to be finished before compiling this volume. As you've probably gathered by now, some of my stories take years to complete. This one, however, only took about a month.

I'd read an article about the flooding down in Louisiana last August and how caskets from a local cemetery were spotted floating down the flooded streets, and I was struck with the simple image of an old man staring at his front door. I saw him sitting in his foyer, waiting for his wife to return. Waiting while the churning floodwaters invaded his home to claim him. But why? That question nagged at me, as the best questions are wont to do, and over the following days a story took root.

Thing is, this story didn't pan out at all like I thought it would. When I began writing the story, I expected it to be a sappy, gothic love story, about a lonely old man given one last chance to see his wife. And that's what it was going to be until I realized Jonathan had a gun in his hand. That's when everything changed and the story took off in its own direction. The only real thing you can do in a situation like that is to follow it, see where it goes, and hope everything turns out okay. Sometimes we writers are just recorders. All we can do is listen while the stories tell themselves.

"Radio Free Nowhere" was conceived from years of driving between Pennsylvania and Kentucky, playing roulette with the radio stations in the area of West Virginia, just south of the Mason-Dixon line. When you're deep in the Appalachia Mountains, sometimes your only choices for radio stations are country, more country, hellfire and brimstone courtesy of various AM signals, and periods of intense static. Sometimes the static is all you have, and there have been many times when I've wondered about what we aren't hearing—or worse, what we don't realize we *are* hearing.

This story was the result of those experiences, coupled with the idea that we're all obsessed with our own curiosities, often to our own detriment. And those dark hands emerging from the water? Those came from the shadows of my dreams. If you've read this far, you've probably noticed I have a thing about hands. Hands creep me out. Especially when there are many of them, their bodies unseen, unknown. Submerging them in the murky waters of a forgotten lake seemed kind of fitting.

I wrote "The Otherland Express" back in 2014 for Troy Blackford's anthology, *Robbed of Sleep*. The story took root from a tweet that Troy sent out earlier that year about waiting for a bus. Unfortunately I couldn't locate the tweet in time for this to go to print, so you'll have to take my word for it.

Anyway, the story was originally titled "The Wrong People," about an unemployed man who catches the wrong bus and discovers it's filled with people who are *off* somehow. Their skin doesn't fit, sagging in weird places, and some of them have to keep readjusting their faces. The story played out in my head like an episode of *The Twilight Zone*, but when I tried writing it, the protagonist fell flat. I didn't care about him and I didn't care about his plight, so I scrapped the story and decided I'd give myself a week before telling Troy I'd have to pass on the anthology opportunity.

A few days later, I read a news article about a teenager who'd left home to meet a stranger from the internet, and the rest fell into place almost immediately. The story's protagonist transformed from a middle-aged fellow down on his luck to a confused, heartbroken teenager. Suddenly he had more of a reason to be on that bus, and the weird people did, too. I'm glad he made it to his destination—and with a new face, too.

I almost gave up on "Saving Granny from the Devil." I started writing it in 2009, set it aside, and proceeded to return to it once a year, trying a different approach each time until I found the right groove. Some stories are like wine—they need to ferment for a while before the flavor is right.

The story wasn't supposed to be fiction at all, but instead an essay about my late great-grandmother. Unfortunately, Old Scratch kept popping up in the narrative, and in 2013 I finally decided to let him speak. The result is the most personal thing I've ever written, blurring lines between fiction and non-fiction.

Many of the events in this story really did happen, including a pair of neighborhood bullies locking me inside an old dog kennel. I was a budding artist in my younger days, *Bedknobs & Broomsticks* is still my favorite Disney film, and Granny really did suffer from a series of strokes in the last decade of her life. I didn't make a deal with the devil to save her, but she did claim she saw a man in black beckoning to her from across the street. That image has haunted me for most of my life.

One more thing about "Saving Granny:" the incident with the monkey really happened. I swear.

"The Darkness Between Dead Stars" is another tale that went through a series of growing pains before finally standing on its own, and was almost scrapped several times. Typically, I'll have a title, beginning, and end in mind before I begin a work on a story. I like to know what I'm writing about from a thematic point of view, and to have a goal post in sight. This isn't always the case, though, and this story is an example of that. I began writing this story with an ending; I spent two years figuring out where it began, and what it wanted to be called.

As I recall, the original plan was to begin the story with a failed entry into the Martian atmosphere that left Maxwell's craft adrift in space. That version would've dealt more with the psychological ambiguity of his predicament, leaving the reader to question if what he was experiencing was actually happening. I didn't care for that direction and scrapped it. My second attempt took a more traditional approach, beginning with Maxwell on earth, his selection, training, and so on. I wanted to keep the story at a reasonable length, so that idea was scrapped as well. By my own admission, I often struggle with writing "short" stories.

Another idea (which never made it to paper) was the possibility of Maxwell's placement in the program being part of a greater conspiracy, orchestrated by a religious cult that worships the stars. Along with being somewhat ridiculous (okay, *entirely* ridiculous), I didn't like how that approach provided answers. My ending was always intended to play with existential uncertainty and the impossibility of knowing, leaving the reader with a question he or she would have to contemplate themselves.

I liked the idea of someone else telling the story, as if to say, "Hey, this is no bullshit. It really happened." Having the story told through the eyes of a witness, rather than over the shoulder of a potentially unreliable narrator, provided more credibility to the circumstances leading up to Maxwell's demise, and ultimately improved the story's effectiveness. I'm quite happy with the way it turned out. As for the title, I was reading a lot of Thomas Ligotti at the time, which might explain the bleakness.

The antagonist of "Human Resources," a mysterious fellow named Charles Boid, has a funny history in my fiction. This story is actually the third in which he's appeared. Way back in 2005 during my senior year of college, I wrote a short story for one of my English classes titled "ZZ." The story was supposed to be in the style of Borges (but read more like Lovecraft), about a computer programmer named Charles Boid who creates a website through which visitors can communicate with eldritch beings "lurking beyond the code."

I expanded Boid's history a few years later in a story titled "The Termination of Charles Boid" which I wrote for a Halloween contest. Boid remained dormant for nearly a decade after that, until Terry M. West contacted me about contributing to an anthology he was putting together. That anthology was *Journals of Horror: Found Fiction*, and the collection had a simple premise: horror stories told through "found" methods, like letters, notes, emails, and so on.

Boid didn't appear until I started writing the email that would become "Human Resources." Since I work in a corporate office, the "found" method of a formal email resignation seemed like a good starting point, and once I realized I was dealing with someone who'd been exposed to He Who Lurks Beyond the Code, I knew Boid wouldn't be far behind.

We probably haven't heard the last of Boid and his digital gods. Time will tell. Boid be praised.

Out of all the stories in this collection, "House of Nettle and Thorn" has the longest revision history, spanning over a decade of drafts and title changes. I got the idea while sitting in a college class (Statistics, I think) and overheard some classmates talking about a teacher who'd seduced one of her students. By the end of the day I had a few notes and a tentative title, "Papercuts," but a deluge of essay assignments kept me from starting that story. By the time I finished college, I'd put the story on a list of unfinished ideas and moved on.

A few years later, after social media took over the world, I revised the concept to address online relationships. I'd read a great story by Neil Gaiman titled "How to Talk to Girls at Parties," and I wanted to tackle the same premise but from a more mature, darker angle. With that in mind, I changed the story title to "Girls from the Internet," hoping to channel the campiness of 1950s horror and sci-fi films.

Things didn't quite work out that way, though. About halfway through the story I realized that title wouldn't work, as the tone I wanted to capture just wasn't happening. The story wanted to go somewhere else, and in more uncomfortable ways. I resisted the urge to scrap the story (although I did put it on hiatus for almost a year) and finally followed the protagonist to his demise in the basement of that creepy house. The end result is "House of Nettle and Thorn," a story that reads like an episode of *Tales from the Crypt* and is vastly different from how I originally envisioned it.

Karen Singleton remains one of my favorite characters because of how she came to life. "When Karen Met Her Mountain" began as a vivid dream, playing out almost like a film in my head. The opening scene of the story remains largely unchanged from its dream counterpart, with exception to a few minor details. I struggled with this one for a while, experimenting with different approaches before finding the right groove.

Originally, Karen was going to be a mute character, with the voice of her father speaking for her, but I couldn't quite get that version to work. She needed more personality than that, and silencing her would've done her character a great disservice. The final version of Karen's tale eventually came together in a single twelve-hour writing session one sweltering August day. I found inspiration in the exploitive revenge film *I Spit On Your Grave* and the claustrophobic horror of *The Descent*.

I loved the idea of a severely damaged character having to find their inner-strength (or in Karen's case, an inner-psychosis) in order to overcome insurmountable odds, and how tapping into that strength forces them to become the very thing they're fighting to survive. It's a feral duality of nature, defeating the beast by becoming the beast.

"The Harbinger" went through a number of title changes, and it predates all of the other ULT stories by a couple of years. I began writing the story under a different working title, "Eldritch Cabal," back in 2007. I envisioned the story as an ode to Lovecraft's "The Shadow Over Innsmouth," told through a series of letters about a mining town overtaken by a powerful evil found deep inside the earth. Unfortunately, the approach didn't appeal to me very much—you can only do or show so much in a letter, and it's really not my style anyway—so I scrapped it.

A few years later, I read a news article about sightings of "black-eyed children," which put me in mind of the pouting "Time-Out" dolls that haunt a lot of country gift shops. "Ugly Little Things" seemed to be a good description, so I used that as a working title for a while. The story was originally going to be about a small bed & breakfast haunted by the dolls, but the idea kept growing, and then in early 2013 I rediscovered those old story fragments from "Eldritch Cabal" and everything fell into place.

I changed the title for the sake of avoiding redundancy, but I kept

Maggie's dialogue about the dolls being vessels for all the negative things we bury within ourselves. This resulted in the overall theme of the collection, with each story being another horrible thing hidden behind the face of a doll.

And now to address the elephant in the room: where did the story's climactic ritual come from? I always pictured Maggie Eloquence as a matriarchal figure, birthing and protecting her young within the nest she'd made of the town. The ritual's concept was one of the most disgusting things I could imagine, with echoes of the original plan of offering her aborted children in sacrifice to a dark being. I wanted the ritual to be something more than just sacrilegious. I wanted it to be transcendent and repulsive, something *vile*.

The birth of Dalton's dolls is the result. We probably haven't seen the last of them, but that's a story for another day.

ACKNOWLEDGMENTS

I know you're itching to close this book and move on to the next, but maybe I can keep your attention for just another minute (or three). These stories—hell, most of this book—would not exist were it not for the encouragement and support of a few folks. Normally this is where the lights go up and the curtain closes, but I want to hold things up for just a minute. These people deserve the spotlight as much as I do. So, from the bottom of my black heart, I give my thanks:

For Erica, who picks me up when I'm down, dusts me off, and sends me on my way. My words always fail me in the most spectacular fashion whenever it comes to expressing my gratitude for having you in my life. Thank you, my love. For everything.

For Amelia, my Book Wife, who drags me through the nine circles of Editing Hell time and time again, knowing I can take it. And I do, with a pained smile on my face. Thank you, my friend.

For Mercedes, my dear friend, for cheering me on over the years and encouraging me to keep going even when I wanted to quit. You honor me with your words, and I'm blessed to know you.

For Joe and Monique and everyone else at Crystal Lake Publishing who believed in this book. I'm forever grateful to be a part of the Crystal Lake family.

For Becky, my agent, who was instrumental in facilitating this new edition and keeping the fires burning. May she be showered in good food and edibles. Especially edibles.

For Tony, Eryk, Brian, and Nikki, for being so supportive over the years. I love you guys dearly—even if you're all sort of weird and write about deeply disturbing things.

And finally there's You. The person holding this book. Thank you for spending your money and time to read my work. Your support makes things like this possible.

All right. I think that's about it. It's time for you to move on to your next book, and for me to step back into the shadows. That's where I work best.

Todd Keisling
Womelsdorf, Pennsylvania
April 20th, 2017
March 12th, 2025

PUBLICATION ACKNOWLEDGMENTS

"Radio Free Nowhere" first appeared in *Exquisite Death*, In Ear Entertainment, copyright © 2013 by Todd Keisling

"When Karen Met Her Mountain" first appeared in *Miseria's Chorale*, Forgotten Tomb Press, copyright © 2013 by Todd Keisling

"The Otherland Express" first appeared in *Robbed of Sleep*, copyright © 2014 by Todd Keisling

"House of Nettle and Thorn" first appeared in *Dead Harvest*, Scarlet Galleon Publications, copyright © 2014 by Todd Keisling

"Human Resources" first appeared in *Journals of Horror: Found Fiction*, copyright © 2014 by Todd Keisling

TODD KEISLING is the two-time Bram Stoker Award®-nominated author of *Devil's Creek, Scanlines, Cold, Black & Infinite,* and most recently, *The Sundowner's Dance,* among several others. A pair of his earlier works were recipients of the University of Kentucky's Oswald Research & Creativity Prize for Creative Writing (2002 and 2005), and his second novel, *The Liminal Man,* was an Indie Book Award finalist in Horror & Suspense (2013). He lives in Pennsylvania with his family.

SHARE HIS DREAD
Bluesky: @toddkeisling.com
Instagram: @toddkeisling
www.toddkeisling.com

CONTENT WARNINGS

All stories contain foul language, varying forms of violence, and other elements as follows:

"A Man in Your Garden": *Intoxication, nightmares, dread, and malice.*

"Show Me Where the Waters Fill Your Grave": *Grief, marital loss, natural disasters, hydrophobia, antlophobia, ombrophobia, and the undead.*

"Radio Free Nowhere": *Sexual suggestion, West Virginia, death, and the undead.*

"The Otherland Express": *Grief, relationship loss, parental abuse, homophobic slurs, and mutilation.*

"Saving Granny from the Devil": *Grief, regret, loss, bullying, homophobic slurs, medical trauma, and animal death.*

"The Darkness Between Dead Stars": *Dread, astrophobia, asphyxiation, hypoxia, and decompression.*

"Human Resources": *Ritual mutilation, suggested suicide, suggested murder, corporate bureaucracy, and esoteric uses of technology.*

"House of Nettle and Thorn": *Strong sexual situations, depictions of sexual acts, discussions of rape, relationship loss, mutilation, and botanophobia.*

"When Karen Met Her Mountain": *Suicide attempts, grief, loss, mutilation, unhinged rage, brutal murder, and relationship trauma.*

"The Harbinger": *Dolls, pediophobia, West Virginia, implied infanticide, elderly trauma, medieval torture, sexual situations, human sacrifice, and depictions of occult rituals.*